P9-CQP-590

THE RUSTLERS
OF WEST FORK

A HOPALONG CASSIDY NOVEL

BANTAM BOOKS BY LOUIS L'AMOUR
Ask your bookseller for the books you have missed.

LOUIS L'AMOUR

THE RUSTLERS OF WEST FORK

A HOPALONG CASSIDY NOVEL

Afterword by Beau L'Amour

BANTAM BOOKS
NEW YORK • TORONTO • LONDON • SYDNEY • AUCKLAND

THE RUSTLERS OF WEST FORK

A Bantam Book / June 1991

Previously published as *Hopalong Cassidy and the Rustlers of West Fork* by Louis L'Amour (writing as Tex Burns).

All rights reserved.
Copyright 1951, renewed © 1979 by Bantam Books.
Afterword copyright © 1991 by Louis and Katherine L'Amour Trust.
No part of this book may be reproduced or transmitted in any form or by any means, electronic or mechanical, including photocopying, recording, or by any information storage and retrieval system, without permission in writing from the publisher.
For information address: Bantam Books.

Library of Congress Cataloging-in-Publication Data
L'Amour, Louis, 1908–1988.
  [Hopalong Cassidy and the rustlers of West Fork]
  The rustlers of West Fork : a Hopalong Cassidy novel / Louis L'Amour.
    p.   cm.
  Original title: Hopalong Cassidy and the rustlers of West Fork.
  ISBN 0-553-07325-7
  I. Title.
PS3523.A446R8   1991
813'.52—dc20   91-1969
                                                       CIP

Published simultaneously in the United States and Canada

Bantam Books are published by Bantam Books, a division of Bantam Doubleday Dell Publishing Group, Inc. Its trademark, consisting of the words "Bantam Books" and the portrayal of a rooster, is Registered in U.S. Patent and Trademark Office and in other countries. Marca Registrada. Bantam Books, 666 Fifth Avenue, New York, New York 10103.

PRINTED IN THE UNITED STATES OF AMERICA

BVG   0 9 8 7 6 5 4 3 2 1

THE RUSTLERS
OF WEST FORK

A HOPALONG CASSIDY NOVEL

CHAPTER 1

SIX-GUN SALVAGE

Hopalong Cassidy watched the old banker count the money with careful fingers. Fifteen thousand dollars was an amount to be handled with reverence and respect. As he watched the mounting stack of bills, Hopalong saw them less as the long green bills they were than as the cattle they represented—the cattle and the work. Into that stack of bills was going money that had grown from days of cold wind and rain, nights of thunder and lightning, of restless herds poised for stampede, of rivers and washes running brim full with roaring flood waters, of dust, blistering sun, and the roar of rustlers' guns.

Into that pile so flat and green went more than money. Into that pile went months of brutal labor, the brindle steer that had killed a horse under him down in Lonetree Canyon, and the old mossyhorn who had fouled Lanky's rope on a juniper, putting him three weeks in bed with a broken leg. And into that pile went the kid from Toyah, who had ridden up to join them so full of vitality and exuberance, only to have his horse step into a prairie-dog hole while running ahead of a stampede. They had buried what was left of the kid and sent his hat and gun to a brother in El Paso.

"There she is, Hoppy," the banker said at last. "Buck will be mighty glad to get shut of that debt, I know. He's a man who takes bein' in debt harder'n any man I can think of, an' he's sure scrimped an' cut corners to have that much in three years!"

"Yeah," Cassidy agreed, "Buck's right conscientious about most things. He don't like to get into debt in the first place, but you know how it was with Dick Jordan. When he fell heir to that ranch out West he sold his cattle an' remuda to Buck, knowin' if there was one man around he could trust to pay ever' last red cent it was Buck.

"Came at a good time too. Buck had been talkin' about more cattle, an' with the additional range he could use, it would be a positive shame not to have 'em. Otherwise, he never would have gone into debt."

"You takin' this money West yourself?" The banker's shrewd old eyes studied the silver head. "I know Buck can't afford to be away right now."

"Yeah, I'm takin' it West, an' glad of the chance. Old Dick was a friend of mine, too, an' I've heard a sight about that ranch o' his. Rightly, it belonged to his wife. It was part of an old Spanish grant, you know."

"Uh-huh. Helped draw up some o' the papers. Got a daughter now, I hear."

"Had her a long time. Shucks, she was fourteen or fifteen before they left here."

"Say"—the banker turned around in his chair—"who's goin' out there with you?"

I'm goin' alone. Mesquite's off somewhere, as usual, an' Buck can't spare two men. Anyway, it ain't a two-man job."

"Maybe. Things out thataway are pretty lively. Had a letter from a friend of mine out to McClellan. Had his bank held up about three weeks ago, killed his cashier, wounded a deputy sheriff, then lost the durned posse."

"Lost 'em?"

"Uh-huh, just plain lost 'em."

Hopalong slid off the desk and gathered up the money. "Well, Buck will be waitin' for me, so I'd better get into the leather an' ride to the ranch. But don't you worry about this money. I'll see it gets to Dick, as promised."

Tucking the packages of bills into his black shirt and drawing his belt tighter, he hitched his guns into an easier position on his dark-trousered hips and started for the door.

The banker arose from his chair and walked to the window where he could watch Cassidy cross the street. The same trim bowed legs, the broad, sloping shoulders, the lean waist and choppy walk of the horseman. His silver guns were worn by much handling, and his boots were cracked and dusty. Suddenly the banker found himself wishing he was younger and starting West with Hopalong on that ride.

As he started to turn from the window a movement caught his eye, and he hesitated. A man had stepped out from beside the bank and started slowly across the street in Hopalong's wake. If that man had been standing alongside the bank, he might have seen Hopalong take the money, for there was an office window near the desk. The banker frowned. His wife would be waiting supper, and if he got into the saloon he might not get out for hours. . . . Anyway, Hopalong could take care of himself. He always had.

Trouble followed Hopalong Cassidy like wolves follow a snow-driven herd, but few men were more fitted to cope with it than the silver-haired gunfighter. He should have told Hoppy to look up Monaghan, at the bank in McClellan. Well, he could write to him. Maybe Hoppy would have business over that way.

•   •   •

Dusk was softening the line of the buildings when Hopalong crossed the street to the saloon. A poker game was in session when he pushed through the batwing doors, but the players carefully avoided his eyes. They knew each other, and knew the game was fairly even all around. But Hopalong was a specialist at draw. His brand of poker was apt to be expensive for them, and they wanted none of that.

Three men lounged at the bar, all strangers. One of them, Hoppy remembered, had passed him on the step. His casual glance read their brands with a quick, easy eye, and he grinned to himself. Drifting punchers, maybe a shade on the owl-hoot side.

Trail dust lay thick on their clothes, but their guns had been wiped clean, and the cartridges in their belts shone brightly. One man—who had passed him on the walk before the saloon—was a slender young fellow with straight, clean-cut features and a deep line at one corner of his mouth. When he glanced toward Cassidy, Hopalong saw that one eye was half closed by a lowered lid. At first the man seemed to be winking, and then Hoppy realized the affliction was permanent.

The other two also had the look of hard cases. The tall man was round-shouldered and his face carried deep-set lines of cruelty and harshness. The third stranger was scarcely more than a boy, but one already far gone down the hard trails by the look of him.

Drifters were not uncommon, and the range life was not one calculated to make men soft. Such men as these came in and drifted on each morning and night, for Twin Rivers was on a trail much traveled in these months.

"Pullin' out tomorrow, Hoppy?" The bartender leaned his

arms on the bar. "Johnny was sayin' you were headed West to visit Dick Jordan."

At the name all three strangers turned sharply to stare at Hopalong. Their expressions excited his interest and also their apparent familiarity with the name of Dick Jordan. Only a familiar name could have turned them so sharply. They looked away, and the man with the squint eye spoke to the others in a low, careful voice, as though explaining something.

"Yeah," said Cassidy, "we bought his herd three years ago. Buck wants me to ride out there, and that country always did appeal to me. It will be good to get shut of this dust and fill my lungs with that good mountain air again."

"Dick bought hisself a good ranch, I hear."

"He didn't buy it. His wife was Spanish an' the ranch was part of an old land grant belonging to her family. She inherited it, so they just moved out there. They took their daughter with them. She was maybe fifteen years old. Nice kid, but all knees and freckles."

One of the strangers snickered, and Cassidy glanced at them appraisingly. Two of them avoided his eyes, but the one with the bad eyelid met his glance boldly. "Heerd what y' said about ridin' to see Dick Jordan," he commented dryly, "an' if I was you, I'd forget it. That there's a tough country for drifters. They don't cotton to 'em, not none a-tall!"

"That right?" Hopalong said carelessly. "Well, maybe I can help them get used to it."

The tall man answered him, and his eyes were hard as he looked at Cassidy. "You go out there huntin' him," he said insolently, "an' you're sure likely to find him! You're liable to go right where he is!" As he finished speaking he put down his glass and all three walked out of the saloon. On the walk outside one of them spoke, and then all laughed.

Cassidy glanced at the bartender. "Know those fellers?"

"Been around all afternoon," the bartender explained, "an' takin' in a lot of room. The squinty one, he's gettin' his horse shod. Then they're driftin' on, headin' West."

Hopalong accepted the information and turned it over in his mind. Suppose they knew he had the money? They might be honest cowhands just feeling their oats in a strange town, but all Hopalong's instincts told him they were more than that, and men to be reckoned with. Nor was he the man to underrate anyone. Considering the problem, he decided that if they were planning to rob him they would do it tonight, and probably right now. There was nothing to be gained by keeping them waiting. With a plan of the town in his mind, he did a few minutes of rapid thinking, then turned and waved good night to the bartender and stepped outside.

Opposite the saloon a man sat beside a saddled horse. As Hopalong stepped out, the man drew deep on his cigarette, and it glowed with sudden, sharp brightness. Cassidy noticed it with a wry curling at the corners of his mouth. A signal. Who did they think he was? A pilgrim? A soft tailed tenderfoot? He stepped down beside his horse and tightened the saddle girth, watching the man out of the corners of his eyes.

There were only three places men might wait where that cigarette signal could be seen. There was a narrow opening beyond the hardware store down the street. Farther along the entrance to the alley by the livery stable was another, and up the street by the sheriff's office was the third. Nobody but a fool would wait by the livery stable, for the other end of that alley was closed off by the horse corrals. The night was cool, and that puncher across the street could have been there for only one reason, to warn the others that Cassidy had come out. Necessarily, they would have to be ready no matter which way he turned, so one man must be up the street, the other down.

The spot by the hardware store and the alley by the sheriff's office would be the places. One man to stop him and two to close in. He grinned at the simplicity of it. Would the fellow stick a gun into him? Or merely ask for a light to give others time to come up?

Hopalong tightened the cinch, and then, as he put a foot in the stirrup, he suddenly seemed to remember something. He took down his foot, stepped up on the boardwalk, and went back into the saloon. Scarcely aware of the surprised glances, he walked swiftly through the room to the back, and turning, as if to enter the office, he went past it into a narrow passage from which a door opened at the back.

Careful not to allow his spurs to jingle, he walked swiftly toward the sheriff's office. When behind it, he looked up the narrow alleyway between the buildings and caught the dark outline of the man who was waiting there. A hard grin parted his lips, and he moved up behind the man. "Huntin' somebody?" he asked softly.

The squint-eyed man whirled swiftly, his hand dropping for his gun, and Hopalong struck with a work-hardened fist. It caught the man flush on the chin and his knees sagged, letting his jaw down to meet the lifting right. As though his legs had turned to limp rubber, the man slumped to the ground, and Hopalong stepped swiftly past him to the corner.

Across the street the cigarette smoker, having heard sounds of the brief scuffle, was on his feet, starting toward him. He stepped out past his horse. "Bizco?" he called softly. "What's up?"

Hopalong stepped easily into the street. "I am," he said.

It was the youngster of the lot, and the least experienced. Instead of brazening it out, he felt himself trapped, and his own guilty reaction betrayed him. His hand dropped for his gun.

The tall man down the street was already aware that something had gone wrong, and had stepped out from cover and started toward them. When he saw Hopalong Cassidy he knew that somehow their plan had miscarried, and like his younger friend, he grabbed for his six-shooter.

Neither man saw the blur of movement as Hopalong Cassidy drew. His guns came up, spouting flame even as theirs cleared leather, and his first shot was for the tall man, who he rightly deduced was the more dangerous of the two. The shot struck just above the glisten of the belt buckle and the second cut the edge of the first. In almost the same instant Hopalong's other gun had roared, and the younger man went to his knees. He tried a shot that tugged at Cassidy's sleeve. Then he spilled over in the dust, losing his grip on his pistol.

Wheeling, Hoppy jumped back into the alley by the sheriff's office, but all he heard was a sudden pounding of hoofs, so he stopped. Bizco, the squint-eyed one, was gone.

People were crowding doorways and some had ventured into the street. Two men were bent over the tall man in front of the hardware store. Watching narrowly, Hopalong crossed to Shorty. Dropping to his knees, he turned him on his back.

The man was dying. Gently Hoppy eased his position. Now that he was dying, Hopalong felt him no enmity. Nor did he feel much sorrow. A man bought cards in a game like this according to his own wish and accepted the consequences. Sometimes such men lasted for years, and sometimes they went quick and hard, like this one.

His eyes flashed open and he looked up at Hoppy. "Fast!" he gasped hoarsely. "You're too blamed fast!"

He breathed heavily, and Cassidy listened to the approaching feet.

"Sorry," the fellow said.

"What you after?" Cassidy asked.

"Money. Bizco seen y' draw money from the bank."

"What was all that about Dick Jordan? You know him?"

It took several attempts before the man's lips could form the words. "Did . . . did know him. Don't . . . don't y' go out . . . there. Wouldn't stand a chance! They . . . Soper an' Sparr . . . devils!"

"What about Jordan? Is he all right? His family with him?" Cassidy's voice hurried, for the man was dying fast.

If he understood the words he did not reply. The chances were that he never heard them at all, that already he was beyond hearing, beyond listening, beyond even thinking. The wheels in his brain were slowing down now, yet there was time for what he did remember. Hopalong saw his lips stir and fumble with the words, saw them in the vague light falling from the rectangle of a window. "Hadda laugh," his lips whispered. "All . . . knees . . . freckles!" The whisper trailed away and died with its owner.

Hopalong got to his feet and thumbed shells into his guns. "That other one dead?" he asked.

The bartender was one of the men who had been bending over Shorty when Cassidy had come over to him. He still wore his white apron, but he clutched a shotgun. "Answer me! Is the other one dead?"

"Yeah," someone spoke up, "he's dead. Right through the stomach! You could lay a half dollar over the two holes—at least where they went in."

"There was another feller!" the bartender said. "What happened to him?"

"He sloped. He'll carry a sore jaw along with the memory, though."

Cassidy walked back to his horse, Topper. He swung into the saddle and turned the white gelding down the trail toward the ranch. Buck Peters would have questions to ask and he would want to know all about it.

Confound the luck! Rose wouldn't want Buck to start off on any wild-goose chase, but the least smell of gun smoke and the old man began champing on the bit like a fire horse! Hopalong grinned as he pictured him. Buck's reactions were too slow now, but he would admit it to no one, least of all Hopalong.

Peters was at the table when Hopalong came in. Hopalong unbuttoned his shirt and placed the packets of money on the table, and Buck dabbed at his mouth with a red-checked napkin. "Sure took your time! I was beginnin' to get worried."

"What you got to worry about, you old mosshorn? Who does the work around here, anyway? You knew danged well I'd get this money an' bring it back, an' all you had to do was set here an' get fat waitin'. Rose feeds you too good, Buck. You're losin' your figger."

Buck's face fired up. "My figger's my own business!" He glared suspiciously at Hopalong. "What happened? I can smell trouble writ all over you!"

Dropping into a seat, Cassidy forked a slab of beef to his plate and accepted the hot coffee Rose poured for him. Then he told them briefly and quietly just what had happened. He left out nothing except the remarks on the subject of Dick Jordan. While Rose worried and Buck chafed at the bit and talked about outlaws, Hopalong's mind was already away from the table and far down the trail he was about to travel.

If anything had gone wrong, it would be a good thing that he was going out. Dick Jordan was a fine man, a big man, and hard-handed, but just, and noted always for hospitality. His ranch had been a favored stopping place, and no man had ever been turned from his door lacking food. Jordan himself had been a buffalo hunter turned trader. As a boy he had worked for a cattle buyer in the East, and finally he went back to that, but his great desire was to own a ranch. He soon had it, and the Circle J had always worked hand in glove with Peters's outfit in everything.

The dying outlaw had mentioned names. They came back to Hopalong's mind suddenly.

What were they again? Soper an' Sparr. Sparr!

Hopalong put his cup down so hard that some of the coffee slopped over into the saucer. Buck and Rose were staring at him. Sparr!

"What bit you?" Buck demanded, his eyes alert and shrewd. "You got an idear?"

"Me?" Hopalong demanded innocently. "About what?"

"You know what I mean," Buck growled irritably. "I mean this here holdup! This Jordan business! If I know you, you just had a thought—not that it wouldn't feel mighty strange under that silver thatch o' yourn."

Carefully Hopalong lifted his cup and then poured the spilled coffee from the saucer back into the cup. This gave him time to assemble his thoughts a little, and he tried to be casual about the question.

"Is Mesquite back yet?"

Buck's eyes brightened. "See?" he said to Rose. "I knowed it! He's got somethin' on his mind that smells of trouble! If he hadn't, he would never think of askin' about Mesquite at a time like this!"

Cassidy forked another slab of beef onto his plate and piled mashed potatoes around it. "The kid's a top hand in any crowd. Look at the way he worked through the roundup. And who is any better with a rough string than him? He's as good with bad horses as Johnny was. Maybe better!"

Buck stared at Hopalong. "He's good with a gun too. Mean

an' on the prod. I never in my life seen but one hombre as ready for trouble as he is!"

"Now who would that be?" Hopalong demanded innocently.

"You, you wall-eyed galoot! You always did hunt trouble! Most folks could ride through a town without anything happenin', but not you. You go into a place filled with old-maid schoolmarms an' right away trouble busts loose an' splashes all over every-body!"

"This here trip," Hopalong lied cheerfully, "looks like the quietest sort of ride. Dick Jordan may have trouble from time to time, but you know Dick. I'll take your money out there an' deliver it safe."

The thought that had come to him as he ate was far from a pleasant one. The name Sparr had at last struck a responsive chord in his brain. Of course there could be many Sparrs. Soper he had never heard of. But there was one Sparr of whom he knew, and none of what he knew was good.

Like Jordan himself, Avery Sparr had been a buffalo hunter. From buffalo hunting, he had graduated to town marshal of a tough Western town. Indiscriminate killings won him quick removal from that job and he had drifted West. From Ellsworth, to Abilene, to Dodge, to Ogallala, to Cimarron and Bloomfield, and in each one there had been gun battles or killings. A couple of the known ones had been outright murder, and there were some others of which the same had been suspected. His surly nature and ready guns earned him no friends and many enemies.

Then Sparr had dropped from sight. There had been rumors of him around mining camps in Nevada and Montana, and it was said he had fled Calgary after killing a mounted policeman there. If this was the Sparr the dying outlaw had mentioned, he was a ruthless killer.

Hopalong could not imagine such a man on Jordan's ranch.

Dick was not a man to be frightened of a six-gun reputation, nor were the hands he was accustomed to have around him. Probably he was stewing over nothing.

"Daylight will be the time," Hopalong said at last. "I aim to take it easy this trip and not put in any long rides. There will be some rough country to get over, and I want to make it all by daylight."

Buck Peters stared sourly at his friend. "Ain't sure but what I should saddle up an' ride along," he suggested tentatively, avoiding his wife's eyes. "That's a mighty long ride, Hoppy, and could be the Apaches are off the reservation again."

Cassidy chuckled. "What you think I need, a nursemaid? You stay back here an' run this show. I'll get this money to Dick, stay a few days to rest up, then be back here before you know I'm gone. I need a ride anyway. I'm goin' stale with settin' around."

He got up and stretched. "Thanks, Rose. I sure did enjoy that supper. Last home cookin' I'll be gettin' for some time, I expect."

He turned toward the door, then stopped. "Say, Buck, you got that last letter of Pam's around anywheres? I'd like a look at it."

Buck Peters's suspicions were not dead. He eyed Hopalong darkly. "Yeah," he said; "it's in my desk. I'll get it for you." He got up and lumbered into the office. "What you want that for? The town you want is Horse Springs. It's a stage stop an' cowtown."

"I know the town. I was there once. All I want to see is that letter. Seems to me I remember Pam sayin' somethin' about where to go if I came out there."

"Yeah," Buck admitted grudgingly, "there was something like that."

He found the letter at last, and handed it over. Hopalong had seen the letter but once before, and had been told all that was in it. Accordingly, when he glanced at it he had done just that—glanced. Now, with thoroughly aroused suspicions, he looked at it with new eyes. Instantly he felt his pulse jump.

He read the letter through slowly, and then returned to the part that referred to him.

This was of two paragraphs, and the writing was different, somehow, as though strained.

Remind Hopalong of the games he used to teach me. There was one especially that I used to like to play. I wish he would think of this as he reads my letter. Dad often refers to that situation in Dry Canyon when Hopalong joined him. It would be wonderful to see Hoppy again now, feeling like that.

Cassidy looked up at Buck's inquiring eyes. All his resolutions about keeping Buck from knowing went by the board, forgotten in his exasperation. "Buck, we're a couple o' fools! The day this letter came you mentioned it to me, and you said she reminded me of the Dry Canyon affair When I looked at this letter I was thinkin' about that gelding of mine, down sick with the colic, an' I never paid it no attention."

"What's wrong?" Buck demanded.

Slowly Hopalong read the passage aloud, and then he swore. "Don't you see? She mentions that business in Dry Canyon, an' says she wants to see me again, feelin' like that!"

Rose looked from one to the other. "Dry Canyon? What does that mean?"

"Mean?" Buck was genuinely worried now. "Why, four rustlers had Dick Jordan cornered down in Dry Canyon. He was helpless, an' they were aimin' to kill him. Then Hopalong showed up. They turned on him, an' Hoppy downed two of them an' the other two throwed up their hands."

"But what is that to worry about?" she protested. "It's in the past."

"Yeah, but she wants to see me again *like that*! I think they are in trouble, an' need help!"

"Why wouldn't she say so then?" Buck protested.

"Maybe somebody made her write the letter," Hopalong said, "but remember what she said about the games I used to teach her? Well, one of those games was a code game. We used to see what messages we could write by using the first letter of each word as the secret message. Now wait a minute."

He studied the letter with care, and then he said, "What did you make of this part?"

Buck stared at it. "That? Couldn't make sense. Figgered the kid had us mixed up with somebody else she knowed."

Hopalong scowled and read aloud.

"How ever, Long Pete Carroll of Mesa Escabrosa, head of PPY, never did come out. Better call Rod Edwards for us. Lew Brake was through a year ago. He left Pat, that mustang here, but finally came after him.

"Now take just the first letters. H-e-L-P C-o-M-E h-o-PPY.

"See?" Hopalong looked up. "Help, come Hoppy, she says. This next part doesn't make sense because she's tryin' to make the letter sound right. She's got the first two letters of 'better' underlined because she wants to use 'em both. Same thing with the next word. Figgerin' in the same way, what do you get? 'Be Careful.' Then later she says 'Help' again."

"Mighty lousy code!" Buck sniffed.

"Aw, it was just a kid's game I figgered out!" Hopalong protested. "Tried to make it easy for her. Never figgered she'd use it like this."

"When you leavin'?" Buck asked thoughtfully. "If they do need help, you better go mighty quick."

"At daybreak," Hopalong Cassidy said quietly; "an' you can wish me luck."

CHAPTER 2

"GAMBLERS DON'T GAMBLE"

On the third morning Hopalong abandoned the trail before reaching the banks of the San Isidro and walked Topper down to the stream through a maze of rocks. He had no definite reason in mind except the instinctive one of a man on a dangerous mission. He wished to leave no sign, no evidence of his passage. The main trail, while not well traveled, would be marked by more than one set of hoofprints, and his own would merge well enough with them.

To his right bulked the towering mass of Horseshoe Mesa, and off to the south were the rocky parapets of Johnson Mesa. Beyond the pass opening before him lay the wide plains through which flowed the unruly Canadian River.

While his horse drank, he dismounted and filled his canteen from a tiny trickle of water running down from among the rocks. This spring was undoubtedly known to the Apaches but he saw no evidence of anyone having been near it. He scowled thoughtfully. All morning he had been filled with uncertainty and foreboding, his eyes continually straying from the trail to study the country through which he rode.

Without any definite reason, Cassidy had the feeling that all was not well. It was not the utter and complete loneliness of the trail, for this was an empty country at best, nor was it the weather, for the air was warm and balmy, the desert still green and lovely and not yet faded by many summer suns. It was something else, some scarcely to be defined feeling in the air or in his bones.

Somewhere on the trail ahead of him was Bizco, yet it was not the outlaw who worried him. Rather, it was the Apaches. That the Indians were supposedly on their reservation made no difference, for a dozen times in the past they had returned to raiding. Of late there had been rumors heard even in Twin Rivers about the restlessness of the younger braves and their constant irritation with the treatment received from the Indian agents.

This was their country. All this range into which he was now riding had been an Apache stronghold, and no warriors ever lived more ready to fight for their land. More than once their war parties had defied the army, raided ranches, stolen horses, killed army personnel, and then vanished like gusts of wind into the desert.

By midafternoon, if all went well, he should be coming up to Clifton House, the best-known stopping place on the river. It was or had been a stage station for the Barlow & Sanderson line, and he would be sure to get information there as to the Indian outbreaks, if any, and with discrimination he might even learn something about Jordan and the Circle J.

If Avery Sparr was in the Mogollons or the Apache country west of the Canadian, somebody would know it at Clifton's. There had been a gold strike over there, and despite the fact that the discoverer had been killed by Indians, more prospectors and miners were coming into the country. There would be talk of this around the bar in Clifton's, and much might be learned. Finally, after studying the country around him with care, Hoppy mounted again and, fording the stream, turned his horse into the pass.

All was still. The sun was already high in the sky behind him, and its warmth was beginning to creep along his muscles and take away the chill of night. His hard blue eyes studied the pass as he rode, and they returned again and again to the trail. Unshod horses had been ridden here, too, and Hopalong had lived too long in the West to take the Apache lightly.

When the rock walls of the pass opened out again and he saw Chicorica Creek before him he breathed easier. The open country ahead, stretching far to the blue mountains beyond the Canadian, were the grama grass plains, and beyond them, out of sight from here, was Clifton House.

A shout startled him to alertness and he drew up. Then it came again, the long, ringing shout of a mule skinner, followed by the gunshot crack of a whip.

"Fool," Hopalong muttered. "Ain't sensible to shout like that in this here country."

He started the gelding again, knowing, although he could not see, that the unknown mule skinner was down in the bottom of the creek. And then, suddenly, the wagon was in view. It was a Conestoga with a patched canvas top and drawn by six spanking-fine mules. A man and a woman sat on the seat, while a boy of probably fourteen rode alongside on a rawboned buckskin.

As Cassidy approached, still partly concealed by the scattered rocks and brush at the mouth of the pass, he saw the skinner swing his mules wide to start up a steep cut in the bank of the creek. The boy on the horse preceded him, shouting back to the wagon and its driver. The mules went into the cut fast, and just as the wagon pulled over the lip of the bank, a shot rang out.

Hopalong saw the puff of smoke over some rocks, and in the same instant a half-dozen Apaches broke cover and started for the wagon on a dead run. The boy and his horse were down, but as his own rifle leaped from its scabbard, Cassidy saw the mule skinner whip up an old Sharps.

Then Hopalong's rifle came up. He sighted quickly, held his breath, and squeezed off his shot. The Winchester leaped in his hands, and the foremost Apache left his horse and hit the ground in a tawny, trail-dusted heap.

The mule skinner must have fired in the same instant, for a horse went sprawling. But more than the dropping of the man and horse, the Apaches were surprised by the sudden attack from their flank. Cassidy rode forward, drew up, and fired again, dropping his second Indian.

Snapping two more fast shots, he slammed his rifle home in the boot and went down the hill at a dead run. The Apaches broke for the rocks, and he raced after the first one, intercepting him just as they reached the rocks. With savage desperation the Indian lunged his horse straight at Hopalong and, knife in hand, leaped for him!

Cassidy had drawn his right-hand gun, and as the Indian lunged with the knife, he swung the heavy barrel. The wrist cracked and as the Indian fell, Hopalong's plunging horse went over him, drowning his shrill cry and hammering it into a choking moan.

Swinging his horse, Hopalong cantered back to the wagon. The driver was helping the boy from under his horse. "You shore showed up at the right time, mister!" the boy said. "That hoss had me pinned down. I was dead meat for certain!"

The driver of the wagon was a dark, sullen-appearing man whose face was now a sickly white. Reaction to fear had left him shaking. "Thanks, mister," he said, holding up a thin hand; "that was shore a help!"

The man's eyes were taking him in now, and Hopalong surmised in them a cool curiosity and some calculation. "You handle them guns right good," the man said. "You from around here?"

"Driftin'," Hopalong said. "Figured I'd see some o' the country west. Over toward the Mogollons."

The man's face stiffened, but he said carefully, "Good country to get shet of, an' you can take that friendly. I know this country. Been ranchin' over near McClellan for the past couple o' years. Just gettin' back from Colorado with my wife an' boy. But you stay away from those Mogollons unless you—"

His voice broke off sharply, and he touched his lips with a nervous tongue.

"Unless what?"

Cassidy was walking his horse alongside the man as they started for the wagon.

"Nothin'." The man avoided his eyes. "But thanks again. You probably kept us alive back yonder. Won't ferget it, neither." He looked up. "My name's Leeds. My brand's the Circle L, six mile out of McClellan. Look me up."

Hopalong was intrigued by the man's comments on the Mogollons. "Headin' for Clifton's. Might's well tag along, I guess. That's my spot for tonight."

"Good grub," Leeds said, committing himself to nothing.

Asking questions was the worst way to get information in this country, as Cassidy well knew. He was reticent himself, but most Westerners were inclined to be even more so. Especially in some neighborhoods where it paid to know nothing and say nothing. Yet in hopes of breaking down the man's resistance and of leading him into some admission or comment, Hopalong talked from time to time on cattle, range conditions, the nutritive value of grama grass, and the probable chance of water from deep wells.

It was the boy who finally interrupted him. "You got a fine

horse there," the boy said, "mighty fine! He shore don't size up like no mustang to me."

"He's not," Cassidy explained. "Hombre north of here has him a horse ranch. Good friend of mine. He gave me this horse for a favor I once done him. Topper is a cross between an Arab mare an' a big Irish stallion this friend of mine owns. He'll walk faster'n most horses trot."

"I'd like to get me a horse like that!" The boy was all admiration. "I seen him comin' down the hill, runnin' like the wind!" He looked up at Hoppy. "My name's Billy. What's yourn?"

At the question, Hopalong saw the driver turn his head slightly. His interest was obvious, although he knew the West well enough to ask no questions. "My name," Hopalong replied genially, "is Tuck. Most folks call me Ben."

They talked quietly until the wagon drew up before Clifton House. Hopalong had already taken in the situation. Four saddled horses stood at the hitch rail, and this was obviously a busy place. A wagon stood nearby with mules hitched to it, and several men loafed about. Their eyes went from Leeds to Cassidy and back again.

One of the men, a rawboned fellow in a torn shirt and dirty gray sombrero, walked over to speak to Leeds as the mule skinner swung down. The fellow had buck teeth and a tied-down gun.

A Mexican stable hand walked toward Cassidy. "Got any corn?" Hopalong inquired. "Give him a bait of it if you have. I'll be movin' on tomorrow."

"Si, señor." The Mexican also noticed the tied-down guns and the rifle, which Hopalong took from the scabbard.

Leeds and the man with buck teeth were watching him, and Cassidy ignored them as he went by and entered the long, low-raftered room of Clifton House. Two men stood at the bar and several were gathered about a table playing draw. Hopalong eyed the group with interest. Draw poker was his game, and this looked like a chance to sit in.

"See any Injuns?" The speaker was a big, dark-faced man who needed a shave.

"Uh-huh." Hopalong jerked his head toward the door. "Leeds an' me had a brush with 'em. Mebbe six or eight. Don't know for sure."

"Git any?"

"Four, mebbe five."

Leeds had come in with his companion.

"That was good shootin', Leeds," the big man said. "Didn't know you was that good."

"I ain't. Tuck got three of 'em. He's good with his guns. They'd of had us shore, me with that old single-shot Sharps. I got one, but they'd of been all over us afore I could git loaded up. The boy was down, pinned under his horse."

"Looks like you come along at the right time," the big man said. "Tuck, your name is? Mine's Sim Thatcher. I'm ranchin' west of here."

"You picked yourself a rough country, from all I hear," Cassidy said.

"Figurin' to stick around?" Thatcher asked. "If you're huntin' a ridin' job, drop around to the T Bar. I could use a good hand."

"Mebbe later." He grinned. "I ain't broke yet."

They all chuckled. "I'd be careful of that horse o' yours," Thatcher said. "This is a country where good horses disappear mighty fast."

The room was suddenly still. Leeds's companion straightened slowly and turned his head to stare at the big rancher. If Thatcher noticed the stare, he gave no evidence of it. His attention centered, Hopalong listened an instant, judging the silence.

Then he said, "Horse thieves? Where I come from they use a rope to stop that."

"What some of us aim to do here." Thatcher was talking, but not to Hopalong alone. He was talking to the room, and he had an attentive audience, even if they did not appear so.

"Somebody in this country?" Hopalong suggested casually. "Or is it somebody driftin' them to Mexico?"

"Both," Thatcher replied. He tucked his thumbs behind his belt and Hopalong noted that he wore one gun, belted too high. "Mostly right here in this country. I reckon those Texas range detectives for the Association could find plenty of missin' stock back in the mountain meadows. It's about time the ranchers got together an' put a stop to this rustlin' of stock. Hunt"—Cassidy saw one of the card players look up—"you with me on this?"

Hunt looked from Thatcher to the bartender. Then he swallowed. "I ain't lost no stock. Well," he added, as if agreeing to an understood fact, "not much, anyway."

Sim Thatcher stared at him, his face stiffening. "So that's the way it is? Well, there's plenty around that don't feel that way, and once the shootin' starts it'll be either with us or against us!"

A slim, cool eyed man with a thin black mustache looked up gravely and seriously. "You'd do better, Sim, to talk quietly to the men you speak of. If Sparr hears of this talk, he might not like it."

Thatcher stood his ground stubbornly. "I didn't accuse Sparr. I haven't accused anybody, but when the time comes, I'll name names."

"That wouldn't be Avery Sparr now, would it?" Hopalong asked casually. "Seems I've heard of an Avery Sparr."

"*Heard* of him?" It was the buck-toothed man. "He's the slickest, fastest gunman around this country! Or any other, if'n y' ask me! I'd say he'd make Hardin or any of them back water if it came to that!"

"What's he doin'? Ranchin'?" Hopalong asked casually. "Seems whenever I heard of him he was a town marshal with a careless gun, or backin' some gamblers."

"He's ranchin'," Sim Thatcher replied; "partners with a Montana man name of Jordan. This Jordan, he come out here an' shortly after, this Sparr hooked up with him."

Leeds turned toward the door. He seemed anxious to get out and away. Sim Thatcher stared at him and started to speak, but the door closed after Leeds and they heard his rapidly retreating footsteps on the hard-packed ground. Nobody spoke for an instant, and then Sim nodded after him. "He keeps some good stock around."

The buck-toothed man turned slowly. "Meanin'?" There was a menace in the question. "Leeds is a friend of mine."

The room was suddenly still again, and judging the two, Cassidy was suddenly worried for the big rancher. Yet it was not his place to interfere, nor would he.

It was the rancher himself who used judgment where Hopalong had expected none. "Why, nothin'," Thatcher said quietly. "I was thinkin' o' those mules he drove up. Mighty fine! Best mules I've seen this side o' Missouri!"

Coolly he ignored the gunman, his broad back turned to him.

After a minute the door closed, and Hopalong noted the man had left. Quietly he said, "That hombre's a friend of Leeds. Looks like he might be gun handy."

"He is." Thatcher's voice was dry. "That's Johnny Rebb. He's a gunslinger all right. He rides for Jordan's outfit."

"Johnny Rebb, is it? Where'd he get the name?"

Thatcher's chuckle was dry. "Like most of that crowd. Names come easy to them."

"How's the trail to Horse Springs?" he asked. "I'm ridin' that way."

" 'Bout like it has been." Thatcher measured him. "That job's open, friend." He nodded toward the guns. "Especially if you use those like I figure you do."

Hopalong shook his head. "Maybe later."

Sim Thatcher turned to go. "Well," he said quietly, "if you go to Horse Springs you better watch both your horse an' money."

Hopalong watched him go, then drifted across to the poker game. He was aware of the cool eyes of the gambler on his face, but he paid no attention. Cassidy's shrewd blue eyes watched the dealing of the cards. This gambler was smart, and he had clever fingers. He was winning, but very slightly, and he would emerge from this game some few dollars ahead. Too many would-be card sharks went all out for a big killing and either frightened off other suckers or got themselves shot.

This man would win and win again and again, not taking too much at any time, but always keeping ahead of the game. Such men often leave games with the other players not even aware the gambler was among the winners.

Finally he heard one of the players call the man Goff. Cassidy filed that bit of knowledge away and drifted down the hall and into the room he had taken for the night.

A quick inspection of the room showed him a crudely made bunk with a cowhide bottom. He would be using his own bedroll. There was one window that looked out toward the barn, and it was small, yet a man could get through it if need be. The door had a bolt on the inside, and he shot it home, then unbuckled his gun belts and placed them on the chair near his bed. He took one gun from the holster and put it down under the blankets, where it would lie alongside his leg. He had known of men being murdered in their beds because they could not lift a hand as far as their pillow.

He slipped off his boots and was ruefully studying a hole in the toe of his sock when there was a light tap at the door. He slid the remaining gun from its holster to his waistband and moved swiftly to the door. "Who is it?"

"Goff." The voice was low. "Figured we might have a talk."

Hopalong shot back the bolt and opened the door with his left hand. Goff stepped in. He glanced at the gun in Hopalong's waistband, then smiled. "This is a friendly visit."

"Sure it is," Cassidy agreed, "an' it'll stay friendly. You can sit on the foot of the bed."

Goff moved across and seated himself, crossing his legs. His trousers were carefully brushed, his boots polished like mirrors. He drew up one trouser leg lightly, then hung his hat over his knee. "Just meet Leeds during that Apache battle?"

"Uh-huh."

Goff had come on his own initiative, so he could do the talking. Hopalong waited.

"Nice country west of here—if you know the right people."

"Uh-huh. Most country is like that."

"From Texas?"

"From a lot of places. What's on your mind, Goff? You've opened, an' I called you. Now what have you got?"

Goff laughed. "Smart!" he said, smiling. "I like that. Men who don't tell all they know are few and far between."

"When I was a boy," Hopalong said quietly, "I used to hear that a fool's tongue was long enough to cut his throat."

"True." Goff hesitated, studying the end of his cheroot. He watched Hopalong; then he said, "I should know you, friend. I know most men who wear guns the way you do, but somehow I don't quite place you."

"Then maybe there's one you don't know."

"Probably there are many, although if anybody suggested

that, I'd not believe him. I've known most of them, Doc Holliday, Ben Thompson, Hickok, Hardin, the Earps—many more."

Goff frowned. "Thatcher offered you a job. Taking it?"

"You heard me tell him. I've still got money."

"He would pay well."

"Where one man," Hopalong said quietly, "will pay well for a gun handler, there's always somebody else who will pay well—or better."

Goff chuckled. "And you want the best price for your work?"

"Wouldn't you?"

"I would." Goff studied him carefully. "But sometimes a man doesn't take everything at face value. Sometimes a man wants to know what he's hiring. Four-flushers have been known to carry two guns, and carry them like you do."

Hopalong's eyes were frosty. "Meanin'?"

Goff suddenly felt chilled. His tongue touched his lips, and the nervous gesture angered him. This man was either dangerous as a poised rattler or he was making a good bluff of it. "Meaning nothing!" he said irritably. "Man, you should know a man can't buy something without knowing what he's getting. Can you produce?"

Hopalong Cassidy leaned forward slightly, his hands resting on his knees. His eyes at that moment were utterly cold and hard. "If a man says he can play a piano," he said quietly, "you got to have a piano handy to prove he's a liar. If a man says he's a bronc peeler, you got to get him in the saddle to find out if he can back up his brag, but if a man walks like a fighter an' carries guns like a fighter, then all you got to do to find out if he's a windbag is start somethin'."

The eyes of the two men held, and it was Goff's that wavered first. It infuriated him, but he was too much the gambler to show it. "You've got something there, my friend. Any man who says he's a fighter and is not, is a fool. He's asking for it." He hesitated, staring at his cheroot. "Are you suggesting that I try you?"

Hopalong's laugh was genuinely pleasant. "Why, no," he said, "because I don't figure you're the man who hires gunslingers. But if you, or anybody, wanted to find out for sure, that would be the way, wouldn't it? Call a man's bluff and see what he's holding. You're a poker player. You understand that."

Goff nodded, his mind leaping ahead. "Yes," he agreed, "I do. And something tells me that the man who calls you would find you holding a full house."

"Maybe. So what then?"

"Why, then," Goff spoke carefully, "I would say that if you want Sim Thatcher's money, hire out to him. If you want to talk to somebody who might pay more, ride on to Horse Springs and tell Mark, who tends bar in the Old Corral, that Goff sent you, and you're looking for work."

"Thanks." Hopalong stood up. "I may just do that."

"If you don't," Goff added as he reached the door, "you might like it better south or west. This country can be very unhealthy for unattached strangers."

"Or strangers who make the wrong attachments?" Hopalong suggested.

Goff smiled. "I see we understand each other." His eyes warmed somewhat. "It pays to learn the customs of a country before taking any permanent stand. The casualties are high for those who make mistakes, and you look like a man who might find the right attachments very profitable."

He opened the door. "If you stay in this part of the country," he added, "we might get together in a game of draw some night."

Hopalong nodded. "We might." His opaque blue eyes lifted. "Ever hear of Tex Ewalt?"

"Who?" Goff stiffened, his eyes suddenly sharp with attention. That he knew the name was obvious, and there were few gentlemen of the green cloth who did not, for Ewalt was one of the cleverest card handlers in the business. A man who knew every trick of the pasteboards ever invented, and a few he invented himself.

"Tex Ewalt," Hopalong said innocently. "I thought you might like to know—what I hadn't learned for myself, he taught me."

CHAPTER 3

HORSE SPRINGS

There are towns that are born hot from the ferment of hell, towns blasted into being on the edge of a cattle trail, the end of a railroad, or the site of a gold or silver strike. Not often do these towns last. They are like some evil plant startled into quick growth by the sin that spawns it, and dying when the price of the sin can no longer be paid. The West has known many such towns, and many a sun-blasted hillside preserves their foundations and ruined walls.

Some towns came to stay, to grow from raw adolescence and become adult, to lose the hard, stark lines of ruthless utility and grow green grass lawns, hedges, and tree-shaded dooryards. Before long old men sit on porches, rocking placidly and talking of the old days. And where once thundering hoofs roared down the dusty streets a child plays with a ball or a dog lies in the dust and sun, sleeping away the warm summer hours.

And there are other towns that are born neither to grow nor to die, but to linger on, fed from some sparse vein of humanity or interest or evil. Such a town was Horse Springs.

First, there had been the spring. A wagon broke down on the site and a man named Teilhet made some Indian whisky of spring water, two gallons of alcohol, a bar of soap, two plugs of tobacco, and an ounce of carbolic acid. It made a full barrel, and it went fast. With his profits he purchased odds and ends from passers-by that could be converted into what he sold as whisky. Sometimes the ingredients were one thing, sometimes another, but the quantity was unlimited and the liquor was potent. Moreover, it was all there was, so nobody complained.

Horse Springs acquired a second citizen who helped Teilhet at the bar, did odd jobs, and stole whatever he could lay his hands on from passing wagons. Surprised in his stealing, he ran to Teilhet for help, and the saloonkeeper, if such he could be called, killed the pursuer with a shotgun blast. The wagon, team, and contents he kept for himself. Johnson, the bedraggled handyman, dug the first grave in Horse Springs's Boot Hill and planted the teamster.

Time passed. The saloon grew to a stage station and fort. It resisted Apache attacks and harbored more rustlers and thieves. A claim or two was filed but came to nothing; the store Teilhet put in did good business with travelers and with the few ranchers beginning to come into the country. It outfitted prospectors, and on occasion provided the murderers who stalked the prospectors in the hills and murdered to recover the outfit. In short, Horse Springs was a place of evil. A place of treachery.

Yet it did grow. A few decent people came, as a few always will, and they stayed, avoiding the hangers-on around Teilhet's saloon. They worked at cultivating gardens, mule skinning, driving stage, or running a few cattle or sheep.

As Teilhet grew older he hired a drifter named Mark Connor to tend bar, and, if anything, Mark was even more evil than his boss, but Mark had learned early what Teilhet learned only at the last. He learned to be his own counsel, to listen much and talk little. Mark became the first agent in Horse Springs for Avery Sparr, whom he had known in Montana.

Horse Springs had grown to a population of a hundred and fifty persons of whom at least fifty were rustlers, thieves, murderers, and others treading the downward path that would end in a hangman's noose, legal or otherwise. Of this town Teilhet was the official king, but behind his back Mark Connor had grown into the power and the command, a fact generally understood but not mentioned. Also understood was the fact that Mark Connor himself took orders, and he took them from Avery Sparr, or from Soper.

Into this town men drifted, and some passed on; some remained. Most of those who remained were thieves or worse; some of them were honest cowhands who went to work on the few scattered ranches in the vicinity. Some were murdered on the trail after leaving town; some were killed in the town itself, although these were relatively few and they died in what, to all intents and purposes, were fair battles.

After a time the town acquired a routine for such matters as strangers with gun skill. Spotted at once, they were divided quickly into three kinds: the few who might be valuable to Sparr, the bluffers and brawlers, and the third element, the officers of the law.

But not even Mark Connor could make up his mind about Hopalong Cassidy.

Tuck, as he called himself, might be the first or the last. He was not the quarrelsome type, although he carried with him an air of wary readiness for trouble that was in itself warning enough.

On that sunny afternoon when first he walked into the Old Corral Saloon he wore a sun-faded red shirt, a battered hat, and worn jeans. His weather-beaten face revealed nothing; his blue eyes were opaque, hard, and casually aware.

Mark waited, his own white, still face unrevealing. He waited, but the newcomer revealed nothing, offered no comment. "Stayin'?" Mark asked finally.

"Mebbe. How's the grub?"

"The best." Mark Connor liked good food and allowed himself a little enthusiasm. "We got a *cook!*"

"Then mebbe I'll be around a while."

"Huntin' a job?"

"Mebbe. Not patic'lar." Hopalong's blue eyes strayed to meet Mark's black, cool glance. "You Mark?"

"Yeah."

"I'm Tuck. Hombre back at Clifton's mentioned you. Goff, his name was."

Mark permitted himself a nod. If Goff vouched for this man he must be all right, for Goff was careful. He was usually careful. It paid to avoid mistakes when you worked for Avery Sparr. "Known him long?"

"Don't know him at all. We talked a little."

The door opened and a man walked in. The back-bar mirror revealed Johnny Rebb. The buck-toothed gunman sauntered to the bar. "Howdy." He nodded to Cassidy. "Rye," he said.

Cassidy glanced at Mark. "Grub?"

The bartender pointed with the hand that held the bar towel. "Through there. It's beef an' beans, but best beans a man ever ate."

"Creosote fire?"

"Uh-huh." Mark's lips stirred in the shadow of a smile. This man knew good food. "You bet! He wouldn't bake 'em any other way."

Cassidy turned and walked through the wide door into what passed for a dining room. There were two potbellied stoves there, both glowing, for while evening was just drawing near, the altitude was a little more than seven thousand feet and the air quickly grew chill.

A dozen tables were in the room, and only one of them was occupied. The man at the table was wearing a gray tweed suit with a heavy gold watch chain across the dove-gray vest, immaculate boots, and a black flat-crowned hat. He was clean-shaven except for a small beard on his chin and a thread of black mustache. His black eyes lifted and glanced at Cassidy, then returned to his dinner.

After a few minutes a small, quick-moving girl came into the room. Hopalong gave her his order, then let his head turn as Johnny Rebb came in and sat down. If Rebb knew the man at the other table, he gave no sign of it.

Cassidy glanced over at Rebb. "This much of a cattle country?"

Rebb shrugged. "The best, if y' can keep peace with the Apaches."

"Any big outfits around?"

"A few. Mostly small stuff."

"What about this Circle J outfit?" Hopalong was aware that the man in the gray suit had looked up casually, indifferently, and was listening without appearing to. "Hear it's big. They run a lot of cows?"

"Some." Rebb did not appear anxious to talk.

"From what I hear," Cassidy continued, "this Dick Jordan is plumb salty. Don't expect the rustlers make much trouble for him."

The room was still for several minutes and then Johnny Rebb said with emphasis: "Rustlers don't make *any* trouble for the Circle J!"

There was more to that remark than appeared, and Hopalong turned it over in his mind. It could mean that Jordan was around and able to handle rustlers, as he had in the past, and it could also mean that the ranch was protected. The man in the tweed suit was interesting, and Hopalong wanted to know who he was.

Meanwhile, as he ate he studied the situation. The Circle J lay well to the south, and the sooner he rode down there and got in touch with Pamela or her father, the better he would feel. Yet it did not pay to ride blind in a country like this, and he knew the hours spent around Horse Springs would not be wasted.

Ignoring Rebb and the stranger in the tweed suit, he sat long over his coffee and did a lot of careful thinking. Then he went to the livery barn to see how his horse was being cared for. Here and there he made comments about the weather and did much listening. He knew how to fit facts together and how to make a complete picture of isolated bits of information. This he was doing now, and the final result was not reassuring.

He had no hope that he would remain long unknown. In the first place, Bizco would be somewhere around, and might even now be reporting to Avery Sparr that Hopalong Cassidy had started West with fifteen thousand dollars for Dick Jordan. Certainly, if he had not already done so, he soon would, and if not, they were sure to meet sooner or later if Bizco had continued on West.

The draw poker session was on when he returned to the saloon, but for once he had no desire to sit in. Johnny Rebb was loafing about, and Cassidy drifted toward him and dropped into a seat nearby. "Leeds go home?"

"Yeah." Rebb looked up, grinning slightly. "He shore was proud o' you. Said you saved his bacon—an' no mistake."

"Got him a good place?"

"Fair to middlin'. He does all right."

"What's McClellan like?"

"Cowtown. Some minin'. Used to be soldiers around."

"Money in town?"

Rebb shrugged. "Sometimes. One big mine over thataway. Big for this country, anyway, and when the ranches pay off, she's loaded."

"Bank held up over there, they tell me."

Rebb's eyes lifted. They were suddenly veiled. "Who tells you?"

"Hombre back down the line." Hopalong jerked his head over his shoulder in the direction of Texas. "Had a letter from there."

"Yeah, there was a holdup."

"Catch anybody?"

Rebb chuckled. "Why, they couldn't catch cold, not that outfit! An', again, maybe they didn't want to."

"Friendly sheriff?"

Rebb was uneasy. He did not like leading questions, but he thought he saw a kindred spirit in this stranger calling himself Tuck. "Not exactly, but he might be gun-shy."

Hopalong chuckled. "Towns with loaded banks shouldn't have gun-shy sheriffs."

"That bank," Hopalong suggested after a minute, "may have more trouble."

Johnny Rebb glanced up. "What d'you mean?"

Hopalong shrugged. "Can't tell. Some fellers might figure"— he hesitated, then let his eyes meet Rebb's—"that now'd be a good time to cash in a six-shooter over there. Right after the one holdup they'd not be lookin' for another."

Rebb scowled. It was a good idea. Was this stranger feeling him out? Who was he? He glanced up and caught Mark Connor's eye, and suddenly he did not feel so good. "Got to light a shuck," he said.

"See you." Hopalong let Rebb rise to his feet before he

spoke again. "Come around someday an' we'll talk about this again. Might be right interestin'."

Rebb hesitated, then shook his head. "I don't rightly figger you, amigo," he said quietly, "but in this country you better not get any ideas. Local folks take care of local business."

Cassidy let his blue eyes show their steel. "Meanin' you?" There was a hint of challenge in the tone of his voice that stiffened and angered Rebb.

"No," he said, "meanin' other folks, who don't take to buttin' in!"

Hopalong went to his room. Once inside he dropped on the bed and pulled off a boot. It dropped on the floor. After a few minutes he pulled off the other and let it fall. Then he took off his hat and leaned back on the bed. He did not go to sleep.

Miles to the south, at the Circle J, Avery Sparr sat on a cowhide-covered divan and stared at the man who was talking. He was a slim, dark-faced young man with one lowered eyelid.

"An' he's got that fifteen thousand on him! He's comin' right out here with it!"

Sparr was a tall, spare man with shoulders narrower than his hips, but rounded and bowed with muscle. He stared at Bizco with shrewd eyes. "An' he got the boys? Both of 'em?"

Bizco was nervous. "Yeah." He touched his dry lips with his tongue tip. "Jumped me from behind, then called the Kid. You know he was green. When he started the ball rollin' it took in the whole street."

"You get this hombre's name?"

Bizco nodded. "He's a two-bit cowpoke from out on some ranch near town."

"What was his name?" Sparr's voice showed his irritation.

"Hopalong Cassidy."

"Who?" Avery Sparr sat up straight. "Did you say *Hopalong Cassidy?"*

"Yeah." Bizco was surprised at the reaction. "You know him?"

Sparr snorted. "Know *him?* Why, he's one of that crazy Bar 20 outfit! The worst one o' the lot, an' poison with any kind of a gun! Sure, I know him! Know of him, anyway. I never had a run-in with him, although some friends of mine did. Those friends," he added, "are in Boot Hill."

Bizco stood silent, but mentally he was congratulating himself on escaping as easily as he had. If Cassidy's name drew that kind of reaction from Avery Sparr, then he, Bizco, had no business fooling with him. Bizco was a shrewd and cunning young man. It had been said that what he couldn't do with a running iron just simply couldn't be done. He knew how to use a cinch ring effectively, too, and had profited by the coming of wire to the plains country by using it also to make convenient designs for branding. A hot wire could burn a brand as well as an iron and could be twisted and shaped into any kind of a brand.

He was adept in his own way. He could read sign, too, and he knew a lot of unusual things about driving cattle by night. But he had no illusions about himself. Nor did he have any urge to die by a gun. He had long discovered that the difference between living and dying was a fast horse—and he made sure his horses were always fast.

Sparr got to his feet. Standing, he towered above Bizco. He was three inches over six feet and heavier than his lean, hard body indicated. Turning impatiently, he strode toward the door across the room.

He was a gray-eyed man with a haggard face, drawn cheeks,

and hard, prominent cheek and jawbones. His hair was brown, thin, and always clung tightly to his long skull. Without another thought for Bizco he opened the door, went through, and closed it behind him. Then, crossing the room beyond, he tapped on another door, from under which a thread of light showed.

A girl's apprehensive voice replied, "Who is it?"

"Sparr. Open up."

There was the sound of a bar being removed, and then the door opened and the girl stepped back.

The room was large and pleasantly furnished. A fire burned on the hearth, but the place was always heated by a potbellied stove. There were books and papers lying about but no sign of a weapon anywhere. The two occupants of the room were the girl and a huge old man, who sat in a chair with his legs wrapped in a blanket.

Dick Jordan was not old as men go, but in the past few months he had aged a dozen years. It had started with the frightening of his team and the plunge they took over a steep bank. He had been thrown free and had fallen among the jagged boulders down the hillside. His pelvis, both thighs, and a collarbone had been broken. The bones had been set, but during the period when he was slowly regaining strength, Avery Sparr had moved in and taken over.

Jordan was a mere shell of his former self. It had been a bitter thing when he realized the accident had left him a hopeless cripple, that he could do nothing to aid either his daughter or himself. Pamela was a slender, beautiful girl of eighteen, and there was no love in her eyes as she looked at Avery Sparr.

"What would Hopalong Cassidy be comin' here for?" Sparr demanded.

Jordan's old eyes fired. "Cassidy? Comin' here?" He grinned

suddenly. "Want to say good-bye now, Sparr? Or are you goin' to wait an' eat lead?"

"Don't be an old fool!" Sparr snapped. "He owe you any money?"

"Him? Lord, no! Buck Peters did, though," he added thoughtfully. "Could be he's bringin' that money from Buck."

Avery Sparr turned to Pamela. In her eyes he caught the glow of triumph. He stared at her suspiciously, his crafty mind studying the situation. He had allowed the girl to write from time to time, not wishing suspicion aroused until he had the ranch in his possession, for his own plans were deep and well laid. In his mind he reviewed the letters she had written, for he had read every one of them. There had been nothing suspicious. Yet he was no fool, and realized that Cassidy's visit might be more than mere chance.

"Don't put any hopes on his gettin' here," he warned them. "And don't make any fool moves. Nobody even approaches this here ranch without me knowin'. Why"—there was pride in the statement—"when a man gits within seventy mile of here in any direction, I know it. We'll know as soon as Hopalong shows up."

"Then he isn't here yet?" Pamela asked. At the first question she had decided at once that Hopalong was in the vicinity.

"Him?" Sparr shook his head, dropping into a chair. "No, he ain't around. That fool Bizco an' a couple of the boys saw him gettin' fifteen thousand dollars from the banker back there in his hometown. They figured to make an easy touch, not knowin' Cassidy."

"Bizco's dead?" Jordan said, grinning widely.

Sparr stared at him irritably. Jordan retained altogether too much spunk for a man in his position, a man crippled and helpless in the hands of outlaws who would strip him of everything. "No, he ain't dead," he replied carelessly, "but he's got him a sore jaw.

Only gettin' now so he can eat proper. The other two didn't make out so good."

Dick Jordan chuckled. "I'd like to see Cassidy an' that old crowd ride in here about now! Or just Hoppy an' Johnny Nelson! Why, the two of them alone would make this bunch eat dirt, an' mighty quick!"

Sparr snorted his contempt. "Don't be a fool! Cassidy never bucked a setup like this in his life. He does all right against two-bit horse thieves an' rustlers."

He got to his feet. "Jordan, I'll have some papers for you to sign come noon tomorrow. Better get your mind made up."

"I won't sign 'em!" Jordan said, but his tone lacked conviction.

Sparr shrugged. He had heard these protests before and knew how to handle them. "You'll sign 'em," he said confidently; "you'll sign anything away rather than have something happen to your girl."

"How do I know you'll play straight when everythin's gone?" Jordan protested. "I should stop now."

"You don't know." Sparr was casual. "You don't know at all. You do know that if you don't do as I say, I take Pamela myself or turn her over to the Gleasons. The longer you delay that happenin' the better chance you got."

He went out and closed the door behind him, and Pamela listened until she heard his footsteps cross the other room and the door close. Then she went swiftly to her father. "Daddy, I sent for Hoppy!"

Jordan stared. "You what? But how?"

"In that last letter. Remember how he used to teach me to read trail sign, and how we played games with codes? I used one of them!"

"But how do you know he even thought of readin' it

thataway?" Jordan said doubtfully. Hope was rising within him. One man against all of Sparr's outfit was not much, but Hopalong— Well, he had done many things that seemed impossible for one man.

"It was a chance, and I took it. But even if he didn't know, when he brings that money here he will guess something is wrong."

"If he gets here."

Dick Jordan was worried now. Secretly, it had been Cassidy who remained in his mind all through his struggle to stay alive and to delay as much as possible the seizure of his ranch by Sparr. Hopalong Cassidy had a penchant for wandering, Jordan knew. Also, the time was approaching when the money Buck owed him was due, and who more likely to bring it West than Hopalong himself? There was every chance that he would come, and he was shrewd. He saw much that other men missed. He would, Jordan was sure, immediately realize that all was not well on the Circle J.

Yet, why hope for the impossible? Hopalong was only a man, even if trail-wise and Indian-crafty. As much as Dick Jordan hated the man who had moved in on him when he was sick and helpless, he did not sell that man short. Avery Sparr had learned his lessons in a hard, fierce school. He coupled the shrewdness of a cunning lawyer with the utter ruthlessness of an Apache. On every hand Jordan saw evidences of his careful planning. And with him was the immaculate, intelligent, and attractive Soper, the man who fronted for Sparr in most of his contacts with outside people.

Soper inspired confidence and friendship wherever he went, and the steel-trap brain beneath the smooth, friendly surface was not at all evident to those who did business with him or knew him but slightly. The two made a combination that was difficult to touch, and where the loophole would be found Jordan could not guess.

Had he been on his feet and able when Sparr first began his plan to take over the vast holdings of the Circle J, much might have been avoided. Crippled, and in the shadows between life and death, he had been helpless.

Avery Sparr had come to the Circle J as a drifting rider, and, as all such, he was granted the hospitality of the ranch. He came to spend the night, asked to stay on for some hunting, then helped with the roundup. Hands were few and hard to get in this Apache-ridden country, so his help had been gratefully accepted.

Sparr's reputation was known to him, but the man was quiet and friendly without pushing himself forward. Then Charley Kitchen, Jordan's experienced and able foreman, was killed in a gun battle at Horse Springs. Nobody at the time thought to connect it with Sparr's presence, for the two had apparently no connection. Johnny Rebb and Bizco had been the killers, and how the fight started nobody knew, but Kitchen had been caught in a cross fire and killed instantly.

Three days afterward four of the oldest hands on the ranch had been ambushed, supposedly by Apaches. Avery Sparr's presence then had seemed a favorable thing, and he had stayed on, refusing wages, but doing a cowhand's work. Then had come Jordan's accident, and almost without realizing it, Jordan had transmitted orders to the men through Sparr.

While Jordan hovered between life and death, and while Pamela was worried sick and busy with nursing him, Avery Sparr had quietly taken over. On the flimsy basis that Jordan had given him orders for the crew, he declared himself foreman, stated that Jordan had made him foreman, and defied anyone to call him a liar. Among the crew of the Circle J were some hard hands, but the toughest of them had been killed in the ambush and none of those left dared challenge the truth of Sparr's statement.

At first he had been merely efficient. He had come to Pamela time and again to ask about her father and offer to help in any way. The distraught girl thought him only friendly until too late. Her first realization of what was happening came when she found that both Bizco and Johnny Rebb had been employed by Sparr. She ordered them fired, and Sparr protested. When she insisted, he agreed, and she had seen no more of them for several days. In those days three of the older men quit. They were paid off by Sparr and sent on their way. One of them talked loudly at Horse Springs and was found dead in an alley a few hours later.

Quiet hung over the ranch. Jordan was better, but he was now aware, for the first time, that he was to be crippled for the remainder of his life. Only then, weeks after Sparr's plan for controlling the ranch had been conceived, did Jordan become aware of what had happened. And he was helpless to do anything. He tried sending a message to the sheriff, and it never left the ranch. Pamela tried to go herself, and found the house guarded, and was not allowed to leave.

Prisoners in their own home, with a half-dozen more of Sparr's tough hands on the ranch, Avery Sparr came to them himself and in a quiet tone told them the situation.

He was in the saddle. If they did what he asked them and obeyed orders without question, they would live. If not, they could die. Alone, he hinted to Pamela that her help in his plan would insure her father's safety. To Jordan, Sparr promised protection for Pamela if he would agree to everything.

Yet Sparr was well aware that Jordan had powerful friends. At first he considered merely selling off the stock and taking the money, but the ranch tempted him, and he decided gradually to take over the whole place. But he wanted no investigation later. He wanted to give the whole procedure the appearance of legality so his future ownership could never be questioned.

He let word go out that Jordan was giving him a working

partnership and might later sell out to him. He kept reports of Jordan's poor health circulating in the right quarters, and holding off carefully, he wore Jordan down with threats, pressure, and bullying until the man was almost willing to agree, just to be free once more.

It was a lonely country with few white men about. All was serene and smiling on the surface at the Circle J. Few passers-by noticed anything unusual about the place. Dick Jordan was very ill and not seeing visitors. His daughter was nursing him and rarely left his side.

Avery Sparr walked back into the main room of the ranch house and seated himself. Cassidy would surely come by Clifton House, and Goff would spot him at once. Still, he had better get word to Goff.

Johnny Rebb drifted back to the ranch at noon and hung up his saddle. He was thinking of the man named Tuck. Sparr had some tough jobs planned, for Sparr wanted money. Rebb gathered that Sparr intended to buy the ranch, or a larger piece of it than he was said to have. He wanted to do this for a reason. Maybe this man Tuck would be a help.

Avery Sparr looked up when the buck-toothed gunman came into the room. "Boss," he said, "hombre sprung one on me t'day. I figger he was feelin' aroun' to suggest the two of us stick up the McClellan Bank. Tough-lookin' blister, packin' two guns."

Sparr shook his head. "We don't need any more men." An idea came to him, and he looked up sharply, his eyes pinpoints of steel. "What was his name? What did he look like?"

"His name was Tuck," he said. "Silver hair, blue eyes that git so cold you figger they'd bore right through you if you looked at him long, an'—"

Sparr was on his feet. "Did you say silver hair? A slope-shouldered hombre?" Sparr's eyes narrowed at Rebb's puzzled nod. Then he said swiftly, "Get Bizco, an' keep him out of sight, but let him git a look at this hombre! An' do it right now!"

"Sure, boss." Rebb shifted his hat in his fingers. "You figger he's the law?"

"Law?" Avery Sparr spun on his heel. "I only wished he was. I figger that hombre is *Hopalong Cassidy!*"

CHAPTER 4

HOPALONG GOES WHOLE HOG

The gelding was feeling the corn Hopalong had fed him and wanted to get out and go. With Horse Springs behind him before the first light began to gray the eastern rim of the mountains, Hopalong had taken a dim trail north, then cut over to the old Mangas Trail, and after a careful check to see if he was followed, he headed south until he reached the old stage road.

Careful study of that trail for several minutes of riding found an outcropping of sandstone in the middle of the trail, and Hopalong used this as a bridge to cross without leaving tracks. Once beyond the stage road he let Topper out to a fast trot and worked his way swiftly through the rocks and trees.

The ride to the Circle J was a long one, and he hoped to make it without discovery, yet he had an idea that Avery Sparr welcomed no visitors and had the trails carefully watched. The route across the wide plain south of Horse Springs would have been much easier and faster going, but Hopalong preferred the relative security of the mountainside, where his passage would be sheltered by the towering trees.

The morning air was clear and pleasant, and every breath was like a long swallow of fresh, cool mountain water. As he rode, there returned to his mind fragmentary bits of lore and casual comments about the country. Without maps or books of information, the western man became a skilled observer of detail, and his descriptions of people and places were extraordinary in their clarity and attention to particulars.

A cowhand from Texas might know the exact appearance of a town marshal in Montana, or of a rancher. A rider might see some twenty head of cattle during a morning's ride and remember each one in detail much later. Not only did such men without books develop remarkable powers of memory, but of description as well.

After a short rest at midmorning, Hopalong saddled up again and pushed on toward the south. Crossing the shoulder of a mountain that headed a deep, wide canyon, he looked down the canyon to see a thin plume of dust on the plain, some two thousand feet below and several miles off. Fishing his glasses from his saddlebag, Hopalong studied the figure with care. The rider was much too far away for any detail, or even to distinguish the color of his horse, but it was definitely a man, and he was headed south at a direction that, if unchanged, might intersect his own. In other words, there was every chance the rider was headed for the Circle J.

Had his own absence from town been noted? Was this rider heading for the ranch to apprise Sparr of the fact? Yet apparently nobody in Horse Springs had guessed the rider named Tuck was Hopalong Cassidy, so why would they go to such trouble? Nor could they know he was headed south. Cassidy started the gelding again and moved on under cover of a fine stand of ponderosa pine, but now he allowed his route to angle deliberately toward the east and the other rider. It would be a good idea to know just who was on the trail, and why.

From descriptions given him long ago by Jordan himself, he knew the trail to the Circle J, so a few hours later he was surprised to discover the rider he had observed earlier was not holding to the trail. Leaving it shortly after he must have passed Coyote Tanks, the strange rider was crossing the wide canyon north of Elk Mountain at an angle that would lead him right to the mountain itself, instead of following a trail east to Elk Peak.

Thoughtfully Hopalong studied the man, who was riding a horse with a nice swinging gait, from his position on the flank of a mountain north of the canyon. Then, riding farther east, he cut the rider's trail and swung down. The shoes of the horse were obviously new. It was a hoofprint he would remember, as a bank cashier might remember the signature of a depositor. He got back into the leather and headed south and slightly east. Sometime later he would investigate that rider and discover where he went. For the moment it could wait.

Elk Mountain, he recalled, formed a long wall that was the north line of the Circle J holdings. They were bounded on the south by the West Fork of the Gila and on the east by the Gila's main stream. The headquarters house lay in a forest park between the West and Middle Forks of the Gila, a position easy to defend from Apaches, and scenically beautiful.

He was on a wide flat north of Cooney Canyon when he glimpsed several steers and, riding closer, saw they were all Circle J stock. Yet scarcely a mile farther along he came upon a heifer, freshly branded with a Circle S!

S, for Sparr? Hopalong scowled thoughtfully. He rode east toward the main stream of the Gila and crossed the northeast corner of Black Mountain Mesa, then struck a well-traveled trail heading south. From time to time he checked the cattle he encountered, and soon the picture was growing plain. The older stock was all Circle J; the younger stuff was Circle S. Changing a J to an S would be no real problem, and apparently Sparr had figured on that, but for the time being he was simply branding all the new stock with his own brand. In that way he would have no altered brands to worry or be questioned about. It was simple, it was big, and it could be successful, given the situation that apparently existed.

Hopalong crossed the Beaver, leaving Circle J range behind. The day had been long and the travel rough, although Topper was a fast-walking horse and excellent on mountain trails. He made a quick and cold camp in a circle of boulders off Corduroy Canyon and, up at daylight, headed south once more. He had been riding for scarcely an hour when he spotted a horseman ahead. They were fairly close and Hopalong lifted a hand. The rider drew up and waited, his Winchester across his knees. The man was Sim Thatcher, the owner of the T Bar ranch, who had dared to express himself freely about horse thieves at the Clifton House.

"You got here, I see." Thatcher was level-eyed and careful. "Headin' south or huntin' a job?"

Hopalong chuckled. "I've still got that money, 'spite of Horse Springs. Looks a bit more private here," he said. "Mebbe we can talk a mite."

"Mebbe."

Thatcher reined his horse off the trail. His eyes were steady, and they missed no move of Hopalong's.

"Touchy folks in this country," Cassidy suggested. "You havin' much trouble with those rustlers an' hoss thieves?"

"Some."

"All since Sparr come into the country?"

Thatcher studied him coolly. "If you want me to call Sparr a hoss thief, you ain't goin' to have no luck," Thatcher said quietly. "If I ever feel like doin' that, it'll be to his face—with a gun in my hand."

Cassidy chuckled. "From what I hear that might be a good idea." His eyes scanned the peak of Black Mountain opposite them. "Ever have any trouble when Jordan was on the Circle J alone?"

"Not a bit!" Thatcher said positively. "Dick Jordan shaped up like a good neighbor. I liked him, an' I liked that foreman o' his, Charley Kitchen. Too bad he got killed."

"Kitchen dead?" If that was so, it explained much.

"Gun battle. He was killed down to Horse Springs. Got in a mixup with a squint-eyed rider named Bizco, and when the shootin' started it was mostly done by Johnny Rebb. That's a trick o' theirs, to start trouble an' have some hombre stationed to one side cut in."

"I'll remember that. So Kitchen is dead? Was that after Sparr came on the ranch?"

"Uh-huh, shortly after. The four of their boys, the oldest an' toughest hands on the ranch, got themselves ambushed down on the Little Turkey. Story was the 'Paches got 'em. It could be true."

"But you don't think it is?"

Thatcher shrugged. "I got my own ideas. I keep my own advice."

Hopalong nodded to himself. It all added up. But what about Dick Jordan? He framed the question.

"Jordan? He was hurt bad in an accident, crippled up, I hear. Nobody seen him or that purty daughter of his for a couple o' months."

Hopalong started his horse suddenly. "Let's move. I don't like settin' still too long. How far to your headquarters?"

"Mebbe five mile by trail. I'm back o' the Diamond." Thatcher studied Cassidy. "You seem to know this country."

Hopalong shrugged. "Rode through north o' here once, some time back. But I've heard about it. After Dick got the Circle J he told me about the ranch an' the lay o' the land."

"Then you know Dick Jordan?" Thatcher demanded sharply.

"I should smile!" He turned his head. "Time and again I've been workin' for his old neighbor Buck Peters. I'm Cassidy."

"*Hopalong* Cassidy?" Thatcher stared at him. "You don't say! Well, now. Come to look at you an' I should have knowed! I've heard stories about you, dozens o' them from Jordan an' that daughter o' his. They set a lot of store by you."

"That's why I'm here. Partly that. I figured they were in trouble."

Thatcher's face grew solemn. "Maybe. An' maybe makin' trouble for other folks. I never believed bad o' Dick until just recent, but takin' in that Avery Sparr was mighty bad."

"Know this hombre called Soper?"

"Arnie Soper? Sure do! Nice young feller. He never gives anybody trouble. Nice-lookin' too. Never packs a gun, but even on that hard-case outfit they leave him alone."

"What's he look like?"

The description was perfect for the man who had been in the dining room at Horse Springs. Cassidy nodded. "I've seen him." He scowled. Bizco had linked Soper and Sparr closely together, and so had the dying gunman. Who was right? The dying man had even implied that Soper was the more to be feared of the two, and such men do not fear lightly.

Suddenly a half-dozen riders cut down from the trees and reined in, facing Cassidy and Thatcher with the road barred. Sim Thatcher's face was dead white. Hopalong noted this from the corners of his eyes and surmised the riders were enemies. They were a tough-looking crowd, and his eyes slid from one to the other in swift appraisal.

"Howdy, Sim!" The speaker was a big, broad-chested man in a faded blue-checked shirt, his heavy jowls unshaven. "You don't look pleased t' meet us!"

"Should I be?" Thatcher's voice was cool. "I know you, Barker."

" 'Should I be?' he says!" Barker laughed. "An' he says he knows me! Well, now! Seems like a good time to git better acquainted, don't it? Thatcher"—Barker leaned forward—"you been told to mind your talk! You been warned before to keep your nose out o' business that ain't yourn! Now you git taught a lesson!"

"Howdy, Barker," Hopalong said quietly.

The big man glared at him suspiciously. "Who're you?" His little eyes gleamed. "A new hand, Thatcher?"

"Not of mine," Thatcher said quietly. "He's a drifter. He's not in this."

Hopalong felt a sudden warmth for the big rancher. Frightened the man obviously was, for they were badly outnumbered and outgunned, yet he still tried to keep Cassidy out of a fight that was not his.

"Well, he's along, so he might's well see it, unless he wants to buy in. Do you?"

Hopalong's opaque blue eyes shadowed a little and he kneed the gelding a step forward. "Buy in?" His voice was suddenly soft and deadly. "Sure! I want to buy in, Barker! I want not only a piece of it, I want all of it!" He pushed his horse forward.

Barker's face turned dark with angry blood. "You talk that way to me?" he demanded, astonished. "Mowry, get hold of this hombre."

A thin, hatchet-faced man started his horse forward. Hopalong's blue eyes flared. "Stay where you are!"

"Tough, ain't you?" Barker sneered. "Well, by the—" His hand dropped for his gun butt, and Hopalong's pistols sprang to his hands. Both guns thundered, and Barker's half-drawn pistol slipped back into the holster. Slowly, like a great, limp sack of meal, Barker slid from the saddle and hit the ground. Mowry stared at a bloody hand furrowed deep by Hopalong's second bullet. Mowry's pistol lay in the dust. The other men sat still, their faces shocked and astonished.

"You played hob, stranger!" Mowry stared at him, his eyes ugly with hatred. "You sure played hob!"

"You hombres are on T Bar range," Thatcher said suddenly. "Better start ridin'." His Winchester was in his hands, and his eyes were cold.

"You heard what the gentleman said," Hopalong added. "Pick up that buzzard meat an' light a shuck."

"You played hob!" Mowry repeated. "Wait'll Avery Sparr hears of this!"

Cassidy chuckled. "You tell him. Tell him quick. An' tell him that Hopalong Cassidy is comin' callin'—peaceful or otherwise, any way he wants it."

"Hey!" One of the riders whispered to Mowry. "That brand on the gelding. That's the brand I seen down to Silver City on that kid's hoss!"

CHAPTER 5

CHALK UP TWO FOR CASSIDY

Sim Thatcher stared after the retreating riders, astonishment mirrored on his face. "Man, you threw that gun mighty fast! Barker there was supposed to be a gunman!"

"Was he?"

Hopalong thrust the still-smoking pistol back into its holster, then thumbed a shell into the other gun. After which he withdrew the first pistol and reloaded it also. "Sparr keeps some gun-handy men around, don't he?"

"He does. An' you saved my life, Cassidy. That bunch aimed to kill me the way they've killed some others. If I had my bet, I'd say some of that bunch were those who ambushed those riders of Jordan's, an' Barker one of them."

Thatcher's face was grim with triumph. "That'll give them somethin' to think about! Nobody ever faced 'em successfully before. All the time they've been comin' it high an' mighty around town an' over the range, they've done about as they pleased. Been two or three killin's aroun', an' they plumb scared out most of the honest men. Each one is afraid if he bucks 'em he'll be next."

"Lost some stock?"

"Some, but only small stuff. This outfit's deeper than that. I don't know what they've got in mind, but it won't be little."

"Know anythin' about that bank robbery over to McClellan?"

Thatcher looked quickly at Hopalong. "Know anything? No, I don't, but I've done some thinking. Those hombres got away slick as a whistle, an' believe me they weren't just ordinary thieves! They had a plan, an' a mighty shrewd one!"

They rode on in silence until they came to the adobe ranch house of the T Bar. Diamond Creek flowed along a small canyon nearby, and there was little at the ranch but the rambling adobe house, the stables, bunkhouse, and corrals. However, they had been solidly constructed around a square and there was a huge log gate, carefully balanced, that closed off the central square from the outside.

The house was L-shaped, and with the bunkhouse it formed the end and two sides of the square, while the stables and corrals formed the opposite end. As the stables were also constructed of adobe and there were heavy plank troughs within the corrals, the place was admirably situated for defense against Apaches.

"Come on us three, four times," Thatcher said, as Hopalong washed his hands in a tin basin. "We drove 'em off each time. Lost a hand one time, though. He was caught outside. I been here ten years," he added, "an' don't aim to leave, short of they carry me. And I reckon what's left won't be worth the haul."

The dining room was long and low-raftered, warmed by a huge fireplace and a potbellied stove. "Need a fire up here, even in the summertime, usually. Nighttime she cools off."

A sturdy Mexican woman came in and began piling dishes on the table, and a few minutes later several hands trooped in and dropped to their seats. One and all, they merely glanced at Hopalong, then began eating. The food was good and wholesome. Hopalong had not realized how hungry he was, but the slab of steak he took was huge, and he returned for another helping when the platter went by him. The potatoes, beans, and rice were equally good.

When he pushed back from the table, Sim Thatcher chuckled at him. "Don't you be cashin' in so soon!" he said. "This here Mexican woman I got has learned one trick north of the border. She makes first-rate apple pie!"

Hopalong promptly slid his chair back to the table and filled his coffee cup. One of the hands looked up.

"Seen Barker t'day," the hand remarked. "He was sort of scoutin' the ranch. I reckoned he might be huntin' for you. All of us, we aimed to start out, when we seen you comin'."

"Hope you got a good look at him," Thatcher said, "if you aim to remember him. You won't see him no more."

If he had shouted for attention he would have received it no faster. Not even the arrival of the apple pie distracted their attention. They stared from Sim Thatcher to Hopalong Cassidy, then back at Sim. A big redheaded puncher with a huge Adam's apple was first to demand an explanation.

Coolly, ignoring their pleading eyes, Thatcher cut into the apple pie with his fork. It was all of two and a half inches thick, and juicy. Hopalong's mouth watered, and he went to work on his own. Each slab was a quarter of a pie. Few Western ranchers ever considered cutting a pie into more than four pieces.

Thatcher chewed quietly, then stirred his coffee and tasted it. The punchers stared at him sadly. Finally the redhead spoke again. "Aw right," he said, "I give in. What happened?"

"Barker," Thatcher said, smacking his lips over the pie, "had some words with us. My friend here declared himself in. Then Barker made a mistake."

Thatcher lifted his cup. He drank from it, then replaced it and picked up his fork. "Well, of all the half-baked storytellers!" Red yelled. "What *happened?*"

Thatcher chuckled. "I said Barker made a mistake. Well, he sure did. He reached for his gun." The rancher glanced ostentatiously at the clock. " 'Bout now they will be plantin' him in Circle J's Boot Hill."

They stared at him. "You mean—you beat him?"

"Not me," Thatcher said. "My friend here. He drilled our friend Barker right through the tobacco sack with one gun an' burned the gun out of Mowry's hand with the other. Then he sat there in his saddle an' let those other hombres ask themselves whether they wanted to gamble or not. None o' them did. About that time I had my rifle out, an' Hopalong here, he suggested they pick up their meat an' mosey."

"Hopalong?" The redhead leaned forward, staring at Cassidy. "Hopalong Cassidy, from the Bar 20 outfit?"

"Used to be Bar 20," Cassidy agreed. "Now I'm driftin'."

"Hope you stick around here awhile," the redhead said grimly; "there's a gent name of Sparr you should talk to."

"Give him time," Thatcher suggested. "He told Mowry to tell Sparr he was visitin' up that way soon, an' to roll the welcome mat out or come a-shootin', as he liked!"

"No!"

"Sure did."

Thatcher studied the remains of the pie that stood down the table and looked thoughtfully at his plate. Hopalong waited, and when Sim Thatcher drew back with a sigh, he promptly reached over and picked up his second piece. Thatcher grinned at him. "Couldn't eat any more if I had to! This ranch sure feeds good! If I was huntin' a job, I'd go to work here."

Hopalong grinned but said nothing. Then he turned to Red and the other hands. "Seen anything of that kid of Jordan's lately?

Pamela, her name is. Last time I saw her she was all knees an' freckles."

Red grinned. "That must have been a long time ago," he said. "Right now I'd say she's about the purtiest thing on two feet this side o' the Pecos! Pert an' purty, an' ever' inch of her woman, b'lieve me!"

"How's her right, Red?" Thatcher grinned, and the other punchers chuckled.

Red's face flamed, and he looked ruefully about, then at Hopalong. "Aw, don't listen to these fellers! Always hoorawin' a man!"

A tousle-headed puncher looked up and winked at Hopalong. "Red took her to a dance one time, an' outside the dance he tried to kiss her. Man, did she ever wallop him! He went around lopsided for three days!"

Thatcher glanced over at Hopalong as he lit his cigar. "You mean what you said? That you're goin' over to the Circle J?"

"Yeah. Maybe tomorrow."

"Want we should go with you?"

"Nope. I'll go alone. However," he added, "if you know a way to get fairly close without bein' seen it might help. Once I'm up close I don't mind."

A gray-haired puncher glanced up. "There's a couple of ways, both of 'em rough rides. As the crow flies it's maybe fourteen mile from here to headquarters on the J. The reg'lar route goes up the canyon o' the West Fork for maybe six mile above the hot springs. Then the trail runs north through the woods for nearly three mile an' turns west to the park where headquarters lies.

"But there's a trail t'other side of West Fork that goes up Little Crick an' crosses at the meetin' o' Whitewater Crick an' West Fork. Cabin right clost there. When you reach that cabin you are exactly six mile west o' headquarters. Stick to the breaks along the north side o' the fork an' you can git right clost."

"Ain't that where Pamela rides sometimes, Red?" Thatcher asked.

Red nodded. "Used to, an' I reckon she still does. They'd not be afraid o' her ridin' thataway, even if she'd leave her pa. West o' there lie the Mogollons an' Jerky Mountains, an' believe you me that's rough country."

"They don't come any worse, Hoppy," Thatcher assured him. "That country west of Jackson Mesa an' the Jerkys is mighty rough, an' she rises higher an' higher. There's a pass back in yonder called Turkeyfeather, but none of us have ever seen it or even know where it lies. Just trapper talk, maybe."

The older man shook his head. "There's a trail in there, Sim. I never crossed it, but I've talked to them as has. Snow Creek trail cuts down from the north an' almost peters out, but she goes on like a game trail until she crosses the Mogollons into the Silver Creek trail to Alma. If a feller wanted to right bad he might get through Turkeyfeather Pass an' hit that trail by holdin' north of Whitewater Baldy."

"Well," Thatcher said, "you won't have cause to head thataway. But if you can take that trail up Little Crick an' cut over to the cabin, I'd say you had a better-than-usual chance of gettin' to the Circle J headquarters without bein' seen until you're within a few hundred yards."

Hopalong nodded. Carefully he went over in his mind all he had heard. He had the retentive memory of a Western man, but he was taking no chances. Upon what he had just heard his life might well depend, and even more than his life, the lives of Pamela and her father. It was during just such discussions that Western men acquired most of their knowledge of a country, and with a meticulous knowledge of what they had heard and seen, their directions often became marvels of detail.

In this case the old cowhand had not gone into detail, but before the night was over Hopalong intended that he should. That country west of the Circle J headquarters interested him. He was one man and alone against Avery Sparr and his outfit of killers, and, skillful as he was, he had no intention of playing the fool. With luck he might get in touch with the Jordans, and if Dick was able to straddle a horse they might run for it into that maze of canyons and mesas west of the Circle J ranch house.

"Whatever you do," Thatcher said as Hopalong picked up his hat, "don't pull out before breakfast. That cook raises chickens. She's got real eggs!"

Awake with the first break of dawn, Hopalong put his hands behind his head and stretched to full length in the bunk. It was good to lie in bed for a while and not have to be up and moving. Lying in bed, he had discovered, was a good way of thinking, if a man didn't go back to sleep.

During his long talk with the old cowhand he had elicited minute details of that route and all he knew about it. The old man liked to talk, and Hoppy had learned that it paid to be a good listener. He listened and he learned. Moreover, he got a rough idea of how many hands there were on the ranch.

"There's maybe twenty, comin' an' goin'."

The old man looked shrewdly at Hopalong. "If you have to light out o' there fast, head due west. Those hombres will sure as shootin' split two ways. One bunch will head for the crossin' nigh that cabin I told you of, an' the others will ride due north of Jackson Mesa to the crossin' of the Middle Fork. That way they'll figger they got yuh cut off. Instead, you head due west past Lily Peak an' hole up back in the Jerkys. If they chase you into them mountains they are bigger fools than I figger." The old man had knocked out his pipe. "But watch out for 'Paches!"

Reaching for the edge of the blanket, Hopalong threw back the covers and swung his feet to the floor. He sat there scratching his ribs for a minute, then yawned, stretched, and reached for his socks. He dressed slowly, and was just drying his hands and face when he heard the triangle clanging for breakfast.

He buckled on his gun belts, checked the guns, and then followed the hands to breakfast. There would be food left, he knew. Grinning, he reflected that being an honored guest had its points—they always saved something for you.

By the time the sun had reached its highest, Hopalong Cassidy had not only the longest part of the day behind him, but sixteen miles as well. Today he was riding a buckskin that belonged to Thatcher, and while not the horse Topper was, it was nevertheless a fine animal and a horse that understood mountains.

Circle J headquarters could be no more than four miles north of him as the crow would fly, but between them lay the deep canyon of the West Fork, and he had half a mind to attempt a crossing and save time. On the other hand, he knew that some knowledge of the country west of him would be a help if he had to run for it, so he continued on along the prescribed route.

It was midafternoon by the time he reached the trail to the cabin, and for the first time he felt uneasy. He had been told that this route was known to the outlaws and occasionally used by them. It might be watched, and to ride down the trail would be foolhardy to say the least. Accordingly he pushed on and found a trail that led down from the rim into the canyon of a branch of the stream.

Turning north off the trail, he rode alongside the stream or even in the shallow, rushing water for almost two miles. Once, coming to a fall of several feet, he was sure that he would have to turn back.

Yet, surprisingly enough, it was the horse itself who found the way around the falls. Hopalong had reined in with the water rushing by the horse's legs, and evidently deciding to take the matter up itself, the buckskin turned right and picked its way carefully, now in, now out of the stream through a maze of rocks to the stream bed below the falls.

Suddenly the mouth of the canyon gaped before him, and from the west another stream flowed, coming in at precisely the point where Hopalong's stream and one from the northwest combined. He had emerged from his canyon slightly upstream from the crossing, and now he found a route out of the canyon, and rode up and stopped the buckskin under the trees.

Getting down, he carefully rubbed dry the horse's legs, for the water had been very cold. After rubbing warmth back into them, he tied the horse and walked down toward the cabin. At once he heard voices.

Dropping to his hands, he lowered himself to his stomach in the grass and edged closer behind the trunk of a tree. Past its roots Hopalong could see two men. One sat on the porch of the ramshackle old cabin; the other was astride a horse. It was he who was talking, and he had evidently just arrived.

"Yeah, Barker." There was a low murmur, and then the same man replied, "Yesterday afternoon. Said his name was Hopalong Cassidy."

"He alone?" the guard asked suspiciously.

"Seemed to be," the rider replied. "He was with Sim Thatcher, but Johnny says they met at Clifton's. Cassidy was alone then."

"Hope he stays alone," the guard grumbled. "I heard about

that outfit. You have trouble with one of 'em an' the first thing you know the country's full of 'em. Friend o' mine rode with a hoss thief that Hopalong had trouble with. That young partner of Hoppy's, Mesquite Jenkins, he tracked down the whole shootin' match. He killed Dutch Bill."

"Well, he sure didn't miss Barker! This Cassidy drilled him right through the heart. Had a tobacco sack in his shirt pocket and the bullet drilled right through it. They claim they found some tobacco where the bullet come out!"

"What happened to Mowry?"

"Him? He's snarlin' like a grizzly with a sore tooth! Hopalong shot his gun out of his hand and laid a furrow across the back of it that shore won't heal fast, b'lieve me! He's swearin' he'll kill Cassidy as soon as his hand's well."

"He better hunt him a hole."

"Maybe." The rider turned his horse. "Well, Sparr wanted me to ride over here an' check ever' so often. I'll head back."

"Stick around. I got a deck o' cards."

"Can't. Sparr's mighty restless these days himself. Might just ride out here, and you know what that would mean."

Hopalong lay in the grass and watched the rider walk his horse away. It was a nice-looking paint, sorrel and white. And he walked fast. The guard stood up to watch him go, then loafed down to the cliff over the river and stared at the crossing and over at the far side. Finally he turned and came back. Putting his rifle down, he began to fix supper.

Cassidy started to get up. Then a thought struck him, and he settled down in the grass well out of sight. He could wait. No use capturing the man before supper was ready. He would only have to get it himself. After a while he got up, hitched his guns into place, and keeping the corner of the cabin before him so he could not be seen from within, he strolled down there.

Inside, the guard was growling to himself, and Hopalong heard grease spattering. The man stepped to the door. Hopalong watched him walk off the porch to throw out some water. He stepped up on the porch as the man left it. When he turned, Hopalong was standing there with a gun in his hand.

The guard gulped and stared. "Say, what th—! Who are you?" he demanded.

"I'm Cassidy," Hopalong said quietly; "dropped in for supper. Fixed enough for two?"

The man stood there helplessly. He was a lanky man with his shirt sleeves rolled up to display a soiled red flannel undershirt. His legs were very bowed and he had a droopy mustache that seemed to droop more than ever now. "I—I reckon," he said hoarsely. "You be keerful o' that gun, mister. I ain't done nothin'."

"Then unbuckle that belt an' let her drop," Hopalong replied pleasantly. "I've no mind to kill another man unless you force it on me."

The man let his belt drop, and Hopalong ordered him to turn around, then walked up and appropriated the belt and gun. Stepping to the door, he grasped the rifle and shucked the shells from it. "All right," he said, "get the rest of it fixed, an' enough for me."

While the man cooked, Hopalong sat where he could keep an eye on both trails. The man noticed it finally. "No use to look," he said, gloomily. "Won't be nobody along."

"I hope not," Hopalong assured him. "I might have to shoot you so's you wouldn't interfere."

"Don't do it!" the man pleaded. "If'n anybody should come, an' I swear I don't know who or why they would, I'll set down on the floor an' keep shet. I ain't hungry for no lead, mister!"

They sat opposite each other and ate in silence. The man kept glancing up, and when each time he found Hopalong looking into his eyes from his own frosty blue ones, the older man became more uncomfortable. "I ain't tryin' nothin', Cassidy," he said. "I ain't no gun slick an' ain't huntin' no trouble."

Hopalong pushed back from the table. "Look, old-timer," he said sincerely, "if you got a horse, I'd say better throw a leg over him an' light out—south."

"Sparr would kill me!" the man pleaded, his face gray. He stared at Hopalong, his Adam's apple bobbing. "He'd kill me shore!"

"Sparr's goin' to be so busy aroun' home," Hopalong replied, "that he won't have time to chase you. Now you do like I say; unless"—he paused suddenly—"unless you want to do somethin' for me."

"What would that be?" The older man's eyes were cautious. Hopalong waited for a minute, thinking. It would do no harm, and if the message got through it might help. Rightly, he deduced that the guard was not too happy about his present situation and would be even less happy now he knew there was to be shooting—which Hopalong Cassidy's presence guaranteed.

"Ride to McClellan," he said, "and tell the banker that Hopalong Cassidy is on the Circle J and some changes are bein' made. Tell him he was recommended to me by Josh Ledbetter."

"You trust me to take that message?"

"Maybe." Hopalong let his cold blue eyes rest on the older man. "I'm givin' you a chance to get out. This Circle J is goin' to be red-laced hell in another day or so, an' men are goin' to die. You don't look like a bad sort, an' no reason why you should cash in for a thief like Avery Sparr."

The man swallowed, then rubbed his whiskered jaw. "All right," he said, "I'll do it. My hoss is right in the trees."

Hopalong waited while the man mounted, and watched him start. Then he got on his own horse and pushed back into the trees. It was late, and the riding had been hard. He found a secluded copse where he swung down from his horse and stripped off the saddle. In a few minutes he was bedded down and asleep.

With the first light he was up. Not chancing a fire, he ate nothing. Rolling up his bed, he strapped it behind his saddle and stamped his boots well onto his feet. He checked his guns and wiped them carefully. He was now within three miles of the ranch headquarters, and intended to be watching when the crew turned out for work.

This morning the buckskin started off with neck bowed and a step like a dancer. Hopalong warmed to the animal. "Cayuse," he said softly, "you got the stuff. Maybe I can buy you off Thatcher. A hoss that can take what I gave you yesterday and come back in fine fettle this mornin' is a cayuse worth havin'!"

Within sight of the Circle J he swung down and led the horse back into a dense clump of evergreens, where he left it. Then he walked to a low knoll covered with pine and lay down on the pine-needle-carpeted ground. It was frosty, as it was apt to be at this altitude, and despite having no breakfast, he felt fine. If all went well he would have a good breakfast down there. What he wanted now was to see Avery Sparr or Arnold Soper, and see them face to face.

The crew turned out, but slowly. He counted eight men in all, checking them by their dress. One, with a bandaged hand, would be Mowry. Recognizing the wolf in the lean gunman, Cassidy watched carefully where he went. Wounded or not, the man was dangerous. Nothing can be worse than a gun-slick tough whose reputation has been injured. For reputation among such men is not only a matter of pride, but a matter, often enough, of survival.

After a while the men mounted and rode off. Only Mowry and a tall man whom Hopalong had not seen before stayed behind in the bunkhouse. Cassidy watched them go, seeing nothing of either Soper or Sparr. And then, even as he watched, a gray horse cantered into the yard and Soper dismounted. This must be the horse and rider Hoppy had seen near Elk Ridge.

He looked up and spoke to somebody on the wide and deep porch that surrounded the house on three sides. "Yes, left late last night. Stopped in a line cabin on Beaver." Then in reply to a question: "No, I saw nobody on the trail."

Avery Sparr stepped down off the porch. Hopalong knew him at once because of his height. He was a hard customer, and Cassidy gave them both a careful study through his glasses, although he was close enough to have called to them. Sparr said something to Soper, and the man in the gray suit turned swiftly. "Killed Barker?" There was astonishment in his voice.

Hopalong got to his feet and walked back to his horse. He put the glasses in a saddle pocket, then swung into the saddle and walked his horse down off the knoll. The corner of the house was between him and the two men, and he could not be seen from the bunkhouse. He was within thirty feet of them before the sound of the walking horse made them look up. "Howdy, Sparr! Soper!" He gave them time to absorb it. "I'm Cassidy."

Neither man moved. Both stood shocked to immobility. His sudden appearance and his bold approach startled them and left them speechless. "Figgered I'd better come down an' see my old friend Jordan," he said quietly. "Heard you fellers were holin' up here."

He swung down, keeping the horse between himself and them, then walked around in front of it and dropped the bridle. He knew the buckskin would stand perfectly.

Avery Sparr's every instinct urged him to reach for his gun and kill this man, but his native shrewdness restrained him.

"Why, shore, Cassidy!" he said. "Heard the old man speak of you. You'll be sorry to hear he's mighty poorly, mighty poorly."

"Had a run-in with some o' your boys yesterday," Hopalong told him. "They braced me in the trail."

"Yeah, sorry that happened, Cassidy." Sparr was completely at ease now, for already he was scheming ahead, planning, working things out. "We've had a sight of trouble with rustlers, an' my boys are apt to get trigger happy when they see strangers on the range."

Both of them were ignoring the fact that it was Sim Thatcher who was originally braced, and that it had not taken place on Circle J range, but on Thatcher's own land.

"Dick inside? I'd like to see him."

"He'll be glad to see you too," Sparr said quietly; "but it can't be for a couple of hours. He never wakes much before ten, an' the doc wants him to get plenty of sleep."

His cold eyes met Hopalong's and they held for a minute. Then his frozen, hard face cracked in a smile.

"Had breakfast? We just et, an' cook's not cleaned up yet. Come on in."

Anson Mowry stood in the door of the bunkhouse staring in open-eyed disbelief. Hopalong Cassidy here! Being received as a guest! He started for the house, hopping mad, then slowed down. After all, his hand was in bad shape. It would be better to wait, to be careful.

Avery Sparr understood the situation, and with surprising ease he went up the steps first, followed by Soper. It was one of those cases when allowing a guest to come in last was definitely the most polite way. Hopalong grinned to himself, but behind the frosty blue eyes he was thinking fast.

The table was still a litter of dishes, and Sparr waved him to a place. Both men seated themselves, and Sparr called for coffee and breakfast for one. Hopalong looked up as the cook came in, then stopped, his mouth open. Standing in the door was one of the prettiest girls he had ever seen.

CHAPTER 6

BIZCO TAKES
LEAD MEDICINE

Ironically enough, the first thing Hopalong thought of when he saw Pamela Jordan was how Bizco had laughed when he described her as all knees and freckles. No wonder he had laughed, and no wonder the description of her had stuck even in the mind of a dying outlaw, for this girl was slim, trim, and lovely. She was eighteen, but a woman in every sense. Not beautiful, but pretty, and with a strength and lithe awareness the West gives to its women.

On her part she was even more astonished. She recognized him instantly, but somehow she had been expecting an older man. He was a man when she was still a child, yet girls come suddenly to womanhood; so suddenly, on occasion, that it leaves one gasping, and so it had been with her. Three years are not many in the life of a man, but the three years of a girl's life from fifteen to eighteen can mean much.

The man she saw was dressed no differently from any Western man except for the silver guns that she remembered so well. His face, already weather-beaten when she first knew him, was unchanged. If lines had deepened, she was not aware of it. Constant riding had trimmed him down, as it did all these men of the saddle. They rarely carried excess weight. There was visible within him some of that vitality which life against the wind and under the sun and rain builds in a man. He had resistance and strength, and in every move, every change of expression, there was the mark of the man he was.

His smile was quick. "Howdy, Pam! It's been a long time."

She had no idea what the situation was, and for an instant he was worried for fear some inadvertent or ill-considered remark might blow off a lid that Sparr had clamped on, and which Cassidy accepted as the best thing for the moment. A moment later and he knew he need not have worried. This girl had known her own trials, and she had grown with them.

"It's good to see you, Hoppy."

She came swiftly around the table to him and offered him both her hands. He took them and squeezed them gently, seeing the fear, doubt, puzzled worry, and hope that was in her eyes.

"Are—are you going to be around long?"

The question pleased him. It gave him a chance to make a reply he wanted to make. "Why, shore, Pam."

His eyes lifted to those of Avery Sparr.

"I'll be around until your dad is able to be up and around again, running things for himself."

Then he added, also for their information, "Sent word down to the bank at McClellan that I was comin' here. Had some news for your dad from Josh Ledbetter and Buck, but that can wait."

"All right. See you later." She turned swiftly away, and Sparr stopped her with his eyes. "When your dad wakes up, tell him I want to see him. I know Hopalong will want to see him, too, but he'd better be prepared for it. We don't," he said carefully, his eyes cold upon hers, "want him needlessly excited."

When she was gone, Hopalong started in on the food that had been placed before him, glad of the chance not to talk while he gave time to thinking this out. In the past few minutes he had acquired a new respect for Sparr. Whatever the man was planning here, he was not to be stampeded into hasty action that he might regret later. Hopalong had not missed the covert warning to Pamela and her father, and he could guess what Sparr might say when he had that brief talk with Dick Jordan before Hopalong entered.

The situation was in his favor, he knew that. Had Sparr planned to kill him, he would have gambled at once, so obviously there was some reason why he would not be hurried. Too old in the ways of men to be fooled, Hopalong knew that Avery Sparr was not the man to be afraid. He was confident of his own gun skill and had the battles behind him to warrant that confidence.

That he had kept his head this morning showed him to be a thinker as well as a man of action. It is not every man who can be faced with such a situation and not give rein to his first impulse. Avery Sparr knew the value of restraint, of calculation.

Soper was yet an unknown quantity, and of that Hopalong wanted to know more. Above all, he was curious. Why had Soper lied to Sparr? For he had lied. The man had come down the trail at the same time Hopalong had come, yet for two nights he had been somewhere. And he had not mentioned turning off the trail. What was it that lay against or in the north wall of the Elks that interested Soper? Where had he been on those two nights?

The man was unreadable. He was pleasant, and he knew how to make conversation, as he was doing now, talking smoothly and easily of range conditions, growing cattle in high altitudes, and the benefit of late rains on mountain grass. There was no false note in the man anywhere. A big, tough, hard-cased man, old in the ways of the West and of crime, a man cunning as a fox and vicious as a lobo wolf, a man who was definitely out for himself and after— what?

There was no sign of neglect on the ranch. Hopalong had noticed that from the time he crossed the river. The few cattle he had seen looked good, and the stables and corrals were all in good shape. Nothing loose lay around the ranch yard. It gave no evidence that Sparr was planning a quick cleanup and getaway. No, the big gunman planned to stay.

Hopalong sat back from his meal. "Good grub," he said, smiling a little. "This country seems to favor good cooks. Sim Thatcher has a good one."

"Couldn't say," Sparr said. "We aren't exactly neighborly. Been cattle missin', we've lost our share, too, an' some of the small outfits figger we're responsible. Nothin' to it."

"You say 'our'—you mean you're foreman here now?"

"No." Sparr put it to him bluntly: "Partner."

"Noticed a lot o' young stuff wearin' a Circle S. Your brand?"

"Yeah." Sparr felt irritation grow in him. "My brand."

"This partnership—any papers on file? Any notice given?"

"Should there be?" Sparr shrugged. "Plenty of time for that. I'm still in this fairly small. Sort of runnin' the show for Jordan."

"I see."

Hopalong reached for the pot then, and filled his coffee cup once more, taking his time. He would have a chance to talk to Jordan, but Sparr would be present. They would give him no chance to be alone with the man, and to insist would only be to precipitate trouble.

If he was correct and the whole ranch was what they wanted, they would be trying to give the thing an appearance of being legitimate. Therefore they would probably wait until he was off the ranch to attempt his death. Their excuse in that could lie with the killing of Barker. They would send Mowry against him, and someone else, probably the same double tactics that killed Charley Kitchen. Kitchen had been a friend of his. They had been over the trail to Dodge together, the first time for each.

Pamela came to the door. "Father will see you now."

Her eyes went from Sparr, who was rising, to Hopalong.

"He was glad to know you had come, but he wants to know whether all the boys are with you, or if they are following?"

The question brought Sparr up short, and Hopalong saw his face change color. Cassidy concealed his pleasure behind a casual expression. The question had been a neat one, and showed Dick —or Pamela—was thinking. "I reckon Mesquite an' Johnny are already here," he lied. "Only a couple of the others comin'."

"What's that for?" Sparr demanded, alert and puzzled.

"Huh?" Hopalong's expression of surprise was perfect. "You mean you are a partner an' Dick never told you about the young stuff we were buyin' from him for a drive? Deal made months ago," he added, "for six hundred head of two-year-old stuff, some yearlin's."

Avery Sparr was caught, and he knew it. Nothing had been said of this by anyone on the Circle J, yet it might be the truth. If it was not, he was fairly trapped by anything he might say. If it was true, and he had not been told, his status as a partner was questionable.

"Oh? Yeah."

He finally got the words out and pushed from the room, leaving Hopalong with Soper.

This was the man Hopalong wanted to know more about, but he was shrewd enough to leave the opening to Soper. Yet the man on the trail had been Soper. Of that he was positive.

"Odd," Soper suggested suddenly; "there is nothing in the ranch papers about any such deal."

Cassidy took a swallow of his coffee, then put the cup down. It was lukewarm. "Never made a paper deal in my life," he said quietly, "an' doubt if Dick ever made one with anybody he knew." He threw a quick glance at Soper. "Why does it interest you? Another partner, or what?"

Soper stiffened, for once at a loss, even if momentarily, at how to answer the question. Outside, he had allowed it to be known that while Sparr was becoming a partner, he was temporarily managing the ranch affairs for Jordan. However, he had a feeling that that would not go over so well with Hopalong Cassidy. "I've been helping," he said, "with ranch business. Avery and I are working together."

Hopalong grinned, lifting his cold eyes with grim amusement. "You are? Now I figgered mebbe that was so, but wasn't so sure. Of course ever' man has some things he keeps to himself."

Soper was suddenly alert. He sat up a little, taking a quick glance at the inner door. "What do you mean by that?" he demanded.

Hopalong rubbed out his cigarette and stood up. "Now that Elk Mountain country along the north line. I like that. Ever do much ridin' around up there, Mister Soper?"

Soper was enraged and at the same time he was worried. If something about this got to Sparr

"You are right, of course," he said carefully. "There are some things we don't talk about."

Cassidy walked to the door and opened it. "Guess they are about ready for me in there," he said.

"Wait!" Soper got hastily to his feet. "Avery will call you when he's ready."

"I'll go now," Hopalong replied quietly. "If the old man is awake an' ready enough to see Sparr, who he's known only a few months, he sure can see one of the oldest friends he's got!"

He stepped into the intermediate room and closed the door, but even as he did so Sparr came through the other one. His eyes went cold when he saw Hopalong, and for an instant they faced each other there across the narrow room. Hoppy told himself, *If he starts shootin', I got to move right or I'd shoot through that door!*

"Go on in," Sparr said. "I'll not bother you."

Surprised, Hopalong watched him go, and then he stepped through into the room beyond.

Anson Mowry was furious. Hurrying up to the house, he was in time to meet Soper coming out. "What goes on here?" Mowry demanded. "That gunslinger actin' like he belongs here!"

"Take it easy!" Soper said crisply. "Sparr knows what he's doing! And don't worry. You'll get your chance at him, and soon."

"That's all I want," Mowry said viciously, but with satisfaction. "Just give me a chance."

"Horse Springs," Soper mused; "that would be the place. We'll talk it over with Sparr. You, Johnny Rebb, and Bizco."

Mowry's face mottled. "I don't need help!"

"Yes, you do, Anson." Soper was calm. "I know this man. We will take no chances at all, do you hear? None at all! Once a gun is drawn on this man now, he must never get on his feet again. He must never talk again. The whole show hinges on him."

"All right," Mowry agreed grudgingly, "I'll stand by." His eyes glinted. "Cross fire, eh? Three-cornered?" He chuckled. "The livery stable, that would be the place. Maybe two witnesses, and Rebb an' Bizco could be in the shadows."

He walked away, thinking about it. He could claim to have killed Hopalong Cassidy then! That would make them sit up and take notice! Nobody would have to know about the others. Around here a few might know, but not elsewhere. The glory would be his. And, after all, Soper was right. Why take a chance?

For that matter, Bizco had his own score to settle with Hopalong. Too bad Bizco was in Horse Springs—they might start working out the details right away.

Bizco, in Horse Springs, was having his own troubles.

Those troubles stemmed from two dusty riders who had come to town from the west, riding in over the old stage road only a few hours before. Leaving their horses in the livery stable, they had shambled over to the Old Corral and proceeded to open a bottle of Mark's best bourbon. With a drink under their belts they had been looking over the hangers-on without much favor.

One of these young men, frozen-faced and cold-eyed, heard a voice on his left, and he turned to see a lean, hangdog man standing there.

"Them your hosses out front? Them with the Double Y brand?"

"Yeah," Mesquite Jenkins said, "they are."

"Feller from your outfit shore saved my bacon a while back. He come in hell a-shootin' just in time to drive off some 'Paches. He was ridin' a big white gelding."

"You don't say!" Johnny Nelson leaned on the bar to look past Mesquite. "Where was this?"

"At Clifton's, on the Canadian. He was ridin' West."

Mark Connor was polishing a glass, but suddenly he was all ears. This was the man who called himself Tuck, the man Bizco wanted a look at.

"He say where he was goin'?" Johnny asked.

Leeds hesitated. Uncomfortably he had the feeling he was talking too much, but of late he had been chafing under the orders from Sparr. At first, hard-pressed by poverty, it had seemed harmless enough to allow a few horses corral space at his ranch every now and again. Even after the robbery of the bank at McClellan it had not been too bad. But horses had disappeared, and people had seen things, and now few of his neighbors spoke when they met him on the street. A man couldn't live without neighbors. Leeds made up his mind.

"He said he was goin' to Dick Jordan's. Jordan's got the Circle J, south of here."

"Jordan?" Mesquite scowled. "You know him, Johnny?"

"Sure do! Used to run the same brand back in Texas. Knowed him there an' Montana too. Plumb forgot about him bein' down this way, but now I remember. His wife was Spanish. She got a big ranch down here through some land-grant inheritance."

"Old Hoppy! Won't he be surprised when we barge in on him?"

Mark Connor stiffened. Hoppy? Hopalong Cassidy? He cursed himself for a fool. Of course! No wonder Bizco was waiting for a look at him! The story of Bizco's run-in with Hopalong had already gone the rounds of the gang. Even as he thought of that, the squint-eyed gunman came in. With several drinks under his belt he was mean and spoiling for a fight. Nor had he missed the Double Y horses.

Connor was thinking swiftly, and he could see old man Teilhet's eyes on the two. Those old eyes were sharp with awareness. Connor started back toward him, and when he got close the old man hissed, "Get Bizco out o' here! He's spilin' for a fight with them two! They'll kill him sure as cactus has stickers! Them two are Mesquite Jenkins an' Johnny Nelson, o' the old Bar 20 outfit!"

Jenkins had never known the Bar 20, but in Teilhet's mind all of that bunch were associated with the earlier brand. He had just occasion for recalling an earlier visit by Hopalong Cassidy.

Mark moved back up the bar, trying to catch Bizco's eyes, but with the intentness only a drinking man can muster, Bizco had eyes only for the two Double Y hands and the memory of his slugging by Hopalong Cassidy.

Yet he was not drunk enough to be altogether a fool, only drunk enough to be bolder than usual. While he preferred the fast horse to the smoking gun, he had some pride in his own prowess and knew that he was better than most hands who drifted along the trail. For these two he had nothing but contempt, and he chose the younger of the two, Mesquite Jenkins, for his challenge.

He chose him because he was younger, and so believed to be less experienced. None of these thoughts came consciously to his mind, but nevertheless they had a part in his decision. Actually, he could not have chosen worse.

Aside from Hopalong himself there probably did not exist in that time and country two men more deadly with six-guns than these two. If anything, Johnny Nelson, being less easy to prod, might have been the lesser of two evils.

Mesquite Jenkins was a young man with few qualities of mercy, and those few he had been learning only recently, from Hopalong, Johnny, Buck, and others of the outfit. He had grown up with the idea that the world had a grudge against him and every man who moved near him had a chip on his shoulder; accordingly he had acquired his own chip. It functioned easily and often.

"Bizco!"

Mark spoke sharply, and ordinarily that would have drawn the squint-eyed gunman's instant obedience, for it was well known that Connor was the right hand of Avery Sparr. But at the moment

Bizco could think of nothing but that Double Y brand and the fact that he wanted to get even. If he noticed Connor at all, he paid no attention.

"Double Y," he said aloud. "I been huntin' a man from that brand."

The eyes of both Jenkins and Nelson turned toward his. Bizco stared at Mesquite. "I said I was huntin' a Double Y hand."

Mesquite's eyes were cold. With that quick, all-seeing glance that read the brand of a man on sight, Mesquite pegged this one. He saw before him a young man of even, clean-cut features and one slightly squinted eye. That the man had been drinking he also recognized, but he was far from drunk. What he saw that was more to the immediate point was that the squint-eyed man was mean and in a quarrelsome mood.

Mark started to speak again, but something in the poised awareness of Mesquite Jenkins stopped him. "All right," Mesquite said, "you are huntin' a Double Y hand. What then?"

Bizco stared at the young cowhand facing him, unaware of the deadly potential destruction that lay in those cold eyes and quiet hands. Bizco rarely drank much, but when he did, he became utterly vicious, as he was now.

"Why," he sneered, "I'm huntin' a Double Y hand. I'm on the trail of a Double Y hand called Cassidy."

"He'd be glad to know that," Jenkins replied. He took an easy step forward, and Mark Connor shifted his feet uneasily, fascinated by the cold death he read in those eyes. "Mebbe I'd do as well?"

Johnny Nelson moved easily, merely fading from the scene to a spot well to one side, but one from which he could command the room. "Looks like your friend is on the prod," he said quietly but clearly. "Let's all leave 'em alone, huh?" Gently phrased though it was, the hint was plain enough. Bizco ignored it, his only interest being Jenkins.

"Maybe you would!" Bizco hooked his thumbs in his belt. "Maybe you would at that! Your amigo Cassidy dry-gulched a couple of friends of mine."

"Hoppy never dry-gulched anybody." Mesquite's voice was cold and level. "If he killed some friends o' yours, they had it comin'." Mesquite took a step nearer. "Furthermore," he added, "you are a liar, an' you know you're a liar!"

Bizco had been standing wide-legged and mean, awaiting that word. He had known it was coming, and had been ready for it, and with a sudden laugh of triumph his hand dropped for his gun.

Afterward there were those who said that Bizco died twice. The first time from astonishment, the second time from Mesquite's bullet. The astonishment because with his eyes riveted on Mesquite, his hand swept back for the gun, grasped the butt and started to lift, all in the flickering space of a split second, only to find himself looking into the black muzzle of a Colt that had materialized in Mesquite's hand as if by magic.

The black muzzle winked and stabbed flame, and Bizco's nerveless fingers relaxed and his gun slid back into the leather. Slowly his knees buckled and he sagged, then pitched over on his face.

For an instant, with the sound dying in the room and the acrid smell of powder smoke drifting where it had drifted so many times before, nobody spoke. And then Johnny said evenly, "Anythin' about this that anybody don't like?"

The two young men faced the room, Mesquite still with his drawn Colt, Johnny with his hands on his hips. Slowly their eyes searched from face to face, waiting.

"Fair shooting," one man said finally, "if I ever seen one."

"He ast for it."

Jenkins slid his Colt back into the holster and turned back to the bar, ignoring the dead man. "Now tell me," he said to Mark Connor, "what was he on the prod about?"

Mark Connor shrugged. "He had some trouble with Cassidy back up the line. Hopalong downed two of his partners an' slugged him on the jaw. From what I hear," he added, honestly enough, "they tried to jump him about somethin' an' tackled more than they could handle."

"Seen Hoppy around?" Johnny asked.

Mark hesitated. He knew now that Hopalong Cassidy was the man who had called himself Tuck, and he was quite sure that he had started for the Jordan ranch, but he also knew that one gun-handy man could be plenty of trouble, even for Sparr, without three on his hands.

"I don't know Cassidy," he said, "by sight. Lots of fellers drift in an' out."

The two took another drink while a couple of husky town loafers removed the body of Bizco. Then, as they were turning to leave, the door opened and Red walked in. With him was another T Bar hand, and both of them pushed up to the bar. Red was bursting with the news.

"Well, Mark," he said, grinning with grim pleasure, "you won't see Barker no more!"

Instinctively Mark Connor guessed what was coming. He looked up, waiting. Mesquite and Johnny halted as they reached the door and turned to listen. "That feller Cassidy," he said. "Barker jumped the boss an' him out on the trail. Cassidy killed Barker an' shot the gun out of Mowry's hand! Man, is that hombre fast!"

"Where's Cassidy now?" Teilhet asked worriedly.

"Him?" Red chuckled. "Why, he's gone callin'! He took off

for the Circle J to pay a visit to the Jordans. Figgered on havin' a talk with Avery Sparr too. Reckon," he said with satisfaction, "things'll be different around here from now on."

Jenkins stepped out on the porch, and Johnny, with one swift backward glance to make sure nobody was going to gamble on a back shot, followed. Outside, both men hastily got away from the light, then paused in the shadows. "Hopalong's havin' trouble," Mesquite suggested, "an' I reckon we better drift down that way, Johnny, an' lend a hand."

"Why, sure!" Johnny looked down the narrow street in which the only lights showed from the saloons. "At least we can count the bodies!"

Yet his face was grave, and he remembered again the other towns where men of the old outfit had ridden together, and the troubles they had faced together, and the lead they had spent.

A man stepped from the shadows by the livery barn and stood there waiting for them. "Double Y," he said.

They stopped, a little apart. "Yeah?" Mesquite replied.

"I'm Leeds. Want to talk, but it's got to be fast. They catch me talkin' to you hombres an' they'd kill me quick."

"Who are 'they'? An' why would they kill you?"

They moved toward him, and he drew back against the wall of the stable.

"Sparr's outfit. He's got spies all over the country. That bartender, Mark. He's one o' them. That hombre you killed, he was a Sparr gunman. Fact is"—he hesitated—"I done some work for him m'self."

"What d'you want to tell us?" Johnny asked. "An' why?"

"That Cassidy feller. He done saved us all, my wife an' boy an' me. Them 'Paches would have had us in another minute at best."

He hesitated, craning his neck to look up and down the street. "Cassidy's gone to the Circle J," he said, "an' that outfit won't never let him off alive. Not unless they figger to kill him some place else. They don't dast."

"What are they doin' down there?" Nelson wanted to know.

"Don't know exactly, but I figger they are out to steal that ranch from Jordan. He's all crippled up, can't walk nohow, an' he ain't got a gun. I know that much. Heerd talk around amongst them. I do know all the young stock is bein' branded with Sparr's brand, an' he seems to be gradually takin' over.

"Him an' Soper, they have give out that Sparr has a workin' partnership, give to him because Jordan was laid up. Don't you believe it! No man in his right mind would take that lobo into the same house with him, let alone in partnership! Folks are gettin' used to seein' Soper an' Sparr around, so purty quick, when Jordan sort of dies, then they'll be in the saddle. Somehow they figger to get legal title. How, I dunno."

"You must have more reason than because Hoppy helped you for tellin' us this," Nelson interposed.

Leeds spat. "Durned right I have! I'm a poor man, y'see, an' mighty little money comes my way. I'm tryin' to git organized on my place, but it takes aplenty. Well, one o' them Sparr riders come down, the one you killed t'night, in fact. He suggested that my corral would hold a few horses mighty easy, an' that he wanted to leave some overnight. He suggested there might be a little money in it if I kept them, an' a heap of trouble if I didn't. I kept 'em.

"It got worse an' worse. They got to tellin' me where to go an' when, an' my neighbors got suspicious. A man needs good neighbors, an' I seen I was doin' wrong but couldn't get out. If I tell yuh this, mebbe Avery Sparr will git his come-uppance an' I'll be let alone."

After the man was gone, the two waited a minute or two. "That settles it!" Johnny said. "We'll start come mornin'."

"I'm not tired," Mesquite said quietly. "Let's camp on the trail."

CHAPTER 7

CROSS FIRE ON THE CIRCLE J

Hopalong Cassidy had played poker with Dick Jordan, and there are few better ways of gauging a man—if one is a good poker player. As he stepped through the door, Hopalong's eyes went at once to Jordan's face, knowing he would read the answer or some of it there. That Avery Sparr would not have allowed him to enter alone if he expected Hopalong to be told anything was clear enough. Moreover, it showed that Sparr was confident, quite confident of his power here, and his ability to force upon the Jordans obedience to his commands—if the situation was as Hopalong believed.

Dick Jordan looked up, and his hard old eyes glinted. "Howdy, Hoppy! How's Buck an' the boys?"

"Fine, old-timer! You look mighty good yourself."

Hopalong had never lied with more enthusiasm. In truth, Dick Jordan was only a whisper of his once jovial, bearlike self. His huge frame was much depleted, wasted away to a great shell of bones and hide. His cheeks were sunken, and from his eyes Hopalong knew that no physical inaction, the accident, or any other physical cause had done this. For the first time in his life Jordan was helpless.

Hopalong made conversation easily, and in a few casual glances assayed the room. It contained no weapons nor anything that might be used as a weapon. There was no way out except through the door, for the windows here were high above the ground. It would be impossible to get in or out of this room save through the door by which he had entered.

"Hear you got yourself a partner, Dick. This Sparr a good man?"

For the space of two minutes there was no reply. Silence hung suspended in the room, and Hopalong could almost feel the impulses in conflict here. Much of what he did not know he was guessing from the vantage point of his old friendship for Dick Jordan. He knew the great love the man had possessed for his wife and for his daughter, who was not only all a daughter could be, but the living image of the girl he had married so long ago. Danger to her would be fought in every way.

"Yeah, Sparr's a good man." Jordan spoke quietly, and, so far as it went, honestly. "He knows cattle, an' he knows men." In this last Cassidy believed he detected bitterness.

"Soper goin' to be a partner too?"

A spasm contracted the old man's face and for an instant a living, fierce hatred blazed in his eyes. "No! No, he's not! Where'd you get that idea?"

"Oh, just surmisin'!" Hopalong stretched his legs. "Buck wants to pay you for the cattle, Dick."

"You bring the money?" From Jordan's attitude Hopalong decided Jordan was actually hoping he had not.

"Not with me," Hopalong said cautiously, "but I—"

Jordan spoke hastily, as if to interrupt. "All right, if he ain't got it now, he ain't got it." Then he added, more quietly, "If anything happens to me, I want my daughter to get that money, an' if anything happens to her, you an' Buck keep it."

"Nothin'," Hopalong said flatly, leaning slightly forward, "is goin' to happen to Pamela—or to you. Take that from me. Dick" —he leaned forward—"what are you doin' with Sparr on this place? The man's a killer and an outlaw!"

Jordan sighed deeply and refused to meet Hopalong's eyes. "A man can hire who he likes," he muttered, "an' sell out to who he likes. You would do me a favor, Hoppy, if you would straddle your hoss an' ride back to Buck. Then stay there. Pam an' me," he said painfully, "have our own problems. We got to work them out ourselves."

Cassidy got to his feet slowly. "Dick," he said sincerely, "I ain't doin' a particle of good, sittin' here like this, but I promise you, like it or not, I ain't leavin'! I aim to stay right here until things are straightened out an' you are on your feet again."

There was a gleam in the old man's eyes, and Pamela came quickly to Hoppy. "Oh, if—!"

"Don't say it." Hopalong hitched his gunbelts a little. "I ain't so dumb. That old frazzle top of a dad o' yours never was a poker player. He never bluffed me in his life. Ever' time he tried to make like he was holdin' a full house, I knowed it was a mighty small pair!"

Hopalong put his hand on the latch. "So long. I'll be back."

"Hoppy"—Pamela caught his hand—"be careful!"

He chuckled. "I said I'd be back, didn't I?"

He started to open the door, then closed it again. He turned and looked at Pamela. "Can your dad straddle a hoss—if he had to?"

She hesitated, then nodded. "Yes, Hoppy, if he had to, and I think he'd love to."

Hopalong walked slowly across the intervening room. They had told him nothing, or less than nothing, but that they were held prisoner here, he knew. Obviously each one feared to do anything to incur the anger of Avery Sparr for fear that that anger would be vented on the other. Pamela believed she was protecting her father, and he believed he was protecting her. Yet, studying the situation, Hopalong could see no flaws in Sparr's plan had not he, Hopalong Cassidy, drifted into the game.

Sparr looked up quickly as he came through the door, Soper more lazily. "Ain't the man he used to be, is he?" Sparr said, leaning back in his hide-covered chair. "Purty run-down."

"Yeah," Hopalong agreed, "only a shell."

"You pay him for that stock?" Sparr asked casually.

"Huh? Oh no, not t'day." Hopalong was equally casual. "Didn't bring the money out because I had some stops to make. I cached it."

Hopalong could scarcely repress a grin at the expression on Avery Sparr's face. Fifteen thousand in cold cash was a nice item, and knowing the big gunman's greed, he could understand how his mouth must have watered when he heard of it. Now he dared not kill Hopalong without chancing the entire loss of the money— something he was neither ready nor willing to do. Yet he wanted Hopalong dead.

Dropping into a chair, Cassidy reached for the steaming coffeepot and filled his cup. Some doughnuts were on the table, and he helped himself and began to eat, drinking coffee. "Start back t'night," he said, "around about half an hour from now. I'll stick around Horse Springs until the boys get here."

"Have to talk to the old man about that stock," Sparr objected uneasily. "Nothin' was said to me about sellin' any. Y' say some o' your boys are already out here?"

"Should be," Hopalong lied.

"Ain't heard nothin' of them," Sparr interposed. "Mebbe they strayed off."

"Yeah, that could be." Hopalong tried his coffee and then

broke another doughnut. "They sure like to hunt rustlers. Those two"—his blue eyes were innocent—"would rather hunt rustlers than eat, an' both of them are good feeders.

"Ever hear," he asked conversationally, "about the time Mesquite started after the gang that dry-gulched me?" He chuckled. "He'd killed eight out of twelve before I could get back into a saddle. He can read sign like an Injun, an' he trailed that slick horse thief Shanghai all over the country. The old sidewinder couldn't shake him, either, an' finally Mesquite cornered him an' brought him in. He was a good man, a deputy sheriff for a while. The only trouble that Mesquite ever had was gettin' prisoners back alive."

Avery Sparr shifted irritably in his chair, but Soper was listening with interest. He had his own plans, and fighting did not enter them. Not that he was averse to bloodshed if no other way could be found, but he had laid his own plans well, plans that would be much better carried out if Hopalong Cassidy and Avery Sparr eliminated each other. The fewer in at the payoff the better, and while he had made his own arrangements for conducting the elimination proceedings, nevertheless a few gun battles would eliminate not only some of those who might insist on a share, but also considerable expense.

Sparr thought of something that had not occurred to him since Hopalong's arrival. "Say"—he turned abruptly—"you sure come up on us quick outside. Which way did you come? From Thatcher's?"

Hopalong shrugged. "I came in from the north. I'd decided to go back across Circle J range an' look over some of that young stuff, so when I started back for this place I crossed the Middle Fork a couple o' miles west o' Canyon Creek. Seen a shack there," he added, lying cheerfully, "an' there was a hombre inside fast asleep."

Actually, it was the south from which he had come and across the head of West Fork and the Whitewater. It would do no harm to create a little friction among the members of the Sparr outfit, and some discontent.

"Come all the way from Thatcher's?" Sparr demanded suspiciously.

"Uh-uh. Spent the night on Circle J's north range. Near Double Spring."

The places mentioned were carefully catalogued in his mind from the information culled from the old cowhand's talk on the T Bar. Yet as he talked he was thinking of what might be done. From where he sat the corrals could be seen. Two horses from there, and his own. It might be done. The risk lay in how much Dick Jordan could stand, and Hopalong was willing to bet there was enough fight in the old man to keep him in the saddle for some rough and wicked miles. It was upon that fight he was planning to gamble.

It would do no good to take them back to Thatcher's even if he got them away from the Circle J. Despite the fact that Sim Thatcher's place was admirably situated for defense, and built for it, the T Bar was too far away over country too easy to cover If escape was to be made, and he intended to start nothing that could be avoided until Dick and his daughter were safely away, it would have to be into those mountains to the west.

It was all unknown country, and he might run them into a box canyon from which escape would be impossible, yet he knew terrain, even if not this particular area, and he had an idea that he could find a way through to hit that trail to Alma. A lot would depend on obtaining a head start and getting into the hills past Lily Mountain. After that he would have to depend on his own skill in covering their trail and in every trick he could think of to escape pursuit, for without Dick Jordan and his daughter all of Sparr's schemes must fall through.

He arose finally. "Glad to have met you," he said, grinning at Sparr, "and Mister Soper. Maybe we'll get together again sometime. O' course," he said mildly, absently, "if you're still here when I bring the boys after that young stock, we'll see yuh." He looked up, grinning. "Some o' the boys would sure like to meet you, Sparr."

He was at the door before he stopped again, and why he said what he did then he never knew, except that it often pays to keep an enemy confused as to how much you know and what you are implying. "By the way"—his blue eyes went from Sparr to Soper —"either of you know a tinhorn named Goff?"

Sparr frowned, but Soper's head came up sharply. "Sure we know him," Sparr said, scowling. "What about him?"

"What would he be doin' ridin' around the Elk Mountain?"

Soper's face went white, then deadly, as he stared, nostrils distended, at Avery Sparr.

The gunman was half out of his chair. "Goff?" He was incredulous. "Around Elk Mountain?"

"Oh, well!" Cassidy was cheerful. "Some idea of his own, I guess. Gamblers," he added sagely, "are odd folks. Always gettin' ideas about makin' money for themselves. Fact is, most folks are like that. Always ready to make a few extry dollars. Like Johnny Rebb said to me the other night—" He paused. "But that was in confidence."

Avery Sparr arose so abruptly that he tipped over his chair. "What was it Rebb said?" he demanded. His voice was harsh, his gray eyes dancing with a cold and ugly light.

"Oh, he was just talkin'!" Hopalong waved an airy gesture of dismissal. "At that, you can't blame a man for lookin' out for his own interests."

He crossed the hard-packed ranch yard chuckling to himself. That would give them something to think about! If it did no more than worry Sparr, it would help. Better yet, it might take Sparr, Soper, or some of the others off the ranch and leave him a freer hand in getting away with the Jordans.

So far as Hopalong knew, Goff was still playing cards at Clifton's, and Johnny Rebb might be anywhere, and the guard on duty at the ford on Middle Fork might never have slept a wink in his life. Men of criminal instincts and aspirations are men born with and filled with suspicion. They live with the cherished idea that all men are out for their own interests.

They judge others by themselves; hence, seeds of suspicion fall on fertile soil and easily flower into a lot of trouble. And with Soper, Cassidy was quite sure he had struck such soil. The man had obviously been frightened of the construction Sparr might put on Cassidy's remarks and genuinely upset when he heard that Goff was riding in the vicinity of Elk Mountain.

Speaking of Johnny Rebb had turned Hopalong's thoughts upon the buck-toothed gunman. There was nothing about him, really, except those buck teeth, that in any way distinguished him, but somehow the young man's image stayed in Hopalong's mind, and the fact disturbed him. Somewhere, deep within him, some wellspring of memory or some unconscious construction had attached importance to Johnny Rebb. And the fact that he could not guess why disturbed Hopalong and made him restless.

Once in the saddle he started east by north, heading for a route that would put him on the Indian Creek Trail, which was the main-traveled route to Horse Springs. As he rode he studied the country with great care, pausing from time to time and reining the buckskin off the trail to make sure whether or not he was followed. It was not until the third attempt that he actually did spot his trailer. The rider was about a half mile behind him and just coming down into the broken country that was the approach to the canyon of the Middle Fork.

Dropping the buckskin swiftly down the trail to the floor of the canyon, Hopalong started it up the opposite side, then swung it to a narrow shelf of rock he would have hesitated to take with another horse, and rode back to the river. Entering the water, he walked the horse up the canyon, staying close to the edge of the river and the trail that ran along the bank.

Following the river for almost two miles, he finally found a canyon and entered it.

More and more he was admiring the buckskin. The horse had not only courage, but an almost instinctive sense of what was safe and what was not. Once it decided a trail was safe it would push along regardless of the narrowness of the ledge or the depth of the canyon. Climbing up from the bed of the Middle Fork, Hopalong followed a mere eyebrow of trail where for almost half the distance one boot brushed the rock wall while the other stirrup was suspended over space. And the buckskin plodded as if it were walking along a bridle path in a park.

Keeping to the timber and brush, avoiding trails, Hopalong rode steadily west, crossing Canyon Creek without seeing anyone. The country grew steadily more wild and the mountains to the west loomed up sharp and clear against the sky.

Even from here he could see how rough they were and how few passes there must be. Among the jumble of massive mountains three peaks lifted high above the others. All of these, he had been told, were more than ten thousand feet in altitude, and the northern of the three was Whitewater Baldy. He found a hollow among heavy growth where there was grass and made camp.

Picketing his horse, he carefully built a hasty fire from dried and weathered branches under a tree where even the thin smoke from the dry wood could be thinned more and dispersed by the needles of the pine. When he had cooked and eaten a meal, he rolled up in his blanket and went to sleep. It was not quite sundown when he closed his eyes. It was after ten when he awakened suddenly.

Instantly he was on his feet. Rolling his bed, he saddled up, strapped on his bedroll, and swung into the leather. The buckskin humped its back irritably, but not very seriously. "Take it easy, Buck," he whispered companionably. "You'll need that energy before another rest, b'lieve me."

An hour was used in covering the six miles back to the ranch house, but once there he swung down in the trees where he had stopped that morning.

The air was clear and cold, sharp and fresh as cold water, and every breath felt like he was actually drinking. The air smelled faintly of pines and wood smoke, and there were lights in the house and also in the bunkhouse. For several minutes he waited, studying the layout anew, and then he worked his way around and behind the corrals, eased past them to the wall of the bunkhouse, and looked within. Anson Mowry sprawled in his bunk, half asleep. The tall hand Hopalong had seen earlier was at a table playing solitaire and facing the door. There was no one else in sight.

Huddling against the log and adobe wall, partly concealed by the corner ends that jutted out from the wall, Hopalong waited and listened.

"Hey, Anse! Wake up! What happened around here t'day? Where'd ever'body go?"

Mowry spoke drowsily, half asleep. "Cassidy was here. The one that shot Barker."

"Here? Is he loco?"

"Naw! You should o' seen the way they invited him in! Like he was their rich uncle or somethin'. Sometimes I think this whole outfit got throwed on its head." Mowry sat up and fumbled for the makin's. Hopalong could see him only slightly, as his body was partly hidden behind the card player. "I gotta notion to drag it."

"Huh! You never had it so good! They feed good here, good money, an' durned little work. I ain't a-scared of this here Cassidy. Anyway, he's Sparr's problem. Let the boss have him."

"Mebbe."

"Or Johnny Rebb."

"Rebb?" Mowry's voice was edged with contempt. "What makes you think he's good?"

"Ever see him throw a gun?" The card player looked up casually. "B'lieve me, Anse, an' you're my friend. Don't you ever stack up against him. That long-haired, homely galoot is fast!"

"Aw!" Mowry was irritated. He got to his feet. "You talk like a crazy man! Who'd you see him with?"

"Remember"—the tall cowhand lifted a bone-ribbed face of sun-tanned leather—"I was at McClellan. That was skittish, mighty skittish! But not Rebb! He stood there cold as ice, talkin' easylike, an' no more worried than nothin'." Then he added, "It was him killed Duke Brannin."

"What?" Mowry whirled. "Him?"

"Uh-huh. I've knowed it three, four months. Brannin an' him had trouble up Utah way. Rebb lit out because Brannin had friends an' he didn't. Duke Brannin follered Johnny an' cornered him at Lee's Ferry. I come up a few minutes after, an' folks said Brannin never had a chance."

Anson Mowry scowled, and Hopalong could share the gunman's feelings. It was good to know these things. Usually, gunmen are well known, but such a one as Johnny Rebb, young and comparatively unknown, could be dangerous.

"Funny he never said nothin' about it. You sure?"

"Practic'ly seen it. O' course I'm sure. It's just that Rebb ain't one o' these talkative hombres. I wouldn't be surprised if he was slicker than the boss."

"Say!" Mowry turned. "Does the boss know that?"

"Uh-uh. Don't think so."

"Maybe Rebb is lucky. The boss was friendly with Duke Brannin."

Mowry sat down on the bunk again and rubbed out his cigarette with a bootheel. "All right, shut up an' let me sleep. Wake me up at one."

"I'll wake you at twelve!"

The card player gathered in the pasteboards and riffled them, then shuffled and cut. Finally he began to deal. From the bunk came a slow snore, then another.

The card player turned his head to glance at the bunk. "Look at that hombre!" he muttered, half aloud. "Already asleep!"

"Yeah," the voice was low, "an' he needs it, so don't wake him."

The card player's head swung around, startled. The hand that had dropped to the gun butt froze. Then, carefully, the fingers spread and the hand lifted. Hopalong Cassidy stood inside the door and to the left of it. In his hand was a Colt. "If you want the last sound you make t' be a yell," Hopalong suggested, "make it Otherwise, unbuckle your belt an' lower the gun real gentle to that table top."

The outlaw was sweating now. He swallowed once, then slowly and with infinite care unbuckled his belt and did as he was told. He had straight black brows that lay like a bar across his forehead and from beneath them his eyes stared, cold and hard, above his lean, hard-drawn face.

"Now turn around," Cassidy said, and motioned with his gun barrel.

The tall man hesitated. "Don't slug me with that gun," he

said. "I ain't aimin' to cause you no trouble—not now." He bared his teeth in a wolfish grin. "But wait'll we git together again, Mister. I'll peel yore hide for this!"

He turned around, and Hopalong walked up to him. Taking his wrists, he bound them solidly behind him. Then he gagged and bound him thoroughly, with occasional glances at Mowry, who slept soundly, and with a glance once toward the house.

Anson Mowry was asleep and dreaming. He was dreaming that he had Hopalong Cassidy at the end of his long gun and was about to squeeze off a killing shot. And then something hard pressed into his stomach, and he opened his eyes to find Cassidy staring down at him from hard blue eyes.

"One whimper out of you," Cassidy said, "an' I'll bend this over your noggin!"

Mowry lunged to get up, and his mouth opened for a yell. The gun muzzle jerked up hard in his solar plexus and he gasped for air. Coolly, Cassidy slammed the gun barrel behind his ear, and Mowry folded. Glancing over at the bound outlaw, Hopalong said quietly, "This hombre won't take anybody's word for anything."

When Mowry was bound, Hopalong left the bunkhouse and walked at once to the corral, where he led out two horses and swiftly saddled them. He had sized up the horses that day and knew just which ones he wanted. He worked swiftly and surely, with a minimum of effort, every move deft and sure. Then he led the horses to the side of the house and went up the steps.

The first person he saw was the Mexican woman who did the cooking. *"Buenas noches, señora,"* he said softly. "We'll have no trouble with you, either."

"¿Cómo?"

"You heard me. Now open that door." He gestured with his pistol. "I'm takin' the Jordans away where they'll be safe."

"Take me too!" she pleaded.

"I'm sorry. You stay here, *chiquita*. Later I'll come back an' clean out this nest of rats."

She opened the door for him, but at the opposite door she shook her head. There was a heavy bar across it and the bar was padlocked in place. It did not fasten to the door, however, and was mostly for show. Hopalong rapped on the door. "Pamela! Dick!"

Feet ran inside, and then Pamela, in an excited, unbelieving voice, called out, "Hoppy? Oh, Hoppy, is it you?"

"Yeah. Open the door."

"I can't. Only the bar on this side. He has the door key."

"All right, take down the bar an' then get your dad ready. We're ridin'."

Hopalong stepped back and kicked the door at the lock. It did not budge. He kicked it again, and swore as he barked his shin on the bar. Coolly he walked back to the yard and picked up an ax. Two well-directed blows and the door flew open. Dick Jordan, who had not yet gone to bed, was struggling to get erect, grasping a heavy cane. With Hoppy on one side and Pam on the other, they got him to the door. "Get me in a saddle," he said hoarsely, "that's all I ask. I can still ride! Anyway, if I die I want to die in the saddle!"

The Mexican woman had disappeared, but as the old man was firmly seated and Hoppy came running back from the house with a brace of guns for the girl and her father and two rifles, she appeared with a burlap sack stuffed with food.

Hopalong grinned at her. *"Gracias, chiquita!"* he said. "You're a woman after my own heart!" He pinched her fat cheeks, and she struck at his hand, embarrassed.

Hopalong swung to the saddle and they started swiftly. Behind them the woman called after them, *"Vaya con Dios!"*

"Go with God!" Pamela whispered to Hopalong. "We'll need to!"

Suddenly there was a clatter of horses' hoofs and a shout of laughter. Into the ranch yard poured a column of laughing, shouting, drunken, or half-drunken riders. Rushing to the bunkhouse, they flung out of their saddles. "Anse! Slim! What d' yuh think—!" Their question was drowned in confused shouts, and Hopalong swore.

"I'll follow," Hopalong said hastily. "Pam, you know this country better than I do. We're ridin' for the Mogollons. We'll try for Turkeyfeather Pass and the old Snow Creek Trail for Alma. Lead the way, an' keep movin'!"

"All right!"

He heard the sound of their horses fading into the woods and over the pine needles where they would make no sound. He slid his Winchester into his hands and lifted it to his shoulder. Then he fired five quick shots, as fast as he could work the lever on the rifle. He knocked out the light with the first shot, smashed the door with the second, and put the third and fourth through the window, and another into the doorstep. Then he wheeled his horse and rode swiftly after the girl and her father.

Once he glanced up at the stars. It was barely past midnight. They had six hours of darkness, and six hours in which their tracks could not be easily distinguished. Pamela was setting a good pace, and once Hopalong closed in beside the old man. "How's it, Dick? Can you make it?"

"Durned right I'll make it!" He watched Hopalong feeding shells into the rifle. "Like old times, Hoppy! It shore is! Wish Buck was with us!"

"Yeah"—Hopalong Cassidy nodded, remembering other times and places—"but I'd rather have Mesquite right now. Or Johnny or even Red."

"Mesquite?" Dick Jordan scowled. "Didn't know him. But I heard that name today."

"You what?" Hopalong was incredulous. "You heard somethin' about Mesquite?"

"Yeah. Had him a gun battle at Horse Springs. He killed somebody there. Didn't get the straight of it."

Hopalong moved up beside Pamela. "Know this trail?"

"Yes, I know it very well. I used to ride this way when we first came out here, but I was never past the Jerkys. Do you know it?"

"Only hearsay. We'll just have to take a chance and trust to luck." Far behind them there were yells and shouting. "I'll drop back. They might stumble on us, but what they'll probably do is split an' head for the fords of the two streams." He slowed his buckskin. Then he remembered. "Pam! Did yuh hear who it was Mesquite shot?"

"Mesquite? I don't know him. I never heard the name, only I did hear that Bizco was killed last night in Horse Springs."

Hopalong Cassidy dropped back, grinning. Suddenly he felt better. It was all right to go it alone, but when there were men like Mesquite and Johnny around—well, it was better to know they were here. And Bizco was dead! Whatever had led him to tackle a curly wolf like Mesquite?

CHAPTER 8

THE FLIGHT INTO THE MOGOLLONS

Several times Hopalong drew up to listen. Inside, he was seething, but he kept his excitement under the restraint of a cold, clear mind that carefully gauged all their chances and kept his thoughts clear for swift adjustment to circumstances. The fact that the outfit had returned to the Circle J, evidently from a spree, was unfortunate. Yet if they had to come back at all, he was glad they had come back drunk. From the sounds there was much heedless rushing around, and every second counted now. Moreover, there was a good chance that at least some of their tracks would be trampled out.

His thoughts leaped ahead to the problem before him. Too experienced to sell the outlaws short, he knew it would be but a matter of a few hours until he had on their trail a bunch of the most relentless manhunters in the West. Avery Sparr would be in a rage, but he was not a man to do things without thought. He would split his forces and ride at once for the two crossings of the rivers. Finding no guard at the Middle Fork, he might assume that that had been the direction chosen. If he did, there was every chance time would be gained through his error.

As soon as they had a few more miles between them and the

ranch, Hopalong would take the lead and leave tracks toward the crossing of West Fork. Then, on the first cold ground they could find, they would swing due west into that maze of mighty mountains that made up the rugged Mogollons. And then he would need every bit of his experience to lose the pursuers. That they would eventually find his true trail, he knew. Yet every hour—every minute, in fact—was another step toward escape and security.

Alone, the problem of escape would still have been great, but encumbered by a crippled man and a girl, it seemed impossible. Dark forest closed in around them, the pines a wall of blackness on either side. Their horses walked soundlessly over a thick carpet of pine needles, and at times the trail broke into the open, where stars shone brightly in the midnight blue of the heavens. The air was cool and fresh, and there was no wind. Far behind them there was still an occasional yell, but already they had some distance with which to work.

The black nine-thousand-foot bulk of Lily Mountain loomed on their left and the shoulder of Jackson Mesa to the right. Not far ahead was the trail to the West Fork crossing. Hopalong moved the buckskin ahead and deliberately led the way into the trail. He knew that every instant on this trail was thick with danger. At any time the hard-riding pursuit might close in upon them, but he also knew that a false trail must be set, and this was the best way to do it.

His buckskin's hoofs clicked stone after they had been riding for several minutes, and off to the left stretched a white, clean expanse of sand rock. This would be the logical place to leave the trail, so Hopalong did not leave. The men behind him were old hands at this game, too, having many times lost posses in close pursuit. From now on he would need every faculty, every fragment of experience, every bit of lore he had ever learned or heard of. He pushed on, and then they dipped into a sandy place and here he turned left. When they had gone a mile, he stopped them.

"Catch a breath," he said. "I'm going back to cover the trail."

He slid away into the darkness, knowing exactly what he would do. As they turned off the trail he had observed several head of cattle taking their midnight stretch near the wash where they turned off the trail. Now he rode around those cattle and started them into the wash, walking them over the sand for a hundred yards or more to destroy as much sign as he could. He had just left them when he heard a clatter of racing horses on the trail and then heard them slow up near the sandstone ledge.

"Here?" The voice was unfamiliar.

"No!" That was Mowry, furious at his second failure with Hopalong. "We'll ride on to the crossing. No chance to follow him by trail sign now. The chances are he'll run for the crossing. Remember, he's got to get out of this stretch by crossing a river."

"He might go west," somebody hazarded a guess.

"He ain't crazy," Mowry replied sharply. "If he went west he'd be trapped. There's only a lot of blind canyons back there and no way through that wall of mountains. No, it's got to be north or south."

"Wish Sparr was here!"

"What could he do that we ain't doin'?" Mowry was irritated by the comment. "Don't worry! We'll find that silver-haired devil!"

Hoppy sat quietly, whispering to the buckskin. The riders went on by, walking their horses now. Then, when they were well past, he turned and started back up the wash, only now he rode with extreme care. The deepest sand was tiring for his horse, but also it was sure to leave no definite tracks that could be read easily. There would be evidence of something passing, but in the soft sand, where grains would fall into the hoofprint and destroy the outline, there was small chance of any sign being left that could be identified either as to nature or time.

"Let's go," he whispered, as he rode by Dick and Pamela. "Don't talk."

Ahead and to the left loomed the raw backbone of the Jerky Mountains. Ahead of him, and upon which they soon came, lay a branch of Clear Creek that flowed north from the steep flanks of Lily Mountain. They reached this stream a little above its junction with the main creek and crossed there, pushing on west and a little north. The land was heavily timbered and rugged in the extreme. For a time they wound their way, with frequent changes of direction because of natural obstructions, through thick pine forest.

With the ridge of the Jerkys on their left and slightly ahead and the stars above, keeping direction was no great problem. From time to time Hopalong stopped and listened, but there was no sound except the occasional hoot of an owl and the distant howl of a coyote. Before daybreak, in a hollow behind an enormous slab of rock, Hopalong drew up and swung down.

Pamela slid from the saddle and went at once to her father, and between the two of them they got him from the saddle. His face was drawn but his eyes were bright and hard. They seated him on Hoppy's bedroll against the wall of rock.

"Don't be frettin' about me, Hoppy." His voice was firm. "I'll stick it. Think only about gettin' us away. This here fresh air is what I need, although," he admitted with a wry grin, "I ain't been ridin' much lately."

Working with swift and deft hands, Hoppy broke small dead branches from the lower trunks of the pines, and with these he built a quick, carefully shielded fire. Once it was going and he had water on, he went away from it and looked back. The great slabs of rock around the camp and the pines concealed it very well.

Back at camp he found Pamela hastily slicing some bacon from a slab put into the bag by the old Mexican cook.

The earth was slightly damp and it was chill. Walking about, Hoppy gathered more sticks, watching Dick Jordan without seeming to do so. Without doubt the man was very tired. The months of lying in bed or sitting in the chair had taken their toll, and the ride had been a hard one. Mentally, Cassidy calculated the time. There was small chance of any successfully organized pursuit until daylight. Yet it would not do to depend on that trail being concealed. Somewhere even the best of woodsmen must fail in that attempt. All he could hope to do was to gain time. And there was little of that.

At a guess they were but ten miles from the ranch by a direct line. They had ridden at least five miles farther than that, but by day the followers might come much faster. Eating now, they would rest only a few minutes and then push on. There was both water and grass here and the horses were making the most of both. With luck, if Dick could hold out, they need not stop again for three or four hours, and then but briefly.

Already they were in very rough country that offered many avenues of possible retreat, and these might confuse the men sent out by Avery Sparr, but starting with their coming move, they must use every stratagem to confuse the pursuit.

Already the sky was faintly gray, and the spires of the pines etched a dark fringe along the sky all about them. The small fire blazed cheerfully, and the wood crackled. Hopalong leaned back on an elbow, watching the girl, smelling the faint, aromatic pine smoke and the stronger, richer smell of bacon frying.

Firelight danced shadows on the flat face of the rock, and Dick Jordan leaned back, his strong-boned face relaxed and at rest, with the firelight glistening on cheekbones and brow, leaving a deep shadow on one cheek and temple. The light caught tiny gleams from the shells in his gunbelt and found highlights in the worn black of the polished leather holsters. Tired now, and half asleep, Jordan showed his age, and Hopalong stirred restlessly, worried about the old man.

Pamela was suddenly up and taking coffee and a plate to her father. Dick awakened, and he smiled quickly, but Hoppy knew the smile did not fool Pamela, who realized only too well how tired her father must be. Hopalong watched her with curious eyes.

Not too many women had entered his life, for it had been a life of hoof and horns, of guns, saddles, and the hard ways of the frontier. Pamela was somehow strange even while familiar. There was only the ghost of the girl he remembered and to whom he had told stories. Now she was self-possessed and sure. Young she might be, but at eighteen on the frontier a girl was a woman, and many a girl was married at sixteen.

She was slender and tall, but beautifully shaped, and her rough, sun-faded wool shirt showed the ripe roundness of her bosom and the beauty of her arms and shoulders. Her face was brown from sun and wind, and the sun had picked a few freckles from her skin. She seemed to become aware of his study and turned suddenly to smile at him, and Hopalong was strangely embarrassed. She arose at once and handed him coffee, then a plate with bacon and a few beans. "We'd better eat them all," she said; "no use carrying that jar."

"Yeah, the lighter the better. Know anything about this country west of here?"

"No." Her voice was low and the tone rounded. "I've heard a few things from friendly Indians. There's a mesa beyond Iron Creek, and the pass you mentioned is this side of there. But we'll be safe nowhere until Avery Sparr is dead."

"What about Soper?"

"He's worse. I don't know why I say that, either. It's an

impression you get after a while. At first I liked him. I believed he would help us, but sometimes I would surprise him looking at me, or at my father, and something in the way he looked gave me the shudders."

"Outside they like him. Thatcher thought he was all right."

"They don't know him." She considered what she had said, then added, frowning: "I shouldn't say that, for I don't know him either, not the least bit. I think that's what frightens me."

"Where did Sparr find him? They don't fit together, somehow. Sparr's western. Soper is not."

"I don't know. But Soper knows a lot. I think he is a college man. He talks very well when he wishes to, and he can be very much the gentleman."

Hopalong got to his feet and went after the horses. When he came back Pamela had already put out the fire, and gathering those sticks only partly burned she carried them off a short distance and scraped sand over them, hiding them from sight. With care, Hopalong worked over the site of the campfire, spending precious time in concealing its remains as well as possible.

Jordan grinned at him when Hopalong came to get him. "Don't worry about me," he said stubbornly. "I'm good for fifty miles, easy. Just keep movin'. Feels good," he added honestly, "to be in the saddle again. I'm no man to be cooped up. If time comes when I have to die, this would be the way I'd choose. Only I'd like to trigger a gun at Avery Sparr first."

"You stay in that saddle," Hopalong said seriously. "Leave the scrappin' to me."

Deliberately Hopalong turned south. Now he selected the roughest possible country. Great cliffs lifted about them, and they turned into a canyon so deep that it seemed night had come again. The somber columns of the pines ranged along the sides of the narrow trail to which they held and then fell away as they rode across a small park, belly high on the horses. The wall of the forest seemed solid, but Hopalong found a narrow space and pushed the buckskin into it, and they wound around among the trees, turning and twisting, but keeping steadily west of south. Suddenly emerging from the forest, they found themselves on the edge of a wide shelf of flat rock, wind-scoured and lonely. It stretched away ahead of them to the very rim of a vast crack in the earth. Riding out on the rock, Hoppy led the way across to the rim. The buckskin paused and peered over, ears forward, stretching its nose toward the sheer vastness of the space before them.

Then, turning the horse, Hopalong skirted the lip of the canyon until a path showed. Well down the path he saw hoofprints of unshod horses. For a full minute he stared down. A hundred yards from where he sat the trail vanished around a bulging shoulder of rock, yet those wild horses, or perhaps Indian horses, had gone that way. Abruptly he started the buckskin, and without hesitation the horse headed down the trail. Cassidy knew that if one horse started, the others would come, and come they did.

Far below them in a vast blue gulf he could make out the tops of the pines. Across from them lifted the sheer mass of a mountain. And then he was giving all his time to the problem at hand.

The trail was steep and the buckskin braced his feet and walked gingerly. At the turn in the trail it narrowed still more. Now there would be no turning back, for there would be no room to turn. Hopalong sat easy in the saddle and let the buckskin trust his own judgment, which Hopalong had come to respect most heartily. The buckskin was not hesitant. Steadily they went down, deeper and deeper into the vast gulf whose jaws closed slowly above them and around them.

After almost an hour they rode out suddenly into a wide, half-open valley dotted and fringed with clumps of trees. At a lope, to add distance, Hopalong led the way across. His blue eyes studied the terrain before them, and then, turning, he glanced back. He could see little of the trail down which they had come, for it merged into the wall of the canyon and was lost to sight. Slowing his horse, he dropped back beside the others.

Dick Jordan grinned at him. "That trail! Hoppy, if you told anybody about that trail they'd figger you lied! I wouldn't have bet a squirrel could tackle it."

Pamela glanced at the buckskin. "Your horse?"

"Sim Thatcher's. I'd like to buy him, though. He's the best horse in the mountains I ever sat."

Dick Jordan asked, "You think that Mesquite they talked about back yonder was your friend?"

"Yeah. He an' Johnny headed out this way sometime back. They went to Tombstone, but I didn't know they had come north. Once they start somewhere you can't tell where they'll end up. Anyway, I hope it was him, an' whether it is or not, this hombre got Bizco."

"One more an' one less."

"Right. An' they tell me he was one o' those who killed Kitchen."

Dick Jordan's face hardened to bitterness. "Can't figure how I got to be so trustin'!" His voice was angry. "I should have knowed Avery Sparr was up to somethin', but he seemed like he only wanted to help, an' when Kitchen got killed, I needed help. First time we smelled a rat was when Johnny Rebb an' Bizco showed up at the ranch."

A thought occurred to Hopalong. "Say, what do you know about Elk Mountain? I saw a rider—figgered it was Soper—who headed right at the wall of the mountain. I couldn't figger where he was goin'. He was ridin' at an angle, sort of southwest from the main trail to Horse Springs."

"Sure. There's a canyon in there. Mighty narrow, but she's

there. Turkey Spring Canyon. Can't figger what he'd be goin' there for."

"Ranch in there?" Hopalong wanted to know. He had found an opening in the trees ahead and veered right, away from it.

"No. There's a stone tower there, though. Cliff dwellers built it. Mostly fallen down now. I did hear there was some prospector usin' it, though."

Hopalong went steadily right, circled out into the grass, and then doubled back on their own tracks and went around a boulder and into the trees. If he could get Dick Jordan and his daughter to the comparative safety of Alma, secure from either the abuse or bullying of Avery Sparr, then he could come back. After that—his weather-beaten face was grim—after that would come the reckoning.

Ahead of them the country slanted down toward a valley floor visible through the scattered bunches of trees and the boulders. The grass was high here, and green, for it was irrigated by the runoff from the mountains. Ahead of them was a small stream, and Hopalong reined in to let the horses drink. Pamela heard his low exclamation and looked around quickly. Hopalong was on the ground staring at the tracks of some unshod ponies

"Wild horses?" she asked.

"No."

His answer told her all she needed to know. Dick Jordan slid the Winchester from his saddle scabbard. "How many of 'em?"

"Maybe six, eight. Can't rightly make out." Hopalong shoved his hat back on his head and swore softly. Outlaws behind them and Apaches ahead. The question was: which was the worse? The stream ahead of them was the West Fork, and it could not be very far to Turkeyfeather Creek. He studied the situation. As he had it, the tracks were not more than an hour old, at most. Were the

Indians moving on? Or did they have a camp near? And how close behind him was Sparr?

At a rough guess, by the route they must take, they were not less than thirty miles from Alma, but the worst of their trip, even excepting the presence of Apaches, was still before them.

"We'll gamble," he said suddenly. "We'll push on to the Turkeyfeather an' make camp there. We all need rest, an' so do the horses. We'll take a chance on Sparr comin' up with us."

"What about the Injuns?" Dick demanded.

Hopalong grinned. "They'll have to look out for themselves." He took off his hat and ran his fingers through his hair, then replaced the hat, pulling it down firmly in front. "Maybe," he said innocently, "they might run into grief. Never can tell what will happen when you go perambulatin' around in the mountains like this!"

He mounted, and they moved forward cautiously. The tracks were apparent, and the Apaches had probably been following the same route. This might not be, but probably was, a war party, their destination the settlements and travelers in the vicinity of Alma and the mining camps clustered around Cooney.

Below them the green expanse of the valley looked inviting, small though it must be, but Hopalong left the trail and started off at right angles toward a sandstone cliff. It was pink with a white streak of quartz angling across the face and at the base some cottonwoods and sycamores promised water.

Between the trees and the cliff face there was just room for riding single file, and Hopalong led off, every sense alert. From time to time he stopped again, listening. His mouth was dry and he was worried, more so than he would have cared to admit. Not far ahead, while still on the trail, he had seen a buzzard fly up as if disturbed by something moving nearby.

Rounding a projecting shoulder of cliff, Hopalong saw before him a long, narrow valley, or canyon. It headed up among some high bluffs that squeezed that end into a narrow space. On what seemed to be a small plateau were a number of trees and some huge rocks rolled down from the cliffs above. Moving off at a fast lope, Hopalong led the way. The last hundred yards was steep grade and in the open, but they made it to the shelter of the trees.

Hopalong reined in and they looked around quickly.

The plateau, if such it might be called, was scarcely more than an acre in extent, the edge of it fringed with a growth of mixed trees—pine, cedar, sycamore, and cottonwood and much manzanita. Behind that was a space, wide-open and grass-covered. Against the cliffs were other boulders, and a small fall cascaded from a crack in the rock higher up. To the left the canyon narrowed into a mere crack that looked dark and gloomy.

"We'll spend the night here, Dick," Hopalong said, "an' maybe a day or so, dependin' on how things look. I don't aim to get you into any mess-up with Injuns if I can help it."

At a protected spot near the foot of the cliff, with several large boulders and trees nearby, they made camp. Taking his rifle, Hopalong walked back across the open area and went into the trees. He had just reached the edge of the trees when he saw a brown movement in the forest from which they had come, and then several Indians rode into view.

There were four of them, and from the direction they must have been following, instead of ahead of him, so they were obviously another group. While he watched, other Indians came from the opposite direction, and in this bunch there were eleven. He wanted very much to warn Dick and Pamela, but he dared not go back. In any event, it would have meant little. These were hostiles. They had seen his tracks. They knew about where he was.

A moment later he looked around and saw Pamela coming toward him. She dropped on her stomach and crawled at his gesture, and he saw her eyes widen at the sight of the Apaches. *"Mimbreños,"* he whispered. "We'll have trouble."

There was no protest in her and no complaint. She accepted the situation and watched the Indians quietly. Evidently there was some dispute going on among them, perhaps as to whether to attack now or later. Yet sundown was not far off, and no Apache will fight at night.

"Do you believe they will attack now?" she asked him.

He shrugged. "No tellin' what's in the mind of an Injun," he said. "They might. The way I figger, some o' them want to an' some don't. Anyway, we've got as good a position as we could find. I only wish we had more food."

Her glance was quick, startled. "You think we'll be trapped here?"

"Could be." He chuckled suddenly. "Some ways I don't know as I would mind. Let Sparr catch up to us an' fight Injuns. He should make a good 'Pache fighter." He watched them thoughtfully, then asked, "How's your father?"

"Very tired, Hoppy. He wouldn't admit it for the world, and he's been sticking it out, but I don't believe he could have gone another mile. He just sagged when we left him against the wall. He's still not recovered, regardless of what he says."

They watched the Apaches in silence, and then Pamela said suddenly, "How far away are they? Could we shoot them from here?"

Cassidy glanced at her from his hard blue eyes, now lightened by wry humor.

"I reckon," he said. "But no use to ask for trouble. Let 'em start it. Maybe they'll decide to go on an' leave us alone." He studied them again. "They ain't over three hundred yards off."

"Do they shoot well, Hoppy?"

He glanced at her. "Take it from me, some of 'em do. A while back seventy Mexicans surrounded one lone Apache an' he stood off the whole seventy and got away. He killed seven Mexicans durin' the fight and everyone was drilled right through the skull. That's shootin'! I don't blame the Mexicans for givin' up an' goin' home."

The grass smelled good, and his body was tired. Hopalong let his muscles relax and ease deeper into the grass and earth. "You better get back, Pam," he said gently. "Fix us some grub. This looks like a long wait."

"What will you do?" She looked at him worriedly.

"Wait. If they start comin' this way, I'll stop 'em if I can. If I can't, I'll come a-runnin'."

"Well"—she was reluctant to leave—"take care of yourself. You take too many chances."

"Not me." He shook his head. "Only a fool takes chances. That isn't bravery, not one bit. The good fightin' man never takes a chance he can avoid. You have to take plenty you can't help, an' only a fool would go to gamblin' with his life.

"There's only two kinds of fightin' men, Pam. Good ones an' dead ones. You either learn, or you die. When I was a kid they told me I was scared for not walkin' a small log over a high canyon. The other kids all did it, but not me. Now if there had been somethin' on the other side I wanted, I would have gone over after it if there was no other way to get it. I never did see any sense in takin' chances that weren't necessary." He smiled. "There's a sight of difference between bein' brave an' bein' a dang fool."

When she had gone Hopalong wiped his hands dry on his shirt front and watched the woods where the Apaches had disappeared. Suddenly they appeared once more. This time they had made up their minds. They were coming now, all fifteen of them.

Hopalong felt his stomach go empty. He let them come, let them cut distance for him.

From three hundred yards they advanced, loping their ponies, until they were two hundred yards, one-fifty, one hundred yards away. He fired, holding the rifle well down, his sights on the stomach of the nearest Indian. The gun bellowed and leaped in his hands, and instantly he swung the muzzle, held briefly, then fired again. An Indian hit the grass and rolled over; then a second. He fired three times more, and then came to his feet running.

It was all of fifty yards to the circle of boulders and trees near the cliff face. Behind him there was a shrill Indian yell, and he felt the *whiff* of a rifle bullet, and heard the cracking sound as it passed him, and then two rifles spoke from the circle of rocks and he swung around, firing his rifle twice from the hip. Both shots were hits, one knocking a horse rolling, the second taking an Indian in the knee. He turned then and ran for the rocks, thumbing shells into his rifle.

He dropped behind the trunk of a tree and rolled over into firing position. He stared. The grassy area was empty of life and still. There was a dead horse out there and the tumbled body of a dead man, but no sign of anything else.

Pamela glanced at him, her face strangely white and frightened. Dick Jordan was chuckling. "Got one!" he said cheerfully, more alive than at any time Hopalong had seen him since coming to New Mexico. "Think we've stopped 'em?"

"Maybe for a while."

Hopalong turned his head to look out past the towering cliff and the trees toward the way from which they had come.

"They'll come again in the mornin'. We can figger on that. However, there's fewer of them now."

Pamela had turned back to the fire. "Coffee's ready," she said quietly. "Shall I bring yours to you?"

Hopalong turned his head. She was frightened, he knew. Anybody would be frightened in such a spot. But she was not letting it interfere. She was doing her job. Stirred, he rolled over again and looked out into the gathering dusk. It wasn't often you found a girl like that. They were few, mighty few!

He took the cup she offered him, and for an instant their eyes met. Then she quickly looked away. He hastily lifted the cup and managed to burn his lips on the hot coffee. It was no time to be thinking of a girl. The Apaches would be waiting for them. In the morning they would be coming, and probably more of them. So they were not safe; they had only gained a stay of execution. Hopalong Cassidy lifted the cup and tried the coffee again. It tasted very good.

CHAPTER 9

CASSIDY
SETS A TRAP

Firelight flickered on the rock wall and on the trees whose limbs arched above them. A night wind whispered among the leaves, stirring the silvery grass in long, moonlit billows. On the far edge of the firelit area lay Dick Jordan, his face gaunt now and sagging with weariness. Sleep had robbed him of the bold face with which he had accepted his sufferings and the vitality-sapping effort of riding.

Hopalong spoke to Pamela. "He's about all in. I don't know whether we dare risk the ride out of here or not."

"Will it be bad?"

"Worse than we've had it so far, an' today was rough for a healthy man."

"Could we hold out here for a day? Long enough to rest him from the saddle?"

"We may have to," Hopalong admitted, "but I'd rather not. Anyway, he won't get any rest here. He'll be wrought up an' worried. Moreover, a few hours won't help him much. Some way or other we've got to get to a safer place. Worst of it is, if we run they've got us."

"What about Sparr? How far behind do you think he is?"

"Not far." Hopalong edged the unburned ends of the sticks deeper into the coals. "Our trail will puzzle 'em some but it won't lose 'em. Anyway, I'd not mind seein' him show up tomorrow."

"You don't mean it!" Pamela shuddered. "Now that I'm away, the thought of falling into their hands again frightens me. I'd kill myself first."

"No, I mean it. I sure do! You see, if Sparr rides into this valley now he'll run into those Apaches. That means they'll fight. Whatever happens then will be good for us, an' I've a plan in mind if it does happen. Fact is," he added, "I've an idea where he is right now. I could guess it within a mile or two!" He scowled. "I wished I knew for shore that was Mesquite an' Johnny back yonder."

"I remember Johnny. He liked a fight."

"He ain't changed. An' Mesquite, he reads sign like an Injun." Hopalong chuckled. "That's a trick you learn livin' in Apache country. It's a school where the Apaches conduct the examinations an' if you flunk you lose your hair."

"Dad used to say they were like brown ghosts. You saw them and then you didn't, for they just seemed to merge into the landscape."

"It's true. It's gospel, b'lieve me. They know every trick in the books an' if they need more they invent more. I've known of fifteen or sixteen of 'em lyin' not a dozen yards from a man, and him never knowin' they were near until too late. Moreover," he continued, "this is their country. They know it an' we don't."

After a while Hopalong got to his feet, a shadow of an idea stirring in his mind. Avoiding the firelight even in this sheltered spot, he worked around through the boulders and brush and into the tall grass. The Apaches would be camped not more than a half mile away and might be closer. With infinite care he worked nearer and nearer to where he was sure they were. Shortly before dark he had noticed a number of crows hanging about in one area, and he was sure they had been drawn by the encampment.

When he was fairly close to where he believed their camp to be and directly between their camp and his own, he ceased to be careful with his trail, and turned at right angles and started off in the direction of the cliff trail. Once away from the vicinity of the camp he moved swiftly, his mind working as he moved.

Riding into the valley, his quick eye had observed every bit of the terrain, and he remembered a wide shelf of rock bordering a small mountain stream near the foot of the trail. There was a nest of boulders at the trail's end, and he let his tracks go directly to them. In the shelter of the boulders and well out of sight he built a small fire, and when it was going well he added a few sticks of slow-burning wood, and then left it.

Now he took to the shelf of rock, careful to ease his feet down and to make no telltale movements as he crossed the rock to the stream. There he waded for some distance, climbed among the trees, and started back. It had taken him all of two hours, but the effort would be worth it, he knew. He did not return directly to the camp but bore off toward the split in the mountain they had seen earlier. When he drew near he saw the mountain was skirted by a dense growth of trees and brush. He made his way through this to the foot of a talus slope of broken rocks.

Mounting it, he found himself directly before the cleft in the wall, and felt a faint stirring of air on his face. The opening was abysmally black and he could form no estimate of its depth by looking. Finally, picking up a pebble, he tossed it out before him. He estimated the fall at about thirty feet, and scowled. Yet working his way along the crest of the talus slope, his foot suddenly touched another sort of surface. Instantly he dropped to a crouch and put out exploratory fingers. They encountered a shallow depression, free of rocks and smooth—a trail!

Whether it was made by game or Indians he could not guess, but there was nowhere for it to go except to the cleft he had found, and so, without attempting to follow it, he straightened to full height and started off in the opposite direction and camp. There had been a cool dampness in the air from the cleft, and that might mean a cave.

Hopalong was close to the camp before he could see any sign of the fire, for he had chosen the spot well. He stopped close by and spoke. Pamela got up from behind a rock on the far side of the fire, rifle in hand. Her face showed her relief.

"What happened? I was afraid you were lost or killed." Her eyes searched his. "Did you find anything?"

"Maybe."

He lowered himself to the ground well out of the small glow of the fire.

"Better sleep. I'll call you in an hour."

"You mean to keep watch?"

"Uh-huh. I ain't worried about the Apaches t'night, but Sparr has no objections to night fighting. I ain't at all shore but what I prefer the Apaches to him. You get some sleep. You must be dead beat."

Avery Sparr would not so easily relinquish a victory that had been practically in his fingers. A shrewd tracker and trailer himself, Hopalong was not inclined to underrate the big outlaw. Utterly ruthless, the man was also relentless, and he would track them like a lobo wolf. Above all, there were men with him driven by personal feelings, men who hated Hopalong so much their feelings would drive them on even when better sense indicated a halt.

Putting himself in Sparr's place, he knew the man must be puzzled. If Hopalong had headed either north or south the gunman would not have been puzzled, but to head directly into the highest peaks of the range, an area without known trails, with steep cliffs and towering peaks, with deep canyons and thick forests, seemed to ask for a trap.

Hopalong would have doubted there was a trail through here had he not heard the stories of the old cowhand on the T Bar. Yet it was possible that such a trail existed, and he had been told to keep north of Whitewater Baldy. That peak, snow-covered now, gleamed brightly off to the southeast, and almost dead ahead was another peak he had been told was called Willow Mountain.

Sooner or later he was coming to a showdown with Sparr. Tucking another stick into the fire, Hopalong considered that. Fear was no part of him. He disliked killing and avoided it when possible, but there were times when no man could avoid it, and he knew that even if he tried to, Avery Sparr would seek him out. The battle had been joined now, and when this game of hunting and hunted was over, they would settle it with lead.

Finally he awakened Pamela, and was instantly asleep. He slept soundly, yet the slightest sound that did not belong to the night would have awakened him.

Four times during the previous day Avery Sparr's Piute tracker had lost Hopalong Cassidy's trail. Four times he had found it again. Night found them on the lip of the cliff down which Hopalong's buckskin had led the party. Sparr stared at it and swore softly, bitterly.

"He's got nerve," he admitted ruefully. "I'd not have gambled on such a trail without knowin' it."

There were eight men with Sparr, some of the toughest in his outfit. Anson Mowry, despite his wounded hand and aching head, had profanely refused to remain behind. The tall puncher whom Hopalong had bound and gagged was along. His name was Leven Proctor, and he was wanted in three states for cattle theft, bank robbery, and one sheriff killing. The others were Ed Framson, Tony Cuyas, the three Lydon boys from Animas, and the Piute tracker.

"You sure he went down there?"

Framson furrowed his brow, staring dubiously over the cliff. He was a stocky man, solid of chest and shoulder.

"I wouldn't figger a self-respectin' goat would tackle it."

"Cassidy would," Proctor said.

The Indian nodded. "Sure. He go down. Old Mimbreños trail."

"He ain't far ahead then," Mowry said, with satisfaction. "All I want is one shot!"

"Want to tackle that trail now, Anse?"

Sparr gestured at the eyebrow of rock clinging to the cliff's face. In the dusk of evening it was no more than a dark line along the face of the rock.

"You can go now, if you like. Get first chance at him."

Mowry stared suspiciously at Sparr. "I'll wait," he said stubbornly.

"We'll get him tomorrow."

Avery Sparr was confident. His study of the mountains ahead showed him no break that might include a trail out of the basin.

"He's trapped himself."

Ed Framson walked to the cliff edge and stared over interestedly. Hopalong Cassidy did not worry him. For a long time he had believed the stories of him were much exaggerated. What he wanted no part of was a mix-up with Apaches. He had seen what they did to a man when they caught him. This was their country, and he had followed Sparr into it with growing uneasiness.

"See for yourself." Sparr waved a hand over the basin below. "He's got into a hole without any other outlet. He's boxed in for fair."

He pointed to the line of massive mountains that barred the way westward. Across the darkening sky ranged granite shoulders of five great peaks, all towering toward eleven thousand feet. Farther north were as many more that approached ten thousand.

"That's rugged country," Sparr said, "an' she's late in the season. There's snow on the peaks already, and any day now snow can block every pass west."

"There are passes then?"

"Uh-uh. Not through here. Farther north there is, but they're boxed in now. We'll get them tomorrow."

"Maybe." Proctor looked over his shoulder from the fire he had built while the others were talking. "That Cassidy sized up to me like a man who knowed where he was goin'. He wasn't runnin' wild an' free. He was goin' someplace!"

"He's there," Sparr replied grimly.

Nevertheless, Proctor's remark unsettled him. Suppose there was a way out? After all, Cassidy would never have gone into a hole like that unless he believed there was. Sparr contemplated the view from the rim with lessening satisfaction. There was already darkness down there, an utter blackness that showed nothing at all. Stars hung like lamps in a sky that shaded to gray and faint violet at the mountain crests. Suddenly Sparr's eyes sharpened. Far out over that vast bowl of darkness was a tiny gleam, the gleam of a distant campfire. That, then, was where Cassidy and the Jordans were. Then he scowled. There was another vague and indefinite glow farther south. Was it a campfire? He could not make it out. If so, who could it be?

Unknown to Avery Sparr he was now looking upon the small fire of the Apaches which was concealed from everywhere but the heights.

Later, long after he had eaten and when most of them had already rolled in their blankets, Sparr returned to the cliff edge. The fire to the south had vanished and there was a faint glow at the foot of the very cliff on which he stood! This was the fire Hopalong had started and left behind him on his night foray. Sparr shook his head, suddenly worried. Who else was down there?

He halted, stopping abruptly. Then he smiled. Of course! It was a trick to confuse him. Trust a trailwise hombre like Cassidy to think of that!

Dawn found Hopalong lying, not behind the larger rocks that offered the greatest protection, but among some smaller rocks almost concealed by the tall grass and brush. The place apparently offered no shelter at all, yet visibility was good from where he lay and the field of fire extended across the whole of the open area before him. Moreover, he had no need to thrust his head up or around a rock, where the Indians would more than likely be expecting him.

Behind him Pamela was busy over a fire of dry wood, making coffee and warming up a little of the food they had left. Dick Jordan was sitting up, and he had a rifle across his knees. His cheeks looked hollow and his eyes were sunken, but the spirit within him was strong. Almost with the coffee came the first movement from down in the trees. Only a slight stir of grass, but Hopalong knew that an Indian had started toward him. Action had begun, or would soon begin.

He glanced warily toward the mountain trail, bathed now in

the bright morning sun that had cleared the ridge to warm the crest but had not yet reached the basin where he lay. There was no movement on the trail. Unknown to him, Avery Sparr and his men were already in the basin. Light had touched the trail before it reached the basin at all, and their descent had begun at once.

Pamela picked up her own rifle and joined them near the rocks. Hopalong glanced back at the camp. The horses were saddled and out of sight in the trees and rocks, the gear all packed and ready. If they had to run for it they could. Hopalong nestled his rifle stock against his cheek and fitted it well back into the hollow of his shoulder. His eyes were cold and blue as they glinted along the rifle barrel.

Long before Hopalong had gone into position with his rifle, four Apaches had found the tracks made the previous night. Rightly, they had deduced they had been made during darkness, and so figured one of the three they had attacked was trying to escape. After a muttered conference the four moved off swiftly, following that trail. Before long they sighted the ghostly wisp of smoke rising from the slow-burning wood of Hoppy's decoying campfire.

Warily the Apaches halted. Instinctively they sensed something was wrong. Had the three riders they pursued come this far they must surely have gone up the trail. And while they waited, puzzling out this strange occurrence, nine horsemen were riding to the basin bottom and gathering at the trail's end before moving around the trees into sight.

The Apaches moved forward carefully. Avery Sparr, on the other side of the fire in a little hollow, also sighted the smoke. This was one of the fires he had seen the previous night, the last of the three. He swung from his horse and walked slowly forward, flanked by one of the Lydon boys. From around a tree he slowly moved his head, and his eyes caught the barest movement, a flash of brown moving flesh. An Apache!

His hand flashed for his Colt even as the Indian thrust forward his rifle, but the Colt came up spouting flame and the Indian died moving. Instantly there was a crash of guns, and Jake Lydon went down, clawing at his chest and coughing blood from a ruined lung.

At the burst of fire Hopalong, knowing his stratagem had worked, riveted his eyes on the nearest movement he had seen. With the crash of gunfire there had been a sudden end to the movement, and Hopalong gambled. Holding his rifle low, he fired into the grass. He heard the fleshy thud of the bullet, saw the Apache's head lift, and nailed it with a second shot. Two shots answered him, and instantly Pamela and Dick Jordan fired. Unwittingly, they had taken the same target, and the Indian died where he lay.

The firing continued, and Hopalong faded back to the horses. "Come on!" he called in a low voice. "In the saddle! You first, Dick!"

Springing his horse into the lead, he led them at a lope down through the trees toward the trail he had found. Whether or not the cleft in the rock was an outlet to the basin he did not know, but they were in no position to wait. Behind him the gunfire continued, but at a slower rate. The buckskin scrambled up the talus slope, then over the ridge and into the slight hollow behind. Without hesitation the horse turned into the narrow space in the rock and Hopalong slowed it down.

The opening into which he had ridden was no more than twelve feet wide and the rock on each side was smooth as glass. At one time water had roared through here, polishing these walls until not even an ant could have found a foothold on their sheer expanse. The floor of the cleft was hard-packed sand after the first hundred yards or so, and the passage through which they rode widened a few feet, then narrowed until their boots brushed the wall on either side. Then it widened again, and here there was an open space of perhaps an acre in extent with some grass and one lone tree.

Hopalong drew up and turned in the saddle, looking at Dick Jordan. "How you makin' it, old-timer?" he asked, grinning. Yet even as he grinned his eyes inspected the older man carefully. The limits of the crippled man's endurance must soon be reached, for, tough as he was, he could not stand much of this. Even staying in the saddle was an effort. Now firing could not be heard. A stalemate, or the end of the fight?

"I'm all right." Jordan glared at him. "How you makin' it? Don't worry about Pam an' me. Long as you can sit in a saddle, I can, b'lieve me! No Bar 20 or Double Y hand was ever as tough as a Circle J rider!"

Hopalong chuckled. "Why, you wall-eyed galoot! The best man you ever had wouldn't have been fit to drive a Bar 20 calf wagon!"

"Huh!" Jordan snorted. "Lanky was best hand, an' we taught him all he knowed on the Circle J!"

Hopalong chuckled. "Why, Lanky always said he left the J because that bunch of gristle-heeled old-timers was so lazy they wouldn't move camp for a prairie fire! He got tired of doin' all the work over there, so he came to a good outfit!"

"When you two stop fussing, you might tell me where we go from here." Pamela gestured at the steep-walled bowl in which they stood. "Maybe we've lost them, but we can't stay here always."

Hopalong had been letting his own eyes search the sheer-walled area in which they had stopped. No outlet was visible. To all appearances they were trapped once more, only worse. Despite the looks of the place, he did not believe it, for the trail down which they had come had been well used, even if long since. There were no evidences here of anyone who had stopped for long. And there was no reason for coming to such a place. Whoever had come in had gone out, and by another route.

"Give your horses a rest," he said quietly. "Just let 'em browse for a while, but don't get down."

He walked his horse around the bowl, finding no tracks here that could be followed until he reached the far side near the lone aspen tree and a huge clump of manzanita. The tree was scarred and torn, the bark ripped, and even some of the wood torn from the trunk. Claw marks on the tree reached as high as eight feet above the ground. On the lower part of the tree it was plastered with mud and hair. Attracted by his examination, Pamela had followed him to the tree.

"What is it, Hoppy?" She spoke softly, as though awed by the silence of the lonely place or by the height of the towering walls.

"Bear tree. No bear will ever pass it without signin' his mark on it. Generations of 'em go to the same tree, an' they reach as high up as they can reach. This bunch has been mostly grizzlies."

"How can you tell?"

"Size, for one thing." He indicated a track on the ground. "Claw marks for another. Grizzly has longer claws than any other bear. All five toes plainly marked too. That ain't usual with black bears."

He turned and walked away slowly, scanning the ground. Finally he pointed at a dark tunnel into the manzanita. "There's our trail. Let's go."

A double-rutted track pointed the way into the brush, and they followed, bending low in the saddle to stay under the branches and leaves. What they found then was a continuation of the cleft from which they had come, but this one started back into the mountain, trending southwest, while the former cleft had run due north and south and they had followed it going north. Yet before they had gone many yards the trail made an elbow and they started back, now riding northwest. The cleft widened suddenly into a high-walled canyon and on one side there was a mound of talus at the foot of the cliff.

The grass thickened and there was brush, but by following the double-rutted bear track they traveled swiftly. Obviously an ancient, long-used trail, it wound around boulders and fallen logs but kept a fairly general direction. Twice they found fallen trees ripped open by bears hunting for grubs. Then suddenly the narrow canyon ended and they emerged in the open with a creek lying across their trail at least a half mile ahead.

Side by side they started across it. Dick Jordan was not talking, but his face was grim as he sat his saddle. Once he permitted himself a faint grin.

"I ain't pullin' leather, Hoppy, so keep movin'. Whoever won that scrap back there will be on our trail."

"This is the Turkeyfeather, the way I've got it figured," Hoppy said, "an' north of us is supposed to lay Iron Creek. We'll head that way an' try to follow it for a while. Then we cross some canyons an' hit the Snow Creek trail somewhere beyond."

Dick Jordan glanced around, studying the sky shrewdly. "We got another reason to hurry," he said quietly. "It's goin' to snow."

Hopalong felt a chill within him. All day he had felt it coming, but had hoped that he was mistaken. It was early for snow, yet they were very high here, and they must go yet higher in crossing the top of the Mogollons. All day he had been trying to convince himself that he was mistaken about that feeling in the air.

He took the lead now and moved on rapidly across uneven, tree-dotted terrain. Then into a dark forest, out of it, and they were on the edge of Iron Creek. Fording the creek, they struck a dim trail. "This meets the Snow Creek trail," he told them. "It will be faster goin' now."

Now he was watching the back trail again, for he knew they would be pursued, and he was only uncertain as to when that pursuit would catch up. The trail was climbing now, and steadily. The sun that had greeted them shortly after daybreak had disappeared while they were following the trail through the cleft, and now the sky was a dull, even expanse of gray. A cool wind touched his cheek, and he scowled, suddenly worried.

If a storm was coming, their situation could not be worse. They still had high mountains and a ride that would take them the better part of another day at least. As the crow flies it was probably less than thirty miles; by trail it was considerably farther, and with a crippled man— He pushed on, stopping only briefly at a spring on the hill near Iron Creek Mesa.

Something touched his cheek, and he glanced up quickly. Snowflakes!

His whole body seemed stilled by apprehension. They had more than thirty miles to go without heavy coats over a high mountain pass in the face of a snowstorm. And neither food nor shelter anywhere along the trail!

CHAPTER 10

APACHE BAIT HITS CIRCLE J

The fight in the basin had not ended quickly, but had dragged on indecisively until the Apaches abandoned the field. Just when this took place Avery Sparr did not know. There had been eight Apaches alive when the fighting started and Sparr had nine men including himself. However, Sparr did not know the number of Indians he faced, and he fought, after a fast start, with considerable caution. Sparr had killed the first Indian he had seen, but in almost the same instant had lost Jake Lydon.

Hopalong's stratagem was apparent at once. The mystery of the unused fire was explained, and Sparr guessed correctly that a trail had been laid out by Cassidy to lead the Apaches toward him. Knowing that while they fought, Hopalong was making his getaway in safety, Sparr was furious. Outgeneraled, he nevertheless settled down to whipping the Apaches, and finally succeeded. At least three more Indians had gone down, but he had two wounded men of his own.

It was then that he showed his own generalship. "Tony," he said, turning to Cuyas, who had suffered a flesh wound, "take Hank an' start back. Push your horses, kill 'em if necessary, but get to the Circle J an' to Soper. Tell him to rush men to Alma to head off Cassidy an' the Jordans. By usin' relays of horses from the ranches along the way they can make it.

"When they get to Alma they can get more men there from Moralles, an' make a quick check to see if Hopalong's got to town. If he hasn't, cover every trail out of the mountains, but concentrate on Deep River an' the Silver Creek trail. I don't think he could get to the last, but he might, so take no chances. Tell him to get all three—no nonsense. Get rid of 'em! The men doin' the actual killin' get a hundred extra each, an' five hundred for Cassidy."

"Five hundred?" Tony Cuyas grinned. "I'll go myself, amigo!"

"What if they've got to Alma?" Hank Lydon demanded.

Avery Sparr scowled. "Then get 'em! Get 'em out of town! Do it smooth an' quiet, but get 'em—and then get rid of them where they won't be found."

When they had gone, Sparr stood for an instant in thought, then turned to his men. "All right, scatter out and find their trail. I'll give twenty dollars on the spot to the man who finds it!"

He stared up at the bleak sky and swore irritably. It would be tough to get caught in the mountains now, and every mile was a mile of added danger. If it started to snow— Suddenly his eyes glinted.

Snow! What a break that would be! Caught in those high mountains in a snowstorm, Cassidy would never get through. Why, it would be spring before they could be found, and even if they found a place to hole up, they would certainly starve if they did not freeze. Such a solution would solve all his problems and be infinitely the best thing. Yet, even if there was no snow, the chances were fifty-fifty that his men would beat them to Alma. The distance was all of twice as great, but the trails were good and there were fast horses at the ranches the outlaws had been using. Cassidy would be burdened by a rapidly failing crippled man and a girl.

Suppose they did make it? Suppose they got to the law? The deputy sheriff at Alma right now was notoriously inefficient. He would act slowly, and Sparr could always deny their stories and say that Jordan had been affected by his fall and was no longer right mentally. Pamela, he could say, was merely hysterical. Yet while some might believe him, many would not. While with Soper's help he might brazen it out, there was a risk in that which he did not choose to take.

The Piute was coming up the trail. He halted when he saw Sparr and lifted a hand. "Got trail," he said shortly. "You come?"

Sparr's long halloo brought instant response from the other riders, and they closed in around him swiftly. Avery Sparr halted at the cleft and looked into the deep shadows without enthusiasm. "A good place to die," he thought aloud, "if he wants to chance it."

"Not him." Proctor was positive. "He won't gamble on it with that old man on his hands, an' in this weather. He'll head for Alma fast as he can roll."

"That's probably right," Sparr agreed, "but we'll go slow."

Despite the tracks left by Hopalong, Sparr and his men were even longer finding the hidden trail from the bowl than Hopalong had been, and by the time they reached the crossing of Iron Creek snow was falling fast and hard. For the last few miles his men had been looking at him expectantly, and at last Avery Sparr conceded that to push on farther was to take an unnecessary risk. It was time now to go back. If they went farther they might be caught in the same snowy trap he was wishing for Hopalong and the Jordans.

Now it was up to the men from Alma and the snow.

"We'll go back," he said. "I think they are high in the peaks now."

"If they are," Ed Framson said, "they'll never get through! Drifts will be over all the trails within another hour or so. They are just far enough along to get trapped."

Leven Proctor stared at the peaks, gloomy now and black against the dull gray sky. A little chill went through him as he thought of the three riding into those icy peaks—a crippled man, rapidly tiring, a young girl, and Hopalong. Remembering Hopalong Cassidy's cold blue eyes, he was not so sure.

"If any man alive can get through," he said, "that gun slick will do it."

Sparr nodded.

"He's tough," he conceded. "One of the toughest."

Proctor stared uncomfortably at the peaks. What had happened to him, anyway? How did it happen that he, a top hand in any man's outfit, was riding with such men as these? He looked around him unhappily. The memory of the girl and her father stayed with him. For Hopalong he was not concerned. He was a tough man in a tough game, and he knew what his chances were. But old men and girls? Leven Proctor suddenly realized that he was not the sort of man he had hoped to be. Money was all right. Escaping the brutal work of roundups and line riding was all right, but he had never intended to go so far as this.

Mesquite Jenkins and Johnny Nelson rode down the trail to the Circle J almost without interruption. Yet they had fortunately missed the trail with the guarded crossing and found the Indian Creek crossing. They came up to the ranch and halted in the edge of the timber. Nothing could have been more peaceful. A half-dozen horses lazed in the corral, the warm sunshine gleaming on their polished bodies. No one moved about the place, although a slow trickle of smoke drifted skyward from the ranch-house kitchen.

Mesquite started his horse, and the two rode quietly down the trail to the house. They were drawing up before the step when Soper spoke. Until that instant neither man had seen him. "How do you do, gentlemen? Have you had breakfast?"

Mesquite strained his eyes to see into the shadowed porch after facing the bright glare of the sun. He was glad that the speaker, whoever he was, was not shooting. "We had coffee," he admitted, "but we could sure eat."

Soper stepped out on the porch, neat in his gray suit, his smile pleasant. "Get down, then! Get down! Glad to have company."

He gestured toward the bunkhouse.

"Most of the hands are gone, and so are the others. Will you come in?"

Soper's eyes measured them quickly. He knew of the death of Bizco, and immediately placed Mesquite as the killer. It seemed impossible that this young cowhand could be so fast. Yet when Mesquite drew nearer and he looked into those icy eyes and that cold face he felt a momentary chill—a chill that removed all doubts. Johnny Nelson, he guessed, was merely a happy-go-lucky cowhand.

The Mexican woman entered at Soper's call and began putting food on the table. Several times Johnny surprised her looking at them with interest, and her eyes, when they went to Soper, held something else. Could it be fear? Nelson shrugged. It was scarcely likely, for no more agreeable sort could be found than Soper.

"Where's Dick Jordan?" Mesquite demanded suddenly. The

question was sharply asked, and it almost caught Soper off balance, yet suddenly he perceived that a time had come for change.

"Dick Jordan left," he said, "with his daughter and a man called Cassidy. They got away, and Avery Sparr is chasing them."

The two exchanged glances, and Mesquite lifted his coffee cup, his mind working swiftly. Who and what was Soper? He seemed friendly, yet Mesquite was a young man more than usually gifted with suspicion. Yet if he was not friendly, why tell them what he just had?

Soper continued to talk. "There's been a bad situation here," he said gravely, "and personally I know very little about it. Most of my duties have been away from the ranch, handling business with this venture and others in which Mr. Jordan was concerned. He has, you know, some mining interests also."

Jenkins did not know, but he was listening and willing to learn. In the meantime, the food was good, and he was hungry. Johnny Nelson was devoting himself to the food, but his eyes and ears were busy. Above all, the Mexican woman interested him. She would, of course, be a holdover from the old days on the Circle J. She would know all that had happened, and if she would talk, and had a chance to talk, she might explain a lot of things.

The thing was to get the chance to talk to her alone and, moreover, to win her confidence. That she was curious about them, Nelson was aware, and she had seen the brands on their horses.

"I'm afraid," Soper suggested carefully and gravely, "that Avery Sparr has exceeded himself. I rarely saw Mr. Jordan or his daughter unless he was present, and many orders were relayed to me through him, but some of the orders have appeared—well, unlikely, to say the least."

While they ate, several riders had drifted in from outlying parts of the ranch, and Johnny had seen them studying the two horses and looking toward the ranch. Among them was a lean, buck-toothed man who walked around them very slowly, glanced at the house, then disappeared in the direction of the bunkhouse.

"I don't," Soper continued, "even know much about the events here. I know that Cassidy seemed to feel that Mr. Jordan and Pamela were held against their will, and he got them away. From Sparr's actions I would surmise that he was correct, for Avery Sparr went off in pursuit, taking some of the toughest hands with him."

Arnold Soper was thinking as he talked, but he was thinking far ahead of his speech. Avery Sparr might catch Hopalong Cassidy, and if he did, somebody would be killed. If it was Cassidy, then Sparr would return at once to the ranch; if it was Sparr, then Soper would appear as a friend and nothing could be proved to the contrary—at least, he added, not easily. The Jordans might not know anything themselves. Or, he corrected himself, remembering Pamela, not much.

In Mesquite and Johnny Nelson he saw two men who could be used to destroy Avery Sparr, and with Sparr out of the way, all would be well. Of course it would be much better if the Jordans were removed, but by this time Sparr might have accomplished that. Knowing the ruthlessness of Sparr when aroused, Soper was quite sure that he would succeed. Soper hoped he would—and get killed in the process.

If he did not, there were possible tools of his defeat here in these two men. "No need for you two to push on," he suggested. "There would be no chance to catch up to Cassidy now. Not in time, anyway. If Sparr catches him, or even if he fails, he will have to come back here. The way I see it, we're going to have snow, and when it comes all the passes will be blocked. Sparr will never keep on into the mountains then; it would be sheer suicide."

"You think Hoppy was tryin' for Alma?" Mesquite inquired.

"Certain of it. There is no other place to go. Alma has some law-abiding citizens, and of course some that are not. Still, if he got to Alma with Dick Jordan and Pamela, they have friends there, and they would all be safe."

"If I know Hoppy," Johnny said, "he won't be looking for safety! He'll be huntin' Avery Sparr!"

"That's him, all right," Mesquite agreed, "an' he'll not rest until he smokes out every one of this gang."

"You have a lot of faith in him," Soper suggested. Mesquite's words had brought a little chill of uneasiness to him. But why be foolish? Hopalong Cassidy was just a cowhand who happened to be handy with a gun. "Sparr may be the better man."

"I've heard of Sparr," Johnny admitted, "but I've yet to see the man who could stack up against Hopalong." He refilled his cup. "Who's in this with Sparr? Was he the only one?"

"Bizco was killed at Horse Springs the other night." Soper turned his eyes toward Mesquite. "By you, I believe."

"Uh-huh. I heard that was his name. What about the others?"

"Well"—Soper was cautious—"Cassidy killed Barker, but there is another one, Anse Mowry. He is totally vicious, and a man named Proctor. Then Mark Connor, the bartender in Horse Springs, is an old friend of Sparr. Most of the men with him would leave in a hurry if anything happened to Avery Sparr. He's the ringleader."

"How come you got along with him?" Johnny asked casually.

Soper waved a hand. "He needed me, and I believed I might help the Jordans. I did not understand the situation here, but I knew they derived some comfort from my presence. So I stayed on. Also"—he made the remark very casual—"I have interests here myself."

"Another partner?" Mesquite asked.

Soper looked quickly at the cowhand. Had there been any

sarcasm in that remark? But Mesquite was eating quietly and scarcely seemed to have noticed. "Not exactly," Soper said carefully, "but I have interests. I had been doing some selling for the ranch and some buying for myself. I have cattle on this range, under my brand."

"Which is?"

"The Circle S."

Soper's reply was low-voiced, as he did not want the Mexican woman to hear. And he did not think it necessary to add that Sparr believed that the Circle S was his brand, but had entrusted the registration of the brand to Soper, who had filed it in his own name, having his own plans. Every head of stock that Sparr's men branded was branded for Arnold Soper.

"I figured that was Sparr's brand," Johnny said.

"He has no brand. He talked some of filing one, but never did. I think he was mainly interested in stealing stock from Jordan. Some of the men working with him are notorious rustlers."

As Soper sat there, he knew that every word he said would make his life less secure if Sparr was not killed soon. Yet he knew that Cassidy had precipitated the whole situation to such an extent that he must follow through now or not at all. There was every chance that Sparr would catch the Jordans, or they would be killed in the mountains. Hopalong might be killed and might not, but whatever happened, he must be prepared. The return of Avery Sparr must be met with these men, these two who faced him.

"Avery Sparr," he began carefully, "is a dangerous man. The longer he lives the more we all are in danger. He hates Cassidy, and if he catches him will kill or be killed. He will not"—he spoke the words in a flat, cold, emphatic voice—"leave the trail until Cassidy is dead. Therefore, if Avery Sparr rides into this ranch yard, you can take it from me that Hopalong Cassidy is finished."

Mesquite scowled. Despite all his confidence in Hopalong, he was worried. After all, the man had been burdened by a crippled man and a girl, he had gone into unknown mountains in Apache country, and he was being followed by nine tough, hard-bitten men, all of them killers when the price or reason was right.

"Well," he said quietly, "if Avery Sparr comes back here, he can die mighty easy."

Soper nodded. "He should. He is a man better off dead."

He got to his feet. "Take your time eating. If you want to rest, take it easy around the house. No use going to the bunkhouse unless you want to have trouble with lesser lights. Sparr may show up anytime. Just stick around. I'll be back shortly."

He walked outside and paused. Right now he felt very much like a slack-wire walker above Niagara Falls. Death lay with any misstep. Actually, he liked the feel of it. He drew deeply on his cheroot and considered what lay ahead. Mesquite was deadly, and the other man was probably competent, but he himself would be standing in the shadows of the porch with a rifle. He would leave nothing to chance.

As for the others— He would call the bunch from Turkey Springs Canyon, in the Elks. They would handle these. Only four men he had, but picked men. He smiled suddenly. Avery Sparr had been a fool to lay a thing like this in his lap! Where Avery had made enemies, he had made friends, and Avery Sparr little knew how carefully his groundwork had been laid. Two could play at such a steal, and between the gun and the brain the latter must always be victor.

Yet confident as he was, he was a careful and a considering man. So now, even at this stage of the game, with the whole situation far advanced, he went over every detail again in his mind. It was much like playing poker, and the secret of it was never to let your antagonists guess how little or how much you might be holding.

It was a law of survival that one must always adapt oneself to changes and conditions. He who refuses to adapt does not last. He may win credit for being stubborn, but he loses or dies. It was in the nature of Arnold Soper to adapt himself, and his every sense was alert to every change.

Behind him Mesquite stared into his coffee cup and then looked up at Johnny. "Something about this doesn't look so good."

"Nothing about it looks good."

"Maybe this hombre is on the level."

"Maybe—an' again maybe not."

"Let's figger like he's not, then we'll be on the safe side."

"When you read sign," Johnny suggested, "you don't get far if you foller only what you see. A man has got to use his imagination, put himself in the place of the man he's follerin', and see where you would go if you was him."

"This here Soper looks smart."

"Uh-huh. He looks smart, he acts smart, but he takes orders an' does what he's told like a good little boy, all white an' innocent."

"Yuh think so? Maybe. But let's, like we said, play like he's smart. Let's figger he gets wise that somethin' doesn't smell right. Maybe the Jordans were prisoners here. Maybe Sparr is tryin' for a big steal. Maybe this Soper ain't honest."

"Let's figger he's not."

"All right. He can be partners with Sparr, he can work for him, or he can work for himself an' pretend he's workin' for him. If he's doin' that last, he knows Sparr is nobody to fool with. He knows he's double-crossin' a tough hombre who would fill him with lead so quick it would make his head swim if he figgered there was a reason. Maybe he figgers Sparr smells somethin' wrong, what would he do?"

"Try to get Sparr killed."

"Right. An' who better to do it than two wanderin' pilgrims like us? Two gun-handy pilgrims who figger they've a grudge against him."

"He's right about one thing," Johnny said. "We can't help Hopalong now. That chase is too far away. If we can help him, it would be here, or maybe Horse Springs."

"Maybe we better have a look around. Around this house, I mean. An' maybe that Mexican woman can tell us somethin'."

"I'll bet she can."

Mesquite eased back the bench on which he sat and got to his feet. He stepped quickly through the door into the empty room beyond. Johnny, after a quick glance, turned toward the kitchen. Both men worked rapidly, and both were accustomed to reading sign, to observing, that is, and drawing deductions from what they saw.

Mesquite noticed the door to the Jordans' room and stepped through. The first thing he saw was the bar. It was not reasonable to expect a bar on the inside of a door within a house. A quick survey of the room and he was positive of one thing. Two people had lived here. Two beds, a closet full of the girl's clothing, and one partly filled with clothing belonging to Dick Jordan. Nowhere did he find a gun or where one had been.

Why would two people owning a large ranch house with all of a dozen rooms confine themselves to one? Without doubt the Jordans had been prisoners here, and they had evidently had instructions to allow nobody into the room but Avery Sparr or some one or two of his henchmen. That was obvious from the bar on the inside.

Also, Mesquite correctly deduced what he was already certain of, that they had left swiftly and taken few things with them. He returned to the dining room and glanced out. Soper stood by the corrals, looking off toward the mountains. He stood as if listening.

Johnny emerged from the kitchen, his face bright with knowledge. "We hit it!" he said eagerly and grimly. "She talked plenty! She has no use for Sparr, less for Soper. This hombre Soper is peculiar. He looks so nice, but he whacked this Mexican cook a couple of times when she didn't give him fast enough service.

"She says they were prisoners here, the Jordans. Only a few people were allowed to see them. She's afraid of Sparr, but she is more afraid of Soper."

Mesquite nodded. "We've done some good guessing. Now to figger this a little bit. Let's figger Hoppy isn't comin' back." At Johnny's shocked expression Mesquite hastily said, "Not that I think he ain't. I'd gamble my life on it. He's tough to handle. What I mean is, let's figger he ain't comin' back. This here place goes to whoever's next of kin if Jordan's daughter is killed. It don't go to either Sparr or Soper, all right?"

"Uh-huh. So we scotch their snake."

"Right." Mesquite chuckled. "Wouldn't Red an' Lanky be happy to be here now? They'll throw a fit when they find out we tied up with Hoppy after all."

"Hey."

Johnny was looking out the window, and Mesquite stepped to his shoulder. The air was filled with slowly drifting snowflakes. Johnny stared at Mesquite's face, colder than death now. Both men were thinking the same thing. Hopalong Cassidy was in the mountains, high in the mountains with few passes and no winter clothing.

Both men knew how bitterly cold those mountains could be. Both knew how rapidly a man loses the warmth from his body in the biting and icy winds at high altitudes, even under the best of conditions. Hoppy alone was bad enough, but burdened with a crippled man and a girl— "If he don't make it"—Mesquite's voice was low and ugly—"I'll kill every man ever connected with this mess!"

"Yeah," Johnny said soberly. "I'm in on that too."

"I feel like goin' out there, an'—" Mesquite's lips thinned with fury and his fingers strayed to a gun butt.

"No good," Johnny said quietly. "We'll wait. Maybe somethin' will break that will show us our way. One thing we know. Come hell or high water, we clean out this rat's nest or they bury us both on the Gila!"

Arnold Soper stared toward the house. The two gunfighters had not come out yet. Well, let them take it easy. There would be time enough. In the meantime—he glanced at his gold watch—it would be better if the boys in Turkey Spring Canyon were down here. Maybe he could slip away and ride up there, but it was long, almost twenty miles. The snow was falling faster and faster now, and the ground was white with it.

Johnny Nelson came out and took both horses and led them to the stable. Mesquite lounged just inside the door. Arnold Soper still stood before the corrals, watching the snow and occasionally glancing toward the higher mountains.

Mesquite heard the Mexican cook raking the ashes from her stove and preparing to begin a new fire for the evening meal. Yet it was still early and much could happen. Restlessly, irritably, he got to his feet. If he could only get to Hoppy! At least he could be doing something instead of waiting!

He walked back to the window, and he was standing there

watching Soper when suddenly the man started forward and stared toward the mountains. He started to run, ran a few steps, then stopped as two riders raced pell-mell into the yard.

Mesquite stiffened and leaned forward, staring. Neither rider was Hopalong, and from the descriptions neither was Avery Sparr. Yet he could see at a glance that both these men had been hurt and their horses had been run half to death. He went to the door and stepped out on the porch, but could hear nothing of what was said, although both men were talking. Finally a man came from the bunkhouse and took their horses, and Soper went into the bunkhouse with the new arrivals.

Snow fell softly but thickly in an ever-deepening blanket. Johnny walked from the stable and stood staring down at the snow where the two men had stood, and then he walked on to the house. "Bleedin'," he said, "both of 'em hurt. One of 'em opened a wound on the ride.

"Looks like they caught up with Hoppy," he said grimly, "an' Sparr wasn't one of them. That means that Hopalong is still movin' west."

"Or cornered."

"Let's go find out!"

They started for the door and crowded through it. In swift strides they crossed the snow-covered yard toward the bunkhouse. As they reached the door, it opened, and framed in the doorway was Arnold Soper. He glanced quickly from one to the other. "Don't go in there!" he said sharply. "There's no need!"

"We want to talk to those hombres that just came in."

"You don't have to. I'll tell you what you need to know." He stepped outside and closed the door behind him.

"Those men were wounded." Mesquite's voice was flat. He was beginning to dislike Soper, and he had never cared for him.

Only before he had been indifferent to the man. Now he was beginning to resent him.

"That's right." Soper spoke easily. For an instant he had been in a panic. If these two should happen to repeat some of what he had said, it might spoil everything. "Cassidy tricked Sparr. He led some Apaches into Sparr, then slipped away while they were fighting. These men were wounded in that fight. One man was killed."

"Cassidy got away?"

"Yes. And when these men left they still had not found his trail. Of course by now they probably have. They have a Piute tracker with them."

The important thing was that Hopalong was still alive; he was still moving. Mesquite chuckled as he thought of Hopalong leading the Apaches into Sparr's outfit, who were, if anything, worse than the Apaches. That was like Hoppy. He was a man who knew how to fight, and when you started anything with him, he went all the way.

"I think," Johnny Nelson said, "we'll go in and talk to them anyway!"

CHAPTER 11

GUN GHOST OF THE GOLD COUNTRY

Arnold Soper hesitated. For an instant his anger had been about to get the better of him, but he realized the futility of that. Nor could he think of any diplomatic way in which the two Double Y hands could be kept out of the bunkhouse. "Let them alone!" he protested. "Both men are wounded. They need rest."

"They'll get rest." Mesquite's eyes turned to Soper's, and for an instant the two measured each other. Soper's eyes shifted first and he was furious. "You see," Mesquite added, "Johnny an' me aim to keep up with the news around here. Don't we, Johnny?"

"Uh-huh."

Johnny Nelson teetered on his boot heels, his eyes hard but smiling as he looked at Soper.

"We sure do. Figgers to get mighty interestin' aroun' here. An' we sort of figger to stick around," he added, "until Hoppy gets back. If he don't get back, we'll sort of finish what he started —all the way."

The last three words were uttered with his eyes on Soper, and the smooth-talking front man for Avery Sparr felt a strange queasy feeling inside him. There was something about these men

—and Hopalong Cassidy inspired the same feeling—that frightened him. No men he had ever seen seemed more ready for trouble.

Inside the bunkhouse he could hear low voices as the two men talked. Maybe he was worrying needlessly, and nothing would be asked or mentioned that would reveal his own story to be lies. There were always ways out, anyway, for a clever man.

"Talk to them if you like," he said carelessly, "but they are merely hands. They don't know anything, but what they suspect is probably plenty. The short one," he added, "is Tony Cuyas, a half-breed badman from Sonora. The other is Hank Lydon. It was his brother who was killed in that Apache fight."

"Thanks." Mesquite turned to the door. "We'll be seein' you." He opened the door and stepped through, then to the left. Johnny followed. The two men inside the room looked up, and the calm left their faces as they saw the two strangers.

"Who are you?" Lydon demanded. He was a burly bearded man with cruel eyes.

"Couple of passin' strangers with some questions."

Mesquite sized up the two at a glance. Followers, not leaders they were, but still as dangerous to cross as a hungry puma with a cub.

"We're interested in Injun fightin'. All kinds o' fightin', in fact. We'd like to hear the story of this fight."

"We ain't talkin'." Lydon was surly. He did not like the looks of either of these men, and their ease put him on edge. It worried him, and Hank Lydon did not like to worry, for he did not like to think. He preferred to act, and usually the circumstances made his actions a matter that called for no thinking or planning.

"Why not be sociable?" Johnny said easily. He dropped to a bunk and began to roll a cigarette. "We want to hear what happened back up there in the mountains. Must be a good yarn. Who shot you?"

Cuyas looked at them from his yellow eyes and looked away. His own temper was short, for his wound had bothered him. Neither man was seriously hurt, yet both had lost blood and they had made a killing ride to get back in time. Yet it was Lydon who answered with a question. "Who are you? What do you want here, anyway?"

"Just a couple of hands. We got a friend out there." Johnny jerked his head toward the mountains. "Feller named Cassidy. Heard of him?"

Both men lifted their heads, and Cuyas stopped bathing his wound. They stared at the two. "No," Lydon said, "never heard of him."

Mesquite laughed, and the sound was unpleasant to Cuyas. He looked suddenly and warily at Mesquite.

"Don't know heem."

Cuyas spoke in a low voice, his eyes never leaving Mesquite.

"Reckoned you might say that," Mesquite said, "but we figgered we might convince you that talkin' was a good idea. You know you are through here? I mean Sparr an' all their outfit."

"Through?" Lydon's laugh was ugly. "Don't be a fool! Sparr won't have no trouble holdin' this place. If he does"—Lydon chuckled again—"Soper will smooth it down for him."

"They work together, huh?" Johnny suggested.

"What else?" Lydon's smile faded. "You better slope. I don't want no trouble right now."

"No," Mesquite said softly, "it's you two who'll ride out of here. You'll ride out if you're lucky—if you talk. Otherwise, they can bury you when the coyotes are finished."

"You talk mighty big," Lydon sneered. "Can you back it up?"

"Why, sure!"

Mesquite came to his feet as gracefully as an uncoiling snake. He stood there, looking down at them, and suddenly all of Hank Lydon's humor was gone and with it much of his truculence. Not a shrewd man, he yet knew danger when he saw it, and now he saw it all too plainly.

"What you want to know?" he asked. "No use fightin' over nothin'."

"Where's Cassidy?"

Lydon chuckled again. "Ask me somethin' I know an answer to. He just dropped out o' the world. He left about as much trail most of the time as a snake on a flat rock, an' then, when we did find one, we ran smack into a big hole in the mountain an' had to go down a path that was mostly imagination.

"At the bottom we found a fire, but when we closed in on it the Apaches was doin' likewise. There was some scrap, but we come out on top 'cept for Jake. He got one first crack out o' the box. While we was fightin', Hopalong dragged it. When we started back, they still hadn't found the new trail."

Suddenly Johnny lifted his head. He seemed to hear the sound of horses moving, but when he glanced out the window he saw nothing. It was still and quiet, with the snow falling steadily. His thoughts went to Cassidy. Their friend was high in the mountains, and the snow up there would be heavier than here, and the air much colder.

Tonight it would be piercing cold, and if the snow kept up, by dawn the trails would all be impassable. For the first time since he had known Cassidy, Johnny Nelson was worried, really and honestly worried, for this time it was not men with whom Hoppy must cope, but the bitter cold of winter in the icy peaks.

"When you get fixed up," Mesquite said, rising slowly, "pack your duds an' get out. You won't be needed here."

"You tell me?" Lydon sneered. His courage was returning

now, and Cuyas, he noted, had finished bandaging his hand and was standing near the head of his bunk. Hank Lydon knew that under that pillow was a spare gun that Tony always kept for emergencies. This was the first one.

The room was still as the fall of snow outside the window. The fire in the box stove crackled slightly. Lydon shifted on the stool where he sat and the wood creaked. The bunks were rumpled, and several old, shabby-looking boots lay around on the floor. In the corner by the potbellied stove there was a stack of stovewood. A few slivers were scattered around and some spilled ashes where the stove had been hastily cleaned out by someone who had not brushed up afterward.

On the wall there was an old Sharps buffalo gun, and both men wore pistols. Hank Lydon stared up at Mesquite, his big head deep sunken between his massive shoulders, the muscles of his thighs stretching tight the heavy material of his jeans. Cuyas, stocky and alert, stood at the head of the bunk, his body curiously poised.

It was that poised alertness which warned Mesquite. He did not shift his eyes but kept the two of them in his view. "What's Soper aroun' here?" he asked casually. "Is he boss or is Sparr?"

"Sparr." Lydon dropped the word flatly. "Soper figgers he's purty big hisself, but he ain't so big as Sparr. Although," he added, with penetration beyond his usual scope, "if I was Sparr I'd keep an eye on him. That Soper," he added, "ain't a healthy hombre. Sparr, he'd shoot a man down as soon as look at him. Soper, he'd pull the legs off a fly in private—or mebbe a man, for that matter. He's cold-blooded."

"Well, we'll drift." Mesquite let his eyes shift from one to the other of the two. "Remember what we told you. Get out! Don't try nothin' fancy, because it will only get you hurt. Get out while the gettin' is good, because the cleanup has started. This deal is finished. You got an hour," he said, "so get movin'!"

There was, he remembered, a shaving mirror alongside the door. It was right where he could see Cuyas reflected in it as he turned. So with a jerk of his head to Johnny, Mesquite spun on his heel. Instantly Cuyas grabbed the gun under the pillow.

Mesquite had been facing the door when he saw the flash of movement in the mirror. He drew as he turned his body at the hips and fired with the gun flat against his waist. Cuyas took the bullet in the chest with his gun almost level and, sagging at the knees, slowly spilled over on his face. Hank Lydon, his face gray, was frozen in position with his hand on his gun butt, covered by two guns that had sprung seemingly from nowhere.

"Want to finish that draw?" Johnny asked pleasantly. "If you do, I'll holster my gun an' we can start from scratch."

"I had trouble enough." Lydon touched his lips with his tongue. "I'm gettin' out of here. All I want's a chance."

"You've got it."

Lydon got to his feet, glancing at Cuyas. Hollow-eyed, he looked back at Mesquite. "That's shootin', mister. That boy, he always did set store by sneak guns. Proctor used t' tell him one would get him killed someday, an' it shore did."

He got his bedroll and started to the door. Outside in the snow he turned to them again. "Which way shall I ride?"

"Suit yoreself," Johnny said; "anyway you like, only if you get in our way again, by purpose or accident, fill your hand an' come shootin' because we don't aim to bother with you again. If you like," he added, "ride to Horse Springs. Tell that outfit that anybody there who cottons to Avery Sparr had better head for a warmer climate before we start 'em."

As Lydon rode off, the two started for the house once more, and then they stopped. The snow was crushed by the hoof-marks

175

of a half-dozen or more horses, horses that had walked by the bunkhouse in the snow and off up the trail. Unknown to them, these were the riders bound for Alma to head off Hopalong. Soper had started them as soon as they appeared. And he himself had mounted and headed north. It was time, he decided, to get his own men on the job. The hideout in Turkey Springs Canyon had served its purpose.

"Shall we foller them?" Johnny asked doubtfully.

"Let's find Soper. I want to talk to him some more."

They started for the house, walking warily, their eyes alert and their hands ready.

Snow was falling steadily in the mountains, and already Hoppy was having a hard time staying on the trail. Only in places did the growth of brush to left and right show its borders, and often that was misleading when some avenue of trees gave off to right or left that could easily have been a trail. They had crossed Willow Creek and were heading through the trees toward a trail that Hopalong believed he could see ahead of them, a switchback trail that climbed through the mountains. The flakes fell steadily, blotting out all the usual landmarks and shrouding everything in a thick mantle of white. In actual distance they had not come far, but the trail was rough, and of necessity they must come slowly, for at times it was possible to lose the trail entirely, and obstructions were hidden beneath the snow.

The gray of Dick Jordan's beard made him seem even older. He moved his horse alongside Hoppy's. "Sparr won't foller in this," he said. "He'll turn back."

"What I figger." Hopalong studied the old man's face keenly. The man looked beat, there was no question about that. He was dead tired and in bad shape, yet to stop now meant certain death, not for one alone, but for all. "I also figger he won't let it lay like that. He'll try to head us off."

Jordan frowned. "You think so? O' course he could get a bunch of riders around to Alma if he had the horses—an' he's got 'em."

"Could he get fresh mounts along the way?"

"He sure could. Half-dozen hangouts for horse thieves an' rustlers along that route. He could get all the horses he would need. Yeah," Dick Jordan agreed, "I think you've figgered it right. I think he'll be waitin' for us, or somebody will, when we come out of the mountains. If we get out."

"We'll get out." Hopalong considered. "How about Alma? I suppose he has friends there?"

"Uh-huh. That Eagle Saloon is a tough place. Hangout for outlaws an' every kind of rapscallion in this neck o' the woods. I figger we should have burnt that place over their heads long ago."

This was high country, for the trail they rode was now nearing nine thousand feet and the horses were laboring heavily, slowed by the ankle-deep snow. Hopalong kept his buckskin moving, and now as never before he appreciated the true worth of the horse. Breaking trail was a tough job, but there was a heart in the buckskin, and it walked steadily on, twitching its ears to Hopalong's occasional comments.

Now the trees were coming down closer to the trail, and at times it was difficult to be sure where it lay. All three were cold. Hoppy could judge the cold of the others by his own, for he was tough and used to exposure to the elements in all sorts of weather. Nor did the snow give any indication of stopping. This was it, he knew. From now on all trails would be blocked, and if they stopped now they would be snowed in for sure. Yet, short of a brief rest, he had no intention of stopping, for he knew better than the others the gravity of their situation.

His mind, however, was already leaping ahead, trying to foresee what would happen if and when they reached Alma or its vicinity. When he glanced around, he saw behind him two snow-covered figures, and he drew up. For some time he had been hearing running water, and he knew there must be a still unfrozen stream close by. Glancing around, he found a nest of rocks not far away that appeared to be the source of the sound, and turning off the trail he led the way down to them.

Dismounting, he helped Pamela break branches from the trees to make a place for her father to sit, then helped him from the saddle. Dick looked at Hopalong grimly. "Hard to be helpless," he said; "been a fighter all my life, an' now when the chips are down I got to be carried like a baby!"

"Aw, shut up!" Hopalong said roughly, grinning at him. "You like it, an' you know you do! What would you do if you ran into Sparr right now? He's too much for any Circle J man! Now a Bar 20 puncher, or 'most any hand from the Double Y, that would be different!"

"Different? Blazes, Hoppy!" Dick Jordan reacted as Hopalong had believed he would, and was all fire and vinegar in an instant. "You know durned well that outfit o' yours never could stack up with any o' mine! Remember that time we tangled with the Comanches on the Staked Plains? Who pulled Bar 20 out of the soup then?"

"One time!" Hopalong protested. "Just one time! An' after three Bar 20 men had stood off seventy Comanches for two days! You come ridin' up with your whole outfit, an' then you come durned near gettin' yoreselves killed!"

"That scalp o' yours would have been hanging in some Comanche lodge right now if we hadn't come along!" Jordan said.

Then he simmered down. "O' course you did make a fight of it. I'll admit that!"

As he talked, Hopalong was working swiftly. Breaking lower branches from the trees, he got a fire started and then scouted some good-sized chunks from under a fallen log and some huge slabs of bark. When the fire was blazing brightly, Pamela got some water from the creek and started coffee. There was little left, but enough for twice more. Once more, after this.

Meanwhile, Hopalong got their blankets from their bedrolls and with some rawhide piggin' strings made three capes that could be thrown over their shoulders and drawn around their bodies, being laced through a half-dozen holes with the piggin' strings, and tied. Working around through the thick dead grass on the banks of the stream, he found some on the bottom that was dry and untouched by snow. This he brought to the fire, and slipping off Dick Jordan's boots, he put some of the dry grass inside. "Help keep 'em warm," he said. "That's an Injun trick."

"Sometimes I wonder where you picked up all you know, Hoppy," Jordan said. "You always come up with some kind o' trick."

"Keep my eyes open," Hopalong said, straight-faced. "We on the Bar 20 learned how to do that mighty young. That outfit o' yours never could see much further'n their noses. Not unless it was whisky," he added. "They could smell a barrel o' Injun whisky right far!"

Hopalong glanced at Pamela. Her lips were red and her cheeks flushed by bending over the fire. He grinned at her. "You get prettier all the time," he said. "I think this cold weather is good for you."

She smiled. "I've been cooped up too long, Hoppy. I needed to get out. Although not like this."

179

"Don't worry about it." He shrugged off her obvious doubts. "We'll get through."

"What would we have done without you?" she wondered. "I have been thinking of that as we rode along. It seems so strange, somehow, because I knew you when I was just a child, I thought you'd be older than you are. Older-looking, anyway."

"In this country a man doesn't change much. He goes on for years; then all of a sudden he cashes in his checks and that's it."

He nodded toward the peaks. "You know, in spite of the fact that I wish we were somewhere else, I never saw anything much more beautiful than old Whitewater Baldy there."

She followed his eyes toward the huge mass of granite that shouldered brutally against the dull gray sky, its mantle of white blazing like a lighted beacon. "It is beautiful," she agreed. "I wish we were seeing it together, Hoppy, and there was no trouble. That Dad wasn't crippled and we weren't having to go so fast. We could enjoy it then."

They started again within a matter of minutes, but Hopalong had uncovered more of the grass for the horses and they ate a little, and all three drank from the stream. Once mounted, each put on the blanket cape that Hopalong had made for them, drew the laces tight, and tied them. Moving on, they were warmer, but even in that short stop the snow had grown appreciably deeper.

All talking ceased. The horses were laboring heavily now, for they were on the switchback trail. Here the first fall of snow in the higher peaks had frozen over and there was ice beneath the snow. Several times the horses slipped, and Hopalong stopped more often. They continued to climb, and as though inspired by the buckskin, the other horses plodded on gamely enough. Several times Hopalong stopped and walked for a short distance, as did Pamela, resting the horses. Before they could mount again they had to wipe the snow from the saddle. Yet now the snow was dry and not damp, as it had been on the lower levels of the mountains.

A long wind sighed through the trees, and the snow picked up in a little flurry whose particles stung like grains of sand. The sky seemed lower now, and the peaks seemed huge. The wind stirred again, and this time it was followed by another gust. Hopalong dug his chin behind the edge of the blanket and swore bitterly. The trail was bad enough, but if the wind started to blow, up here where the trees were sparse, they might wander away from it and tumble off a precipice without ever realizing they had gone astray.

The air thickened, and he could not tell how much was cloud and how much was snow. But the wind had an edge like a knife, and his fingers felt like stubs over which he had no control. Now they began to feel the cold in earnest. Before it had been nothing compared with this, for with the knifing wind there was the penetrating chill of the higher altitudes. Head bowed into the wind, the buckskin plodded wearily on. Several times the horse faltered, and finally Hopalong slid from the saddle into almost knee-deep snow. Keeping his arm through the bridle, he led the way, slogging wearily ahead, and under his feet the trail still climbed.

Actually, they were probably only a few hundred feet higher. Yet the distance seemed enormous. Step by step he fought on, knowing that to stop could mean death. Once he slipped and went to his knees in the snow, and the buckskin stopped patiently while he got up. In a fog of cold and mental haze he realized they could not go on. If Dick Jordan was not almost frozen in his saddle it would be a wonder. And this last time Pamela had not dismounted.

But he did not stop. Bending his head forward, his eyes on the white snow beneath, he plodded on, his strides catching a strange rhythm of their own so that he became lost in a dull monotony of successive footsteps. The wind howled and he stumbled again, falling on his face in the snow. This time he got up more slowly, and his hands felt like clubs when he tried to brush the snow from them. He turned there, white with snow, and looked back. Through the falling and blown snow he could scarcely see Pamela or her horse, only the darker blob in the dense white around them. Old Dick Jordan still sat his saddle, a grim mound of snow.

Turning, Hopalong started on now. Never before had he called on all his strength so much as now; never before had each step seemed an effort, each stride accomplished a victory. Whether his horse could have carried him he did not know, but he forgot to remount, slogging endlessly on and on. Then he fell again and struggled to get up. Something was wrong when he tried to rise, and his numbed brain fumbled with the problem. Then it came to him. His feet were higher than his head when he fell flat, and that meant they had started downhill!

He scrambled to his feet, feeling a surge of victory within him, and started off swiftly, fighting his way down. Now it was an advantage to be moving: Every step took them farther downhill; every step took them closer to food, closer to shelter, and closer —his face was grim under the mask of cold—to the guns of Avery Sparr.

Suddenly the clouds parted and he saw a star. With a shock he realized it must already be well into the early part of the night, and darkness had come on so gradually through the gray of the clouds that he had not realized. He walked on, only now his eyes were alert for some sort of shelter, not only for them, but for the horses as well.

Finally he gave up. Sounding the snow with a branch broken from a tree, he led the way through the snow toward the root mass of an uptorn giant of the forest. The root mass made a wall ten feet high and almost fifteen feet broad, and at the base of this he pushed away some of the snow. He had no ax, but the fallen tree itself offered what he needed. It was long dead, and in the passage of time several of the limbs had been shattered. Gathering several pieces of a large limb, he brought them back. Ranging them side by side, he used them as a base for his fire. Then he built it with bark and leaves from the under side of the huge tree. Not until the fire was blazing did he go back to Pamela.

Carefully he lifted her from the saddle, feeling her heart beat and her breath warm against his cheek. She struggled to speak, and her eyes opened, and he carried her to the fire. Then he hurriedly stripped evergreen boughs and made a bed for the old man, and returned for him. As Hopalong carried him to the bed, the old man spoke. "Guess the Double Y has it this time, boy. I'm all in."

"So'm I," Hopalong admitted, "but we're over the hump. We're goin' downhill."

Pamela sat up stiffly, but her eyes caught fire at the realization, and she struggled to rise and help him. But Hopalong knew his job and he worked swiftly. The fire was built larger than necessary, but partly because he knew what its psychological effect would be on the two people. Then he went a little way into the woods and cut two poles, which he brought back and thrust into the snow.

He placed a third across the top in the crotches at the ends, and with other limbs hurriedly built an evergreen lean-to that proved not only a windbreak but a fire reflector. Then he led the horses in behind this protection and carefully wiped them free of the snow and rubbed each horse down in turn. By the time he had finished with this he was thoroughly warmed up.

Pamela was on her feet and melting snow for coffee. She smiled bravely at him, looking like nothing so much as a woebegone little girl, and he grinned, then laughed, and walked across to Dick. "Better sit up, old-timer," he said. "You'll enjoy the fire more."

"She feels mighty good, boy." Jordan extended his trembling hands toward the flames, then glanced up. "If I live through this I'll be good for twenty years more!"

"That goes for me too!" Hopalong said. "You better count that twenty years now. We've got the worst of it behind us."

"What if they're waitin' for us?"

"They will be. But maybe they won't be watchin' so good. They won't expect us to make it, an' if I know that kind of hombre, he's lazy an' don't like watchin' no trail in this weather. No, I think I'll have to hunt them up."

Pamela straightened up. "Oh, no, Hoppy! Please don't!"

He smiled at her, but his lips and eyes were hard. "Yeah, I'll hunt them up. This trip over the mountain has got me mad!"

They rested and drank coffee, and Hopalong let his mind trail down the possibilities. He was sure that his guess was good insofar as their trail watching was concerned. It was still rough going down the canyon of the Silver, but they had made it this far. There were mining camps, small ones, along this trail now. None of them would be safe.

They must at all costs push on, and the trail would be guarded carefully by Sparr's men. That much stood to reason. Having gone so far, Sparr was not the man to give up the ship. No, he would be even more dangerous now, not only desperate to save what he was losing, but vengeful because of the trouble Cassidy had already caused him.

From now on the danger of cold would still be great, but less, after a few miles, than the danger of men. And these were men who would shoot on sight. In fact, it was Hopalong's guess that their orders would be just that. Putting himself in Sparr's place, he could understand how desperate the man must be, for he had worked months on this plan and had undoubtedly considered it in the bag, and then, at the last minute, Hoppy had stepped in and was defeating him.

No, the trail would be guarded, and the man might easily have offered a bonus for their death. Desperate now, he would stop at nothing.

Two hours they rested and waited, and then they remounted and started once more, carefully putting out their fire and taking with them only a small bundle of sticks in case another fire was necessary and dry wood not available. The snow let up for a little while, and taking his rifle from its scabbard Hopalong freed it of snow and checked the mechanism. He did the same for each of his pistols. One of them he thrust in his waistband close to the warmth of his body to keep it free of snow.

There was no fire left in the horses now. They plodded, with each step an effort, for the way had been long and hard. Then Cassidy spotted a cabin, but no trail of smoke lifted from the chimney. Pushing on, he saw two more cabins in the next mile. All were makeshift log huts thrown together by prospectors or miners.

The trail now was steadily downhill, and the trees were growing taller once more. Hopalong rode warily, his eyes searching the forest ahead for any tiny gleam of light.

And then, suddenly, he saw it: a lighted window!

Motioning the others to stop, he dismounted and went on ahead through the trees, and when he reached a place where he could see the trail to the cabin he saw there were fresh tracks in the snow. Walking back to Dick and Pamela, he said quietly, "These are some of 'em, I'd bet my last dollar. I'm goin' in. By the look of things there are three there, but I think I can handle it."

His hands were tucked into the front of his coat, warming his fingers against his body.

He dared take no chances on their being numb now.

"Just wait," he told them. "I'll be back in a minute!"

He turned and started down to the cabin.

Pamela stared after him, and Dick nodded at Hopalong. "There goes a real man!" he said. "I'd not like to be in that cabin now!"

"Dad," she protested, "can't we help him?"

"No," he said, "we can't. He knows what he's doin'. Better than anybody, he knows. Just give him time. We would only mess things up for him. Now any bullet is an enemy bullet, and any man who lifts a weapon is an enemy. We'd only get in his way, an' he won't want that."

Careful to allow no crunching on the path, Hopalong walked up to the window and peered through. Three men sat at a table playing cards. All three were tough-looking and dangerous. Drawing his hand from his shirtfront, he stepped around in front of the cabin, and with his left hand he opened the door.

Three heads came up, three faces turned to look. Three startled, momentarily arrested men stared at the snow-covered figure standing in the open door. Beyond him was the night and the snow, the trees ghostly with their gathered shrouds, ghostly as this apparition from the night. He stepped in and the door closed behind him. As it closed he spoke. "Howdy, boys! I'm Hopalong Cassidy!"

As if at a signal, all three grabbed for their guns, a bearlike man with a bald head in his sock feet, an unshaven man in rough miner's boots, soiled shirt, and suspenders, and a younger one with a fancy neckerchief. All three grabbed iron, and Hopalong sprang left, landing lightly on the balls of his feet, his first shot exploding even as his feet touched the floor, directed at the first man to move. His second shot caught the bald one in the throat and he turned around and fell back over his chair to the floor.

The miner sat dead still, his hands lifted. "Don't shoot!" he yelled. "I'm out of it!"

"See you stay that way." Hopalong stepped around the table to look at the big man who lay unmoving amid the chair's wreckage. "Who sent you up here? Sparr?"

"Nobody sent me! This here's my cabin. Sparr sent them hombres up here to lay for you, an' I hadn't no choice. I ain't no gunslinger, Cassidy! What could I do?"

"How many horses have you got here?" Hopalong demanded.

"Three horses an' my pack mule. You ain't goin' to leave me stranded, are you?"

"You can ride the mule. I'm leaving three o' my horses here, but I want 'em here when I send for 'em. Now you drag those hombres into your lean-to an' fix some fresh coffee an' grub. You can figger you are mighty lucky you ain't layin' with those fellers on the floor. Get movin'!"

The miner hastily went around the table and stared down at the bodies. He seemed appalled by the suddenness with which it all had happened, and Hopalong could see at a glance there was no fight in the man. No doubt there were many such who worked along with Avery Sparr simply from fear or from lack of the will to resist, or perhaps for the few extra dollars it made them.

The man touched his lips with his tongue. "You drilled the two of 'em plumb center!"

"Then let's not make it three," Hopalong said quietly. "Make the coffee."

CHAPTER 12

FOUR WHO TRIED

Alma lay quiet under the unblemished purity of new-fallen snow. The Eagle Saloon, as is the way of such places, was brightly lighted and blaring with what they undoubtedly assumed to be music. A half-dozen tough-looking hands, whose last day's work was several years behind them, loitered along the bar, lying to each other about women they had known and money they had spent. At a card table several others loafed, waiting for word that Hopalong had been sighted. None of them expected the word to come.

Behind the bar Chet Bales, no longer riding since he had caught a bullet in his knee that left him with a permanently stiff leg, was serving rotgut liquor to his uncritical customers. Most of these men had done minor chores for Sparr; all of them hoped to do bigger chores for him. Since his arrival the Eagle had been considerably more prosperous than in the past few years. Frowned on by less popular and more cleanly establishments, the Eagle bloomed and grew like some noisome flower in an otherwise pleasant garden.

Dawn was not far away, but none of these men were thinking of turning in, for they had their orders, which were to kill Cassidy whenever and wherever he could be found, and to many of them the five hundred dollars was a sum for which they would gladly have murdered a half-dozen men. Watchers had been posted on every trail leading out of the mountains, and these were relieved at intervals. Yet as the hours drew by and nothing happened, they became more and more convinced that Hopalong Cassidy was either snowed in high in the mountains or dead on the trail. Yet they had their orders, and so they stayed.

As for Hopalong, he led his little cavalcade into town by a back street about an hour before daylight and went directly to the home of Doc Benton, a lifelong friend of Jordan's who had lately come to town. Leaving Dick, now on the verge of collapse, Hopalong turned to the door. Pamela ran to him and caught his arm.

"Hoppy!" she pleaded. "Don't go!"

His face was bleak in the graying light of the coming day and his blue eyes were frosty with some strange light she had never seen in them before. "I'm goin'," he told her flatly and evenly. "You stay here, Pam, an' help look after yore dad. I'm goin' down to meet those fellers at the Eagle that have been huntin' me. I don't aim to disappoint them any."

"Be careful, Hoppy. Please!"

He grinned then. "Why, Pam, you don't need to tell me to be careful! I'm always a right careful sort of gent. Only there's some folks down there that need to be showed the error of their ways. I reckon I need to lead a few of them from the paths of temptation."

The stubble of beard on his cheeks had grown. He felt tough and mean. The miserable ride through the snow, the bitterness of running when he wanted to fight, the feeling that had been building in him against Avery Sparr, who would try to steal from a crippled man and a girl, all had been mounting in him until he knew that sleep or even rest would be impossible until he had faced these men. He knew what he had to do, and he was in the right frame of mind to do it.

At the moment he hoped they would start something, any one or all of them. He felt blazing mad clean through, and the bitterness in him was like gall in his mouth. He did not waste time looking through the saloon windows. He went up the steps then through the door and its slam behind him was like the crash of a double-barreled shotgun. They whirled and stared, all sleep gone in an instant.

Feet apart, he stood inside the door. His eyes were utterly cold, but within him there was a leaping devil. "I'm Hopalong Cassidy." For the second time in a few hours he threw into their teeth the name that was a challenge. "Somebody here want me?"

Riveted to the floor, they stared at him. "Come on!" His voice was cold and deadly, laden with menace. "I heard some o' you coyotes were huntin' me! I heard there was money on my head! Let somebody try to collect!"

Nobody moved. They were caught flat-footed, and the fierceness of his challenge, the daring of him, the sudden appearance when they believed him dead, all served to take their breath away. Nobody moved.

He was beside himself with fury. With a quick stride, he stepped to the bar and grabbed a glass from a man and hurled the liquor into the eyes of a half-dozen of them. Then, spinning on his heel, he grabbed a card table and dumped it over on the floor. "Come on!" he begged. "One of you! A dozen of you! Grab iron an' let's see what you do when you hunt men for money!"

Still nobody moved. Men pawed the stinging liquor from their eyes, but of those around the card table nobody even so much as looked at the scattered money or cards. The room was still, the fire roared in the stove, but nobody spoke. "All right!" Hopalong's voice was utterly cold. "On your feet! You first!" He indicated a man who sat where the table had been upset. "Shuck your guns. Then grab your horse an' get out of town!"

"Huh? In this weather?" The man stared and was about to venture further protest when Hopalong took a step toward him, his elbows crooked for a draw.

"Yeah! In this weather! I crossed the mountains in it—let's see how you hombres like it! That goes"—his eyes swept their faces—"for every man jack of you! Get your horses an' get goin', but shuck your guns right here!"

Cassidy's eyes fastened on the bartender. "Bales," he said. "I remember you. An' you know me. Close this place now, and don't stop this side of Holbrook, get me?"

"Look, Hoppy!" Bales pleaded. "I got a game leg! I got money in this place!"

"That's tough. Nobody has a right to run a business where a lot of murderin', back-shootin' coyotes like this hang out. You know me, Bales! Start shooting or close up!"

Bales gulped and slowly heaved a deep sigh. "Well, it looks like a mighty cold winter here, anyway." He looked slowly around the room. "As of now"—Bales sighed again—"consider the Eagle Saloon closed."

Carefully the men got to their feet and started for the door, and one by one they shucked their guns. One man hesitated, and looked longingly after his pistol. "Cost me a tough month's wages," he said. "Will I get it back?"

"No." Hopalong was relentless. "Next time you earn a gun you may learn to pack it in better company an' for a better cause. Keep movin'!"

Within ten minutes the saloon was dark and still. Running a piece of rope picked up from behind the bar through the trigger guards of the guns, Hopalong slung them over his shoulder. Coolly he walked down to the sheriff's office and banged on the door. A sleepy-looking, unshaven officer in a red flannel undershirt and sock feet came to the door. "What's the fuss, mister? Go sleep it off before I throw you in the clink!"

Without more than a glance Hopalong dumped the guns on the floor. The sheriff stared, blinking his eyes at them. "What th—!"

Hopalong looked up at him, and his frosty eyes made the sheriff back up. "I've just closed the Eagle," Cassidy said calmly. "These guns belong to the hombres I run out of there. Do what you've a mind to with 'em, but don't give 'em back to that outfit or I'll come over here an' pull every hair out of your mustache one by one!"

"You *what?*" The sheriff's face swelled with fury. "Now, see here, young fel—!"

He stopped, seeming to get the gist of Cassidy's remarks for the first time. He swallowed and stared.

"You closed the Eagle?" he exclaimed in amazement. "You took those hombres' hardware off 'em?"

Cassidy was already walking away down the street. An early riser stopped in front of the sheriff and stared at the guns, then at Hopalong's retreating back. "Hey, who was that?" he asked.

Dazed, the sheriff turned to look at him. "Mister," he said reverently, "I got no idea who he is, but b'lieve me he's the toughest hombre that ever come west o' the Pecos!"

When Arnold Soper left the Circle J, he rode due north by the Indian Creek trail toward Turkey Springs Canyon. If ever he was going to act, the time was now. There was nothing more he could do on the J, and in fact his presence there might become infinitely dangerous if any of the men at the ranch or those who were to come would talk to Mesquite and Johnny.

He doubted whether they would get anything out of Cuyas or Hank Lydon, but it was possible. However, in any event the safest place for him was out of the picture completely. His mission to Turkey Springs was simplicity itself. He had four tough men there, and they had already been well instructed in their jobs. They knew where payment was to come from, and all that would remain would be the sweeping up, with guns, of a few odds and ends. They might have to kill Sparr, but that, too, might be taken care of for them.

Avery Sparr was not yet back at the ranch and he might catch Cassidy and in the shoot-out somebody was sure to be killed. Such men do not often miss. In any event, one of his enemies was almost certain to be eliminated. When the returning rustlers showed up at the ranch, Soper started them off at once, for it was to his interests that the Jordans and Cassidy be eliminated.

So, as he started north, the situation looked very good. He could almost surely write off the Jordans and Cassidy. If they escaped Sparr, there were the mountains, and if they got through the snow and over the heights, there were the Sparr men awaiting them on the other end.

Bizco was dead, Barker was dead, and both of them were men to be taken account of. That left, aside from Sparr himself, if he survived, Johnny Rebb—a very uncertain quantity—and Anse Mowry. Both men were dangerous, although he knew most about Mowry. With the others he anticipated little trouble. But it was these three, and after them Proctor, Framson, and Mark Connor, whom he wanted wiped out. And then he would be in the saddle and would have everything his own way.

. . .

Unknown to him, several things had happened at the Circle J. Mesquite and Johnny had some information from the two wounded men, and Hank Lydon had started for Horse Springs with the warning from Mesquite. Mesquite himself, with Johnny Nelson, had followed the tracks of the racing horsemen a way, and then had seen Soper's tracks turn off. Soper had dismounted right off the trail to tighten his cinch, and from the tracks of the new boots they had surmised who it was.

They wanted nothing better than this. Mesquite, a tracker almost as good as any Indian, led the way down his trail. Wherever Soper was going they intended to go too. Snow was falling steadily, and the trail was easy to follow if they did not fall too far behind, but they could afford to ride fairly close, for the snow drew a curtain between them.

Yet it was because of the snow that they lost him. The tracks petered out in an open place where the snow was swept clean by the wind, and it was almost an hour before they found them again. Consequently they were well behind, and now the trail was being covered very rapidly by the sifting snow.

At Turkey Springs the four men were waiting restlessly for orders, and when Soper arrived, he paid each man a hundred dollars on account and told them how the other nine hundred promised them could be made. The Hardy boys, Jim and Dave, came from Mississippi by way of Texas, while the Coyote Kid was a half-breed Kiowa who had teamed up with Oklahoma Tom at Mobeetie.

The four had one distinction aside from downright gun skill— they were not squeamish. They would kill at any time or any place if the price was right. Yet not one of them would hesitate to face any man in a gun battle, and Soper had chosen well, as he knew. In a brief talk he told them that now was the time to get started, then rode on, planning a quick trip to Horse Springs to let matters get settled around the Circle J.

It was his nature to be absent when things were happening, and Horse Springs would be a place where he could be much in evidence and so have a perfect alibi for all that happened. This would fit very well with his serious, honest air and would confirm people in their opinion of him—that he was a nice young man unwittingly embroiled in gun fighting and thievery.

Exactly one hour after he left, two riders drifted into the canyon on his trail and were immediately seen by the Coyote Kid. His call brought the others. "Know 'em?" he asked.

"Looks like the two he mentioned," Dave Hardy said, "an' they are on the list."

"But not important," his brother protested. "Pay no attention."

Oklahoma Tom shrugged. "Why wait?" he asked. "We might as well take 'em while we got 'em. Anyway, they are trailin' Soper."

He hitched his guns into position and walked toward the corrals.

The Coyote Kid had his rifle in his hand. He walked to one side and dropped on a bench at the cabin door, the rifle across his knees. In the past he had found it an unexpected position for shooting, and with practice he had acquired a skill that enabled him to empty the gun into a water bucket without lifting the rifle from his knees. The Hardy boys, ten feet apart, lounged in the open, waiting for Mesquite and Johnny.

Mesquite noticed the man idling by the corral and the somewhat suggestive rifle. "Well, what d' you know?" he said to Johnny. "These hombres are all set up for trouble."

"Must be friends of Soper."

"That means they ain't friends of ours."

"Let's talk to 'em first. Hopalong always advised me against shootin' too quick."

Mesquite drew in his horse and looked down at the Hardy boys, then slid from the saddle. He liked to work with the ground under him, even if it was snow.

"Huntin' somebody?" Dave Hardy demanded.

"Not necessarily. Have we found anybody?" Johnny stayed in the saddle, his eyes alert and eager.

"Funny feller!" Dave sneered. "Where you headin'?"

"Sort of lookin' after that hombre up ahead. Right curious about his friends."

"Meanin' us?"

Johnny examined them thoughtfully. "Nope. Don't reckon any of you was ever friendly to anybody unless you was paid for it. This here looks like a renegade outfit if ever I saw one."

"You talk mighty free, stranger."

"Folks have said that afore, haven't they, Mesquite?" Johnny watched the Coyote Kid. "You know, that hombre on the bench could get hisself shot mighty easy, playin' around with that rifle like he is."

"Who would shoot him?" Dave Hardy demanded. He wanted to get on with it now it had started.

"Why, most anybody who didn't like to have a gun pointed at him."

Johnny reined his sorrel away and although he could not immediately shift the rifle, he left the Kid without a target.

"I figger you hombres better drift. Yore on Circle J range."

"We got a right to be."

Dave Hardy was wondering. He had heard of the Double Y. It was a tough outfit.

"Jordan give you the right?" Johnny asked.

"Jordan?" Hardy laughed harshly. "Why, that ol' fool ain't got no say about anythin'! He's through!"

"Not the way we see it."

Johnny let his horse take three steps forward, which placed him right between the Coyote Kid and Oklahoma Tom. Both could fire on him, but every shot would be an equal danger for the man beyond.

Mesquite was standing free of his horse now, his hands at his sides. Both of the former Double Y hands knew what sort of position they were in and what to do about it. Mesquite, a lone wolf until recently, found his heart warming anew to Johnny Nelson, whom he had learned to like next-best to Hopalong himself.

Mesquite was a fighter, and he knew little else, and Johnny's generalship in getting between the other two amused him. He knew just what it could mean in such a fight. Each of the gunmen would have to exercise very great care to keep from shooting his partner, and that instant of deliberation would be all Johnny would need. Mesquite chuckled, and the Hardy boys looked at him suspiciously.

"Looks like you are fixin' to go someplace," Mesquite suggested. "Get your orders from Soper?"

"Don't know him." Dave Hardy was nervous. He didn't like Johnny's position at all, for in addition to putting himself between the two on the bench and at the corral, his position flanked their own. "Who's he?"

"The hombre who left his horse right there"—Mesquite Jenkins pointed at the spot where the tracks were plainly visible—"while he went inside to talk. He spent some little time too."

"Smart feller, aren't you?" Dave replied, unable to find the exact words to start trouble and no longer sure how much he wanted it. "You huntin' trouble?"

"Uh-huh." Mesquite took another step forward and paused. "You got any? Whether you have or not, I'm suggestin' you give an account of yourselves or drift."

The Coyote Kid was getting nervous, and Oklahoma Tom, full of fight, was tired of talking. He stepped clear of his corral corner and yelled at the Hardys. "What's the matter? We want to kill 'em, don't we? Then have at it!"

His own gun swung up, and Johnny's draw was a flashing, instant thing. In that moment the still, wintry peace of the snow-covered canyon was shattered by crashing guns. A thunder of shots, a pause, and then another shot, and then a final one.

Mesquite had drawn the instant the Hardys moved, and both guns came up spouting lead. Utterly cold, he was one of those men, like Billy the Kid, who have no nerves when under fire. He took a step forward, and as his guns bellowed he saw Jim Hardy back up and sit down suddenly, then grab his stomach and roll over in the snow, moaning and whining.

Dave Hardy had taken the first shot and it had been a near miss, hitting Johnny on the gun belt near the right hip and spinning him half around and off balance. Not only off balance, but out of the shooting for the split second it took Mesquite to get a bullet into Jim.

As Dave started to swing back, Mesquite nailed him with his second shot, and then walked in, hammering lead into both falling men.

Johnny's first shot had clipped splinters from the corral corner, and the second hit Oklahoma Tom in the chest. The bullet smashed through his lung and nicked a rib, staggering Tom, who stood flat-footed and got off a shot that killed Johnny's sorrel but saved his life, for as Johnny sprang clear of the falling horse, rifle bullets roared past his ears from the bench where the Kid sat.

Johnny sprang around, planting his foot as he completed the

turn and slip-shot three fast ones at the Kid. The Coyote Kid felt one bullet go past his face, and he lost his enthusiasm for murder. Leaping to his feet, he sprang toward the end of the house, and as he rounded the corner he whirled and caught Johnny's bullet in his throat. The shooting was over as suddenly as it began. Mesquite had a bullet-burned shoulder and Johnny a dead horse.

The two Hardys lay within inches of each other, both sprawled out and dead. Oklahoma Tom sat against the corral fence coughing blood and dying slowly, while the Coyote Kid was already dead, his rifle lying on the ground a few feet away. Both Mesquite and Johnny walked toward Tom.

Blood trickled over his chin, and he stared at them gloomily. "Never figgered on this," he said, "but I guess I had it comin'." He coughed and spat blood, and his lips fumbled for words. "Wished I knew somebody to tell good-bye, but I reckon there ain't anybody, 'less it's Mabel up at Horse Springs. If you see her, give her my watch, will you? She was—she was—good scout."

"Sure," Johnny said. "I'll make it a point."

Oklahoma Tom's eyes glazed, then sharpened. "No—no hard feelin's?"

"No," Johnny said. "All in the game."

"Yeah."

Oklahoma Tom looked puzzled.

"I guess I threwed a loop over the wrong life somewheres back down the line."

He coughed again, and then coughed harder, and died coughing, with his head against the poles of the corral.

Arnold Soper did not get to Horse Springs. For some reason he was worried, and he disliked to think of what might be happen-

ing at the Circle J. His curiosity and need for knowledge were so
great that he turned around at Coyote Tanks and started back,
heading through Turkey Springs Canyon once more. Thus it was
that he missed Mesquite and Johnny by minutes but walked right
into the shambles they had left behind.

One look was enough to start him retching, and he turned
away. Yet after a few minutes he straightened up with a start and a
sudden sinking feeling. His ace in the hole was gone. These four
men on whom he had expended so much, and upon whom he had
depended so much, were gone. What would he do now?

Swiftly he surveyed the field of possibilities. He himself had
no stomach for shooting. He could shoot and was a good shot, but
the risk was something he did not wish to consider. Bizco and
Barker were dead, and when all was said and done, only two men
remained who might be able to help him, and of those two he was
not at all certain, and with neither of them had he been friendly.
They were Anse Mowry and Johnny Rebb.

Rebb was fairly close to Sparr, he knew. On the other hand, it
was Soper's belief that all men had a price, and in this Johnny
Rebb was included. He decided at once that Johnny Rebb was the
man he must see. And where Rebb was he did not know, but he
must surely be en route to the ranch. Arnold Soper, disgusted and
more worried than he would have cared to admit even to himself,
mounted his horse and started back over the trail to the Circle J.
Three times in the ensuing hour he drew up, and three times he
had almost decided to leave, to run out, to get away, but three
times he shook his head and continued.

It was dark when he paused for the fourth time. There was
no sense in this. Already there had been too much killing. The
chance of a quiet steal was gone, and there would surely be many
questions asked now. It would be better to throw in his cards and
leave. There was nothing belonging to him at the ranch that was

really important. It was silly to go back there, actually. Sparr must be back by now, and somehow Soper felt a foreboding about meeting the big gunman. No, he would go back to Horse Springs, ride outside of town, and catch the first stage west.

He had turned his horse to start back to town when he remembered the watch. It was a keepsake, the sort of thing a person carries around with him for years. It had been given to him for writing an essay on the causes of the War of the Revolution when he was fourteen years old, and although it was not a good watch, he had kept it for a long time. He hesitated, then turned back. Upon such decisions do men's lives rest, for in turning back to get the useless watch he was turning back to his death.

Along the length and the breadth of the Gila River country there was a sort of hushed waiting. Even in areas of the upper river, where nothing was known of events around the Circle J, vague rumors were being bandied about. The Eagle Saloon in Alma was closed. There had been killings in Horse Springs and on the T Bar. Armed men were riding the country, and it was rumored that a cattle war was in the making.

Yet all through the upper Gila country people were aware that a change was taking place. Mesquite Jenkins and Johnny Nelson had come into Horse Springs only a few hours behind Hank Lydon, and Hank had told his story well. The appearance of the two and the death of Tony Cuyas were now the latest topics of conversation, also the Circle J's brief but bitter battle with the Apaches in the high basin country. And in Horse Springs the disgruntled rustler who had left his treasured .45 on the floor of the Eagle was talking.

"Yeah," he said bitterly, "it was Cassidy all right. Dead? That hombre ain't anywhere close to bein' dead! He's the livest corpse I ever did see, an' b'lieve me I've seen a few! He closed the Eagle up tighter'n a drum. Yeah, left the country. Chet just took right out. Said he knowed Cassidy from away back." He shook his head and turned to listen to a query.

"Uh-huh," he said, "the two on Silver Crick got it. They went up to that miner's cabin, an' they was holed up there when Cassidy come in on 'em. They tried to make a scrap of it. They hadn't no luck. Both of 'em drawed black deuces in that game."

Teilhet slowly got up from his heavy chair and walked along the bar to where Mark Connor was wiping a glass. "You better slope, Mark. Stage will be in purty soon, an' you better get your duffel an' hit the road."

"Me?" Connor was shocked. "You firin' me?"

"If you like." Teilhet shook his head. "You been a good man, Mark, saved me lots of headaches, but if you stay, you will be a bigger one. I'm too old a man to close up an' start somewheres else, an' I know what Cassidy an' his crowd are like when they start to unwind.

"You heard him"—the old man gestured toward the rustler—"that is the way Cassidy works. I never figgered Sparr would get him."

"An' if he does?" Connor demanded harshly.

"Come back an' go to work. I've nothin' against you, but this here place is all I got. I can't afford to lose her. You better take my advice an' slope."

"I got money comin' from Sparr."

"Forget it. It ain't worth stayin' for. I'll pay you what you got comin' here. The stage is due in just a few minutes. Don't miss it."

Frightened by the old man's sincerity, Mark Connor stripped off his apron and headed for the back room where he lived. It would be only a few minutes until the stage arrived—ample time in which to pack. He had scarcely closed the door when Mesquite Jenkins and Johnny Nelson came in through the front. There was blood on Mesquite's shoulder and it was noticed at once. Leeds saw it first. "Hurt?" he asked.

Mesquite turned and, recognizing Leeds from his friendly warning, replied, "Burn. Had us a battle."

Sensing the curiosity of the crowd, he added, "Four hombres in Turkey Crick Canyon. Two of 'em the Hardy brothers."

"All dead?"

"We're here, ain't we? They started it." Then Johnny added, "Figger they had a deal with Soper. He visited 'em before we got there. They had a list of fellers to kill an' we were on it. They started right then. It was a bad start."

Teilhet leaned his big hands on the bar. He felt very old now, and wished he had closed the place early. Luckily, Mark was ready to leave. He would not be getting out of town too soon. Too much killing. Maybe he was getting soft in his old age. He had known the Hardy boys—tough lads they were too. But not tough enough for these two, and Cassidy was somewhere around, probably heading this way now. If he made up his mind to it, he might burn the Old Corral over their heads. He was right sudden, that Cassidy, and had a way of making things stick.

West of the Jerky Mountains, Avery Sparr and his weary riders were on the last leg of their homeward trek. Sparr was in the lead, as yet unaware of how badly all his plans had failed and how they were folding up around him. It was getting late, and as he rode he turned over in his mind the various angles. He felt a vague sense of defeat, for he had wanted to get his hands on

Cassidy and had wanted to keep the Jordans a little longer. In fact, he had never made up his mind to killing that girl. She was something, when you thought about it. But women had a way of making trouble for a man.

Ed Framson pulled up alongside him. Framson was a hard case and one of the few whom Sparr trusted implicitly. That was partly because Framson was in every sense a reliable man. Rustler he might be, but his word was good, and he was loyal. He was also tough.

"Never could figger why you let Soper register his brand," he began suddenly. "That puzzles me some, although I ain't long on figgerin'."

Avery Sparr's head came around sharply. "What? Soper's brand?"

"Uh-huh. The Circle S."

"That's my brand, not Soper's. He registered it for me."

"Reckon he lied, Avery. I seen the books. Soper registered that brand in his own name."

Avery Sparr's gimlet eyes went cold and ugly. He had been wrong to trust that smooth-faced rat! He should have guessed there was no good in the man, but Goff had spoken well of him, and Goff was a good solid fellow. Or was he? Maybe the two were working together! "Thanks, Ed," he said quietly. "I reckon I'll have to start cleanin' out the skunks in this outfit."

"There's a few need it." Framson was quiet. "Soper, he's the worst. I figgered it was somethin' you planned yourself. Never figgered he would take a chance on crossin' you. He's right keerful o' that hide of his'n."

They rode for some distance without speaking, and then they saw a rider approaching. It was Sim Thatcher.

Sparr's innate viciousness rushed to the fore. "Why, there's that T Bar coyote now!" he said. "I reckon this is as good a time as any!"

Thatcher drew up, facing the tight group of riders, his face white. "You had better save that," he advised, seeing Sparr's hand on his gun. "You'll need it!"

"What's that?" Sparr's hard face chilled. "What you mean?"

Sim Thatcher was smiling. "Your show blowed up, Sparr. Tony Cuyas tried to throw a gun on those two partners of Hopalong an' got killed. Hank Lydon lit out of the country. There's four dead men in Turkey Springs Canyon that were friends of Soper. Hopalong made it over the mountain safe with the Jordans, an' then he closed the Eagle an' run that whole outfit out of the country. They are scatterin' like rats ahead of a bull snake!"

"You're lyin'!" Sparr's face was a mask of fury.

"No, I ain't. Hoppy killed two of your men on the Silver. He's headed back this way, gunnin' for you. The Jordans are safe in Alma."

Avery Sparr stared bitterly at his big hands. So this was the end! Well, one thing remained. He would kill Soper, and then he would round up all the cattle in sight and drive them over the border. Maybe he was only a cow rustler, anyway!

Yes, there was one other thing he could do. He could kill Hopalong Cassidy, the cause of all his trouble. Yes, that was just what he would do. And he would do it tomorrow.

CHAPTER 13

BLOOD ON THE SNOW

If the gun hands of Avery Sparr could come west by relays of horses, Hopalong Cassidy could go east the same way. Doc Benton started him off with a powerful bay who had been too long in the stable and wanted to get out and go. The trail north from Alma went up the canyon of the San Francisco and through the Plaza. Hopalong pushed the bay hard, and he was working his way over the trail through the Kelley Mountains when he encountered a puncher headed south. The man was riding a fresh steeldust, and Hopalong swapped mounts with him, promising to leave the horse at the Plaza.

At a ranch on the Negrito he swapped again, this time leaving on a fast black horse. And it was the black that took him through to Horse Springs. He had caught three hours' sleep in the cabin on the Negrito, so he swept into Horse Springs early on the morning after leaving Alma.

No horses stood at the hitch rail and the street was empty of tracks save a few from the night before. The Old Corral was open, but Teilhet himself was puttering around inside. He lifted his heavy head as Hopalong came in and nodded to him. His huge, pearlike body seemed to tremble visibly as Hopalong entered. He responded to Cassidy's quick question.

"Blowed town, I guess. They figgered there would be trouble."

"Where's Connor?"

"Gone."

Teilhet leaned his thick hands on the bar.

"Look, Cassidy, I'm an old man. Don't close me up or burn me out. I know how you are when you are on the prod. Leave me be, will you?"

"All right, but stay out of it, understand? One sign that you are givin' a hand to any of that Sparr crowd an' you get what the Eagle got, hear me?"

Hopalong looked up, freezing the frightened man with his glance.

"Seen Mesquite an' Johnny Nelson?"

"Uh-huh. They are in town now. Over to Ma Baker's eatin' breakfast, I figger. If you ain't et, that's the best grub in town. Next to this place, that is, an' my cook ain't around yet."

Hopalong stepped to the door and glanced quickly up and down the street. Snow was falling lazily, but there was no one in sight. Under the thick blanket of snow the outlaw town looked almost beautiful. It was wrong to consider it an outlaw town, he reflected, for it was anything but that. The good people always outnumbered the bad, only they made less noise and attracted less attention. It was a good town, and would continue to be so.

Mounting the black, he rode to the sign that indicated Ma Baker's and pushed open the door. The first person he saw was Johnny, then Mesquite.

Hopalong grinned widely. "Well, if it ain't feather-headed Johnny!" he said. "Who's your partner?"

"Tumbleweed that blowed in. He don't know much but he's

willin' to learn. I been sort of showin' him aroun' some, but he gets into a sight of trouble."

The ghost of a smile came into Mesquite's eyes. "Pay no attention to this pothole rider, Hoppy. He's sore because Ma gave me the biggest hunk of apple pie."

"Pie for breakfast?" Hopalong inquired. "I'll buy that. Nobody ever ate so foolish as a cowhand off the home ranch, but apple pie? I'll tackle it anytime!" He glanced sidewise at them. "What's been comin' off down here?"

They explained, first one talking, then the other. Hopalong nodded at the story of Turkey Springs Canyon.

"I figgered somethin' like that. Soper disappeared down that way one day but I had no time nor reason to trail him. Didn't even know there was a canyon in there. Did you see him? Or Sparr?"

"Didn't see Soper after he left the ranch, an' never have seen Sparr. I reckon he'll be there by now, or close to it. Goin' back?"

"Uh-huh, an' right away."

The door opened behind them and Hopalong looked up to see Johnny Rebb standing there. Rebb looked quickly from one to the other of them, then seated himself. Nobody said anything after their first greeting. Rebb ate silently and got up to leave.

Hopalong lifted his eyes.

"Rebb, yuh ridin' for Sparr?"

The buck-toothed gunman turned a little to face them. Instantly Hopalong heard a clang of an alarm bell in his subconscious. The man in the shabby vest and worn shirt was cool, completely cool, completely poised. "Yeah, I ride for him."

"If you're driftin' back to the Circle J, tell him I'll be down soon. He can wait for me, or meet me on the trail."

"He'll come."

Mesquite Jenkins lifted his cold eyes. "Where'll you be?"

"Anywhere you like," Johnny Rebb said quietly. "Nobody is runnin' me out of this country."

"See you at the ranch," Mesquite said. "I must eat breakfast."

"I'll see you there," Johnny Rebb replied shortly. He turned his back to them and walked out, and the three exchanged glances.

"Salty, that one." Hopalong returned to his food. "There's some tough men in this outfit. Leven Proctor is a cool head an' he's got a few brains. Anse Mowry is poison mean, a killer from away back. Ed Framson I don't know, but he sizes up as a bad hombre—a stayer too."

"Six or eight of 'em?"

"About that."

"Maybe we'll have a scrap like those in the old days. Won't Red throw a fit when he hears about it?" Johnny chuckled at the thought. "At that, we could use his rifle. I never saw a better man with one. Not even Cassidy here, an' he's one of the best."

Mesquite lifted his head and looked at Hopalong. "Say, you know a hombre named Goff?"

"Met him at Clifton's. What about him?"

"He's perambulatin' around some. Can't figger what for, unless he's tied in with that Soper gent. He was talkin' to Leeds the other day. Leeds an' that kid of his had come to Horse Springs for grub. It seems folks down McClellan way don't cotton to 'em very much."

"He's tied in with the Sparr outfit."

"Yeah," Johnny admitted, "but he done us a favor, an' you too. Told us where yuh were, an' that yuh might need help down to the Circle J. So we high-tailed it down there to find that you had hit for the mountains like somebody built a fire under yore tail."

As they talked Hopalong was thinking the situation out. Having such gun hands as Mesquite and Johnny, two of the fightingest cowhands that ever tied on with any outfit, made the situation some different. Instead of going it alone, he was to have two men with him who could more than carry their own weight.

Usually Hopalong preferred to work alone, and did, but any of the old outfit who knew him well were fighters, and he knew when they were in the game they would understand what moves he would be liable to make and would act accordingly. Now, with these two, all the problems were much more simple. It was not enough to regain the ranch for Dick Jordan and his daughter, for all threat to it and to them must be removed. Rightly, Hopalong deduced the next actions of Avery Sparr. He nodded as he considered that angle.

"Look at Hoppy," Johnny said. "He's figgerin' out some devilment against that Sparr."

"More'n you could do," Mesquite replied, grinning. "If you were sittin' there noddin' I'd just figger you were goin' to sleep."

"Sleep!" Johnny roared. "Why, you no-account maverickin' crow bait! Nobody sleeps less than I do! Nobody!"

"Supposin'," Hopalong said, to quiet the argument, "you were a rustler tryin' to steal a ranch, an' you failed. You knew you were blowed up. What would you do?"

Mesquite considered the question. "Probably grab all the cows in sight an' head for the border."

"Much as I hate to admit it," Johnny agreed, "that's probably right."

"The way I figger, I think our friend Sparr has a couple of chores he'll want to do. He'll want those cows, an' he'll want my scalp. Also, there may be another one or two that he'll want. Take those four hombres you downed at Turkey Springs now. They weren't his men any way you can figger. If they weren't, they must have been Soper's.

"You saw Soper headin' that way, or trailed him. I did too. He lied to Sparr about how long he'd been away from Horse Springs, so he must have stopped with those hombres for a while. In other words, Soper was riggin' a double-cross."

"We saw it that way," Johnny agreed. "You think Sparr will go gunnin' for him?"

"Sure he will! I'd bet my shirt on it!" said Mesquite. "Might be a good idear for one of us to get on his trail an' stay there."

"An' it is time we were movin', all of us." Hopalong got to his feet. "Let's go!"

Leaving money on the table, they went out to their horses. There was plenty of snow on the ground, but the air was warmer. Nevertheless, it promised to continue cold, so Hopalong led the way to a store where they each bought sheepskin-lined coats and gloves. Hopalong restocked on .44's, as did Johnny. Mesquite had thoughtfully appropriated all the shells on the two men he had killed at Turkey Springs, so he had plenty of ammunition.

With a showdown imminent and no time to waste, Hopalong led the way straight across the plains, pointing for Coyote Peak and the pass. The black was a good horse and somewhat rested, and he moved right out on the trail. Mesquite and Johnny rode alongside, and three pairs of eyes swept the country from the high slopes of the mountains to the long, flat levels of the snow-covered plain.

South of them things were not standing still. Avery Sparr had returned to the Circle J in a driving fury. Framson, Byrn Lydon, Leven Proctor, and the Piute headed out at once and began rounding up cattle. All of them were pleased, although secretly. They were men of small imagination and the idea of stealing a ranch had been too big for them. Now that Sparr had relinquished the idea they all felt better because of it. Rustling was something they understood, and all were good hands when necessity forced them to be.

Moreover, they knew where most of the cattle were to be found and within a matter of hours had bunched a herd of several hundred head. These they started south toward the crossing of the Gila. If they could get this herd to Mexico they would have a nice stake coming, regardless. Yet it was Anse Mowry, on the ranch with Sparr, who voiced another thought.

"That Cassidy come out here to pay a debt, didn't he?" he questioned suddenly. "Didn't Bizco say something about fifteen thousand dollars?"

Avery Sparr turned his head slowly. "Yeah," he said thoughtfully, "he did, at that. But maybe he paid it to Jordan."

"Mebbe, but I doubt it." Mowry grinned wolfishly. "Fifteen thousand. That's a lot of money, Sparr."

The big gunman nodded. "Fifteen thousand!" he muttered. It was a lot of money. It was enough money to make him forget his failure here. And he wanted Cassidy, anyway. Suddenly he began to think.

Hopalong Cassidy would come back to the Circle J. He would most certainly come here, and while Avery Sparr had no doubts about handling him alone, he had no idea of trying it. No, the thing to do was be careful, lay a trap for Hopalong and let him blunder into it. Mentally he checked off the men he would have, and began planning their placement. As he planned, he felt a sharp feeling of satisfaction.

This time he would get Cassidy, and this time he would clean up all the loose cattle he could find without combing the breaks. But Hopalong Cassidy had upset his plans, and it was Hopalong he wanted.

The plan when made was good. In fact, it was foolproof. When Hopalong rode into the yard at the Circle J he would be finished, and no matter from which direction he approached, the path would be bristling with rifles. "How yuh like it, Anse?" he said, with satisfaction.

"Perfect!" Mowry's eyes glinted. "Only one thing. If he's still alive when they quit shootin', I want to walk out an' fire the last shot! And I want him to know it!"

An hour later, with the men gathered around him, Avery Sparr quietly laid out the whole plan for them and checked every man on his duties. As he talked, Leeds, a dozen yards away, was unloading supplies, bought several days ago, from a heavy wagon, carrying them into the storeroom under the eyes of the Mexican woman. Fixing a piece of broken harness was young Billy Leeds. Passing by the corner of the house, en route to the blacksmith shop for a punch to make a hole in the leather, Billy overheard a few words. Stopping near the porch, he listened quietly to the talk, and then walked on. When he returned, he was bubbling with excitement.

To leave now would be to attract attention and suspicion, not only to himself but to his father. This was the last thing young Billy wanted; what he did want most of all was to warn the man who had killed the Apaches on that day east of the Canadian.

He fidgeted and worried until his father noticed it and glared at him. "What the tarnation's the matter?" he demanded angrily. "If you got nothin' to do, help me with this stuff!"

As Billy grabbed a box and started for the storeroom with it, Leeds glanced at the dispersing knot of men. What were they about now? Whatever it was, it was no good to know about it. The faster he got away from the Circle J the better he was going to like it. Yet from Billy's actions and his suppressed excitement he knew the boy had something on his mind, so he hurried to get the wagon unloaded, and as they rolled out of the yard he turned to Billy.

"Now what are you fussin' about, kid? You got something on your mind."

He spoke not unkindly, and Billy looked quickly at him. He was never sure about this man who was his father. Old enough to know the mission of the men who came and went in the night around the ranch, he also knew that his father permitted it. He was aware that nothing his father could do would make them stop, and although ashamed of his father for not standing up to them, he understood how he must feel. To stand up to them meant to die or get beaten, and after that, what would have changed?

"That bunch"—Billy was not sure how his father would take it—"they figger to kill Hopalong. I heard 'em talkin' of it!"

Leeds sat silent. Cassidy had come to them when they needed help, and he had asked no questions, nor hesitated. Besides, he had already taken a hand in this game. "You know what they planned?"

"Uh-huh. I heard it all."

"They'll be comin' soon," Leeds said. "I doubt if they'll come by Injun Crick, although they may. We'll stop at the cabin corral an' I'll git a horse for you. Then light out for that peak west o' Cooney Tank. From there you can watch all three trails. When you spot 'em—an' be sure it's them—ride like blazes an' head 'em off. But mind you, son, don't rush up on 'em sudden. Not them kind of fellers. You're liable to git your stomach full of lead."

"How will I see from up there?" Billy protested. "It's too far!"

"Not with this it ain't."

Leeds drew a long marine telescope from under the seat.

"Sparr give me this to watch for riders who might be needin' horses fast, so I'd have 'em ready. Now we'll put it to some good use. But mind you, son, watch out for any of Sparr's fellers. They'd shoot you quicker'n a wink!"

How does news travel in the range country? Men have tried to explain it with such terms as the "grapevine"—meaning that one man told another and he still others, and each of them told more, and so on, until the word was passing from mouth to mouth among thousands of people. Perhaps this is the explanation, but whatever it is, the range country knows, as does the veldt of South Africa, the bush of Australia, and the jungles of the Amazon, that once one man knows a thing, all know it. In all the far and secret places the news moves, or perhaps it is not news, but only a feeling of portent, a feeling of something imminent.

For days the stories of the happenings at Alma, at Horse Springs, and on the Circle J had been going the rounds. How it traveled so swiftly no man could say, but Sim Thatcher knew all the stories, and on that day he gathered his hands on his home ranch. "If Hopalong needs help," he said flatly, "we'll give it to him!"

"From what I hear," the old-timer said dryly, "I don't think he'll need it. Not more'n those two lobos he has helpin' him."

Alma remained quiet. Horse Springs remained quiet. Goff was missing from his old hangout at Clifton's, although just where he had gone nobody knew.

At the shack where Hopalong had made the crossing guard cook for him, Arnold Soper at last found Johnny Rebb. He found him sitting alone on the steps, whittling. Soper rode up and swung down. "Good man!" Soper said. "I've been hunting you!"

Rebb looked up without comment. He had never liked Soper and never trusted him. Johnny Rebb was a man born out of his time. He was the perfect type of the feudal retainer of the old days in the Europe of castles and men at arms. If bravery is a virtue, then Rebb was not without it. If loyalty is a worthy thing, then Rebb was worthy, for he had loyalty, even if to the wrong man and at the wrong time.

To Johnny Rebb the cause was nothing, the man everything. He was a born henchman, a born follower.

Despite his utter cruelty, his coldness, his willingness to kill, Avery Sparr had a strain of free-handed generosity, and once in a casual and thoughtless moment he helped a woebegone youngster who had crossed the plains with an outfit of freighters. He fed him. He staked him to a horse (stolen), a saddle (likewise), a gun (the original owner had been too slow on the draw), and a few dollars. Sparr had gone his way, and Johnny Rebb had teamed up with an older man to collect buffalo bones. While hunting, Johnny practiced with the six-gun and proved to have a natural dexterity, which, coupled with unusual speed of hand and eye and days of practice, soon gave him considerable speed.

Of this speed his partner knew nothing, hearing the shooting but not seeing it, as Johnny Rebb was self-conscious. When the bones were sold and the season was over, with ill-advised confidence the older man tried to gyp Johnny. Words led to words, and the wrong words led to guns. The older partner died suddenly, his shocked surprise mirrored in his eyes. He had never managed to start his draw.

Law and order was a new thing in this vicinity, but already was taking itself quite seriously. The town marshal came to arrest Johnny Rebb. His successor was a more sensible man, and Rebb finally left town when he chose. In the following two years five men lost arguments with Johnny Rebb, bringing his total to seven, none of whom had managed to get a gun free of a holster. And then he met Avery Sparr again.

He met him as Avery was robbing a bank, recognized him despite the mask, and when his companions were shot down, Johnny Rebb took up the battle, joined Sparr, and left town with him. Avery Sparr remembered Johnny when the occasion was mentioned, and he knew a priceless loyalty when he found it. Since then, each had stood over the other and protected him in bitter gun battles.

But of this Soper knew nothing, and it is doubtful if it would have mattered. An educated man, a cunning man, even a very smart man, Arnold Soper was morally nearsighted. He was firmly convinced not only that every man had a price, but that the price was cheap.

"This show's about over," Soper suggested carefully, lighting a long black cigar. "We're washed up here. Or Sparr is."

Johnny Rebb shifted his boots but said nothing.

"People know now that he's not on the level. He's made too many enemies. Not even I could save him.

"Cassidy and his friends will be on the ranch soon. Maybe he'll die there and maybe he won't. Regardless of that, it will not be the end of trouble, but the beginning. Avery Sparr tried violence and it won't work. Only one man can get this ranch now— only one!"

"You?"

Johnny Rebb looked up mildly. Possessed of loyalty, Rebb was also possessed of suspicion, and the chief object of his suspicion for a long time had been Arnold Soper. With that in mind, Rebb had trailed him more than once. He had known about the men in Turkey Springs Canyon but waited to see what developed. He had known about the secret conferences between Goff and Soper.

"That's right. I am the only one. I can get this ranch, and I can hold it. I can get possession legally, and I have been working on that angle for a long time. But I shall need a good man to help me, and a man to run the ranch after I get it. As you know, I am no cattleman. As to the market, I am at home. I know prices, and I can sell beef. I know nothing of raising beef or breeding cattle. And you do."

Johnny Rebb crossed one knee over the other. He had an idea what was coming, and he was ready for it. Yet he waited, wanting to hear the man out.

"I need you, Johnny. Together we can make money. Together we can get rich. You could even become a partner, and there's a vast chunk of land here, and we could reach out and take in Sim Thatcher's ranch. We can do things together."

"Yeah," Rebb agreed, "mebbe. But what do I have to do to git in on all this?" He picked a blade of dry brown grass, not covered by the snow. "Where do I fit in?"

"We could have this ranch, Johnny, but there are a couple of men in the way. One of those men is Hopalong Cassidy."

Rebb looked up.

"An' the other?"

"Avery Sparr."

Johnny Rebb chewed reflectively on the grass blade. Not one instant did he give to considering the suggestion or what it might or might not mean to him. He thought only of how foolish Sparr had been to use a man like Soper, even for a little while. Such men were not to be trusted. He spat finally, then said, "No."

Soper stopped in mid-stride. First, he was astonished, and then he was angry. He was astonished because he could not understand anyone being as shortsighted about his own interests as Johnny Rebb; second, he was angry because Johnny Rebb was literally his own last chance. He could not face Sparr alone. Of course, if Sparr made a run for it, there might be a chance, but there were things taking place of which Soper knew nothing.

He did not, for example, know that Sparr's decision was already made.

"No?" he demanded. "What do you mean? This is the chance of a lifetime, Rebb! A chance for money, an assured position in the community! A chance to grow richer and richer, and right here in our hands, and we can swing it. Sparr can't swing it. We can. You and I. And you say you don't want to?"

"I don't." Rebb got to his feet. "As for you," he said carelessly, his eyes cold on Soper's, "I figger you're a two-faced coyote. You'd turn rat on me the way you are on Sparr. You ain't even the shadow of a man. You're a double-crossin' two-bit rat!"

Coolly he spat at Arnold Soper's feet, then turned his back and started toward his horse.

It was too much. The final defeat of his plans, coupled with the contempt of a man he had secretly sneered at, was too much for him, and Soper, he who had abjured violence, suddenly gave way to his temper and jerked a derringer from his pocket. He had never been known to carry a gun, and the fact that he even possessed one he had kept secret.

Yet now he jerked it and cocked the hammer.

The click of the drawn-back hammer was the thing. On the taut, ever-ready gunman's nerves it acted like an electric shock.

In stride, Johnny whirled, and as he turned he drew, and when he drew, he fired.

His wind knocked out by the slugging blow of the .44, Soper took a step back, gasping. He could not understand what had happened to him. For an instant he believed his own gun had burst in his hand, but there it was, and still cocked, and then he looked up and saw the slow trickle of smoke from Johnny Rebb's gun. Puzzled, he stared at it, and then the gun slipped from his fingers and fell into the snow. His eyes followed it, and they saw something else. There was blood on the snow.

His blood!

Realization came to him then, and suddenly with it came a horror of death. It was horror vented in a scream that broke off halfway, but Arnold Soper did not know he had not finished his scream. He did not even know he had screamed. He knew nothing at all, and would never know anything again. Arnold Soper was dead.

Johnny Rebb mounted his horse, looked once more at the body, and then cantered slowly away toward the ranch. It looked like it might snow again.

CHAPTER 14

JOHNNY REBB MAKES HIS CHOICE

Hopalong Cassidy had taken time for a shave and a bath, so he felt better, and much rested. A well-wisher from among the friendly, honest folk of Horse Springs had loaned him a sorrel that, while not the horse his own was, nevertheless was a fine animal. This was a country that liked good horses, and they had them. He rode without talking, content to keep his eyes on the country. They were restless eyes, all too aware what dangers even the most innocent country can hold.

"Mebbe we should see Thatcher," Nelson suggested. "He'd like to get in on this, I bet."

Mesquite looked his disgust. "You want to go after him? Me, I got a date with that Johnny Rebb. They tell me he's mean."

"Salty," Nelson said. "I'd bet on it. He carries himself like it."

"Good man gone wrong," Hopalong assured them. "I talked to him some, but from all I hear, he's Sparr's ace in the hole."

"Reckon we'll find Soper down here?"

"Mebbe. He'll be around somewheres. Leave it to him to make a try somewhere along the line."

"Hoppy"—Johnny nodded off to the left—"somebody's been drivin' cattle recent."

Cassidy studied the trail off to one side, swinging his sorrel over for a closer look. "Uh-huh. Maybe twenty head. Drivin' south."

"Looks like they've started their cleanup," said Johnny.

If Sparr's men were driving cattle, they might find few of them at the home ranch. Hopalong seemed to share this idea with them, for he spoke to his sorrel and moved into a canter. The other two kept pace.

They were abreast of Black Mountain when Hoppy's eye caught a flash of reflected light. He looked quickly, but the light was too far away to be from a rifle. It was well up on the side of a butte out on the plain, probably three miles away. "Somebody's watchin' us with a glass," he said.

"Let 'em watch." Nelson shrugged his shoulders and began to roll a smoke. "They know we're comin' anyway."

A few minutes later Hopalong caught the flash of a fast-ridden horse. "That's funny! He's headin' this way, comin' right to us."

They continued to ride, and they did not talk while they waited. When the rider drew nearer, they saw it was a boy, a slim youngster of fourteen. Then Hopalong recognized him. "Howdy, Bill!" he said, drawing up. "Where you goin' so fast?"

"Been watchin' for you!" the boy exclaimed excitedly. "That Sparr feller, he's got an ambush laid for you! He's got six or eight men, all tough hombres, an' they are all set up an' ready.

"There won't be nobody in sight but Sparr when you show up, but there's to be men in the bunkhouse, the blacksmith shop, the storeroom, and the house itself, an' all with rifles an' shotguns. The minute Sparr gives the word, they cut down on you. They are all laid out there now, hidden an' waitin'. My dad says you better beat it, an' if you want Sparr, ketch him somewheres else!"

"Thanks, Billy." Hopalong looked thoughtfully at the horizon, then back at the boy. "How many in the house?"

"Two. That there Proctor will be there with one o' the Gleasons. The Piute an' another o' the Gleason boys will be in the blacksmith shop, Anse Mowry in the storeroom, an' Ed Framson in the corral. That Lydon, he's to be in the bunkhouse."

"What about Johnny Rebb?" Hopalong asked.

"Never heard. He wasn't there when they planned it."

Hopalong started his horse again and walked it slowly forward, but as he rode he was recalling the exact setup of the buildings at the Circle J. As in most of this Apache country, they formed a small fort in themselves, although not as compactly arranged as those at the T Bar.

The large, rambling old house faced the bunkhouse. Alongside the bunkhouse was the blacksmith shop, and directly across from the shop, and attached to the house itself, was the storeroom where extra food and supplies were kept. Across the end was the barn, a large, shambling structure with a huge loft for hay, and beside it the corrals.

At the opposite end the rectangle was open with a nest of rocks and brush overlooking the whole yard and offering excellent firing positions for anyone defending the area, but an equally good if not better position for anyone wanting to fire upon the ranch buildings.

Into this space Hopalong Cassidy was expected to ride, as he had ridden before, only this time the instant he passed into the rectangle of buildings, even from the brush and trees as he had come before, he would be under the muzzles of a circle of rifles in the hands of men sworn to kill him.

The thought of turning back did not occur to him. Notoriously stubborn, he refused to admit that he could not do what he started out to do, and now his mind was seeking out a way. "You better high-tail it, Billy," Hopalong suggested. "No use lettin' them see you with us. From now on it's our problem."

When the boy was gone, Hopalong said nothing for a few minutes, and then he commented, "Looks like a good chance to round up the whole outfit."

"What I was figgerin'," Mesquite replied. "An' havin' 'em scattered out thataway may be just the best thing ever."

"How d'you figger that?" Johnny demanded. "We can't fire in every direction, can we?"

"Why should we?" Hopalong said. "So far as we know, he doesn't know the two of you are along, so you are to be my aces in the hole. Whatever is done, I've got to ride out into that plaza between the buildin's an' let 'em all see me, but it is the two of you that have the big job to do. You got to get rid of that bunch in those buildin's, or some o' them."

"That hombre in the rocks," Mesquite said, "should be easy for Johnny."

"Why me?" Johnny demanded fiercely. "Why me? Why should I be stuck up there away from the scrap?"

"You are the best rifle shot," Mesquite replied innocently. "Take out that feller—then you can open fire on the windows they'd shoot from."

"What about you?" Nelson demanded suspiciously. "Where will you be?"

"Why, I'll take the house first! You can open up on those houses across from me."

"All right, Mesquite," Hopalong agreed. "I'll take Sparr an' then the storeroom. Mesquite, if you finish in the house, go for Framson in the corral."

They rode more swiftly now, and at Hopalong's word they

split. Hopalong could see that the herd Sparr's men had gathered had reached several hundred head, and it had been driven to the eastern end of the ranch. Evidently they planned on striking east and then south along the North Star road and heading south for Mexico.

The sun was high and the morning ended when Hopalong sighted the house through the trees and slowed down. His mouth felt dry inside and his stomach was hollow, for he knew that when he rode into the rectangle of buildings, he would be encircled by death.

Suppose Johnny failed? Or Mesquite? Suppose something went wrong? There would be nothing for him to do then but to fight his way out of the circle. Any way he looked at it, he was facing the biggest gamble of his life, but he knew he wanted Sparr, and wanted him the worst way. He let the sorrel go forward at a walk, and then lifted his voice in song. That was to be the signal for Johnny to move in on the Gleason who held the rocks.

On the spur of the moment he changed his plans. It was the horse that caused it, for he disliked to think of a fine horse taking a chance on being killed by flying lead. He dismounted alongside the house and then stepped to the corner.

Before him the hard-packed earth was pinkish white, and he could see that despite the comparative coolness the windows were lifted in the bunkhouse. Snow was gone from the small plaza except close to the buildings. The sun glared brightly on the walls and was reflected from the windows. Hopalong Cassidy stepped out from the corner of the building to the edge of the long porch that ran before the house.

"Sparr!" His voice rang loudly in the empty plaza. "Come on out!"

As if on signal, Avery Sparr stepped from the barn.

"You want me, Cassidy?"

Hopalong could see the big gunman scowling to pick him out against the dull wall of the house where it was shaded by the porch. It was going to be tougher for him now, and those men inside the house would not find it easy to shoot at him if Mesquite failed. But Hopalong knew he would not fail. He had never failed.

"Why, sure! Heard you were huntin' me, Avery. Reckoned I'd make it easier for you, seein' as we have a little score to settle."

"You crabbed my game, Cassidy." Sparr walked forward two steps into the open. "Come on out where I can see you!"

Hopalong Cassidy's quick eyes had been gauging the situation. He found he could step out into the open and still not leave himself a target for the men in the house, and that unless Ed Framson shifted fast, he would be blocked off by Sparr's own body. Moving with easy steps, Hopalong walked into the open, and the two men faced each other seventy yards apart. As if eager to draw Hopalong still farther into the open, Avery Sparr started toward him.

Meanwhile, Johnny Nelson had skirted the timber and raced his horse through the snow to the foot of the hill atop which one of the Gleason boys would be waiting. The thick snow, partially shaded by trees, muffled the hoofbeats, and Johnny swung down and started up through the rocks. He was moving swiftly and surely, fierce with eagerness and desperate with the necessity of closing in on this man in time to back Hopalong up, for well he knew the dangerous position into which his friend had stepped. He went up the rocks swiftly, and atop the hill saw a husky man in a sheep-lined coat crouching behind some rocks.

He took two quick steps before his boot crunched on snow and Gleason saw him. His face wolfish, the man dropped his rifle and drew a knife. He lunged at Johnny, eager for the kill. And Johnny Nelson knew that a shot from him would explode the whole yard into a blazing pit of gunfire, where Hoppy would be the focal point. He took one step back, and as the long arm thrust wickedly with the low-held knife, Johnny grabbed the man's wrist and he spilled him over on his head into the piled-up snow and leaves.

The fellow hit hard and lost hold on his knife, but he was tough, and came up with a lunge. No more than Johnny did he wish to spoil the ambush down below, and he was a bearlike man who loved to fight. He closed in swiftly and took a ramlike fist in the mouth that lost him some teeth, and then a right on the jaw that made his skull ring. He ducked his head to get in close and caught a fist and then an elbow. He lunged again, slipped, and his chin encountered a lifting knee.

He went down hard, and Johnny Nelson dived for the rocks and the rifle.

At the very same time as Johnny mounted the rocks, Mesquite reached the house. There were no doors on the back, so he tried a window. It was shut, and either locked or frozen. Hastening, he tried a second and a third. All were tightly closed. Desperate, he was about to round the house and come into the open when the Mexican woman cook saw him. She came quickly to the window and tried to lift it. No luck.

Grabbing a kettle from the fire, she poured it over the middle sash and the bottom. Mesquite shoved and the window came loose. In an instant he was through the window and into the house. Stepping around her, he pushed past into the huge living room.

Leven Proctor lounged against the fireplace, a rifle in his hands. Crouched by a window was the second Gleason, a small man with a wizened rat face. "Drop 'em, boys," Mesquite said softly, "or gamble!"

At that instant the yard broke into a thunder of gunfire and Gleason gambled—and lost. His gun, already drawn, swung around, and Mesquite opened fire with both guns. Leaping from his holsters like a magician's gesture, they vomited flame. Mesquite saw Proctor's face over the darting flame of his guns and saw the tall man swing the rifle and fire. He felt himself stagger and saw Leven Proctor go down to his knees, coughing blood. Gleason was dead over the windowsill, and Mesquite darted for the door.

It was like him that he wasted not a look at Hopalong. He had been given his chores, and he knew what he should do was what he had been told to do. He started on a run for the corral. Framson, about to get into a new firing position at last, saw him coming. His eyes swung one way, then the other, but Mesquite was too close a danger, and he snapped a quick shot at him, felt a bullet smash his shoulder. He dropped his gun, scooped it up, and dodged across the corral. Mesquite circled it, firing between the planks.

Framson went down coughing, got up, and leaped for the corral fence, grabbing the top pole with his hands. He swung himself over and Mesquite stood, wide-legged with lifted guns, and for an instant they looked at each other. And in the cold eyes of Mesquite Jenkins, Ed Framson saw death. He grinned suddenly, feeling the red heat of the bullets he had taken in his body.

"Why, you lucky blister!" he said. "You lucky blister! I'll kill you!"

He dropped, landing miraculously on his feet, his grin wide. "You got me, but I want company!"

His gun swung up, and Mesquite's Colts hammered death into him, knocking him back step by step, until he fell.

Even as Mesquite was crawling through the window and Johnny fighting among the rocks, Hopalong Cassidy was walking out into the open against Sparr. And Avery Sparr, who had never known fear of another man, suddenly felt a strange certainty welling up within him. The battered gray hat, the fringe of silver hair, the frosty blue eyes, the sloping shoulders, and the curious, short-stepping cowman's walk—that was Hopalong Cassidy, and it was death.

In that clear, sun-bathed luminous instant Avery Sparr knew his time had come. It came to him with a flash of realization, such a certainty as he had never known before. He knew he was going to die, and somehow then he knew that it had been in his mind ever since he had first seen this man. All his plans had gone wrong. His big gamble, which until then had been so safe, so sure, all had failed.

Yet in that clear instant of realization, his cold and haggard face revealing nothing, Avery Sparr knew that a man has but one time to die. All other things he can do many times, but he can die but once, and if a man cannot live proudly, he can at least die proudly.

Tall, gray, and bleak, he stopped, facing Hopalong across the thirty yards of distance that separated them. In that instant—such is the way of fighting men—he felt almost an affection for the gunfighter facing him. At least he wouldn't be like Hickok, shot in the back without a chance by a tinhorn, or shot from the dark like Billy the Kid. He could end it out here in the sunshine and take Cassidy with him.

"How d'you like it, Cassidy?" His voice was harsh. "Let's see how good you really are!"

They stared at each other, each knowing well how the other felt, for both were fighting men. No matter how far apart the ways of life, the divisions of color, creed, or living, there is between fighting men an understanding, and such these felt now. Sparr spoke once more before the guns began to talk.

"You know, boy, it's a nice way to go, out in the sunshine, with the sound of the first snow meltin'!'"

His hands dived for his guns, and as if on order, guns began to crash about them.

To men in great moments of suspense, moments of great emotion and action, comes a suspension of time, so that the action of seconds seems to drag to long, long minutes.

Avery Sparr's big hands dropped in that old familiar gesture of death, dropped for the butts of the big guns he loved so well, and, like darting lightning, the guns cleared their holsters and leaped to position, yet in a breathless instant before him, flame shot from the guns of Hopalong Cassidy.

Sparr's teeth bared in a snarl as he took the hammering lead; his cheeks seemed to sink to deep hollows. His hat was gone somehow, and there was the dark, smoky taste of battle in his mouth, and he was shooting, shooting, shooting!

He had no way of knowing in those last gun blazing split seconds of his life that his equilibrium had been destroyed by the first bullet he took, that the second had torn his left arm, smashing the bone and tearing flesh as the misshapen bullet found a way through. He had no way of knowing that the big guns in his hands were hammering into the sun-baked earth and that his own body was knocked right and then left by lead from Cassidy's smoking guns.

Hopalong, his face bleak, stepped around the big gunman as a fast boxer steps around a slow-moving slugger—stepped around and shot him to doll rags, for Hopalong knew that while one tiny breath of life wavered in this man he was a fighter still. Cruel he might be, criminal he might have been, but he was a fighting man.

Once only he paused to flash a shot at a window. Then he

finished the job and left Sparr flat on his face in the sunshine. Wheeling, he ran for the storeroom.

Anse Mowry was there. Anse, who had cursed Hopalong and sworn to kill him. Anse, who was vicious and cruel, but who had watched with amazement as the mighty Avery Sparr went down beneath Hopalong's guns. Suddenly something thick and bitter climbed in his throat, and with a cry of half-animal fear he saw Hopalong wheel away from Sparr and come toward him.

Wheeling, Mowry clawed at the window. Forgotten were all the boasts he had made; forgotten his claims and his meanness.

He clawed at the frozen-shut window, then grabbed a chair and smashed out the glass. With a lunge he dived through, the glass ripping his flesh. He started on a run for the woods, his throat torn with cries of fear.

Sanity had left him, and he had only one idea: to get away, to escape. Suddenly, fearfully, he glanced over his shoulder and snapped a wild shot at the window where Hopalong's face was framed. The long gun spoke, and he turned half around and stretched out in the snow, his boasts as dead as his fears, his blood staining the snow, as red as any man's.

A spatter of shots came from the buildings, and Hopalong sprang back. Somewhere a horse's hoofs hammered and died away, and then the air was soft with sunshine and the smell of melting snow. Hopalong fed bullets into his guns and stepped into the open. Mesquite was coming toward him, limping. "Burned me," he said. "You hurt?"

"No." And then, thoughtful as he always was, "Where's Johnny?"

"Comin'!" Johnny Nelson came down the rocky hill toward them.

"Mowry?" Mesquite asked.

"Dead."

"I got two in the house," Mesquite said, "an' Framson's gonc."

Johnny Nelson waited until he recovered his breath. "The Piute an' his sidekick lit a shuck when Sparr went down."

"How about Lydon? Wasn't he the one in the bunkhouse?"

"My first shot. Let's look."

Lydon lay inside the window, beyond the rustling of cattle.

"That other hombre, the one up in the rocks, I knocked him out, but he got up an' came for me with a knife. He's finished too."

Hopalong picked up his hat, which he had lost in the fight. "One man still missing," he said. "Where's Johnny Rebb?"

"Lit out, maybe?" Nelson suggested.

"Uh-uh. Not him." Mesquite was positive. "He ain't the runnin' kind."

At the sound of approaching horses all three turned swiftly. Mesquite's rifle swung up.

"Hold it!" Hopalong grasped the gun barrel. "That's Sim Thatcher an' his crowd."

Thatcher rode up, his horse shying at the body of Avery Sparr. The rancher stared at him, then turned to Hopalong. "Dead, huh? You did it?"

"Yeah. I reckon two or three got away. The Piute an' one of the Gleasons. No sign of Johnny Rebb.

"Sim, I'm ridin' to Alma to tell Dick about this. While I'm over there I'll pick up that buckskin o' yours. Now look, that's the best mountain horse I ever rode, an' I want him." He paused, and sobered. "Of course he's a mite old, an' a little sway-backed, but—"

"You durned no-account, silver-headed liar!" Sim Thatcher chuckled. "That buckskin ain't quite five yet, and if he's sway-backed I'm the next Emperor of China. Don't start runnin' him down to beat me out of him. I like that horse. He's one of the best I ever saw, but you done me a big favor, Hopalong, so if you don't take that horse as a present, you need never speak to me again. Nor," he grinned, "you don't eat no more apple pie at my place!"

Hopalong rubbed his jaw, his blue eyes twinkling. "I reckon that last argument cinches it, Sim! I sure was figgerin' on more pie!"

Mesquite looked at Johnny Nelson. "Did he say pie? Apple pie?"

"Sounded like it." Johnny looked serious. "I don't believe it, but in the interests of truth an' veracity, not to say science an' history, I figger we better ride over to the T Bar an' carry on a little investigation-like."

Hopalong watched them start for their horses. "Better leave a couple of men here, Sim, if you can spare 'em. I'm headin' for Alma. Also," he added, "you better take all the rest of them back to your spread if they want to protect that pie. There's only one thing those boys do as good as fight, an' that's eat!"

Dick Jordan was sitting up in bed when Hopalong entered the room. "Confound it all!" he bellowed. "These here women sure keep a man hemmed in! They don't give me enough grub to keep a yearlin' youngster goin' an' expect me to get better!" He held out a hand. "I sure am pleased, Hoppy! Fact you're here proves things is better! Leastways, you're still on your feet!"

"Yeah."

Hopalong dropped to a chair and tried to comb his hair with his fingers, conscious of Pamela's presence. They were bursting with questions and it was like him to tease them by ignoring their curiosity. "Looks like a good winter, Dick. Nice fall of snow, some meltin' now, but that's only in the low places. Purty quick she'll snow real hard again, an' we'll have good summer grass. Now—"

"Consarn you, Hoppy!" Jordan interrupted. "Stop that infernal beatin' around the bush! What happened? Where's Sparr?"

Hopalong glanced at Pamela, who was staring at him, avid with interest and excitement.

"Sparr?" he inquired. "Oh? Oh, yeah! Sparr."

"Well, what happened?" Jordan demanded, scowling.

Pamela leaned forward, looking even more charming than usual. "Hoppy, stop teasing! Please, please tell me!"

Cassidy chuckled. "All right. Well, there ain't much to tell. Mesquite an' Johnny had a run-in up in Turkey Springs—"

Quietly he told them the story, adding no unnecessary details, merely giving them the information.

"About all it amounts to is that your ranch is in your hands again and those outlaws are either dead or runnin' for the border."

"You didn't say nothing about Rebb," Jordan complained. "What happened to him?"

"Not a word or a sound. He vanished just like the earth swallowed him. I wanted to leave the same day to come over here, but couldn't. One of Thatcher's boys found Soper. He was dead, had been shot and killed at that guard cabin on the ford of the West Fork. From sign around he figgered Johnny Rebb done that.

"Mesquite trailed Rebb's horse up to the cabin an' saw where he was joined by Soper. Soper evidently tried to kill him because we saw Rebb's tracks goin' away, then where he turned real fast. And Soper had a stingy gun lyin' near by him."

"What about Rebb's trail?"

"He started for the Circle J, but evidently heard the shootin' an' saw the T Bar outfit come up. Maybe he ran into some of the boys who took out, but anyway, he never showed up."

Outside, the moonlight was bright as moonlight can only be on an early winter night. The street was empty of snow, save in a few sheltered places where the day's sunlight could not reach, but in the east the high peaks of the Mogollons sparkled like moonlit diamonds, impossibly, unbelievably beautiful.

In an empty cabin almost a block away from the house where Hopalong Cassidy talked with the Jordans, a man fed a fire in a glowing red stove, and close to the stove he held his hands, and from time to time he kneaded his fingers with care. The room in which he sat was dark but for the fire, but it had the lonely, empty feeling of a room long deserted.

This was the home of one of the men Hopalong had run out of the Eagle. The room's only window opened on the street, and from it one commanded an excellent view of the house where Dick Jordan lay recuperating from his mountain journey.

The man in the cabin smoked a cigarette, then carefully put it out, and sat still beside his fire, waiting with such patience as only the hunter knows. And he was, indeed, a hunter—Johnny Rebb, waiting to kill Hopalong Cassidy.

He had not much longer to wait. Death is rarely impatient and can conjure up a multitude of tiny delays. Death definitely has dramatic sense and understands the rules of suspense, for upon this night Johnny had come to his feet more than once, his gun ready. First it had been the doctor coming out, and then somebody who delivered an armful of groceries, and then a visitor. Hopalong was staying a long time.

He would not stay the night. Johnny Rebb had taken precautions to find out, but it did not matter, for Rebb was prepared to wait a week, a month if necessary. He had a good store of dry wood. He allowed little smoke to emerge, no light to be seen. His supplies had been brought in by night.

Hopalong Cassidy was a careful man. Always a fighting man, he had learned that survival was a matter of intelligence, of knowing things first, and being always ready for the unexpected. Pamela had come with him to the door, and they stood there, talking.

"Will you go back to Buck now, Hoppy?" she asked.

"No." His eyes strayed down the street and rested upon a dark house; rested, then moved on. "No, I reckon not. I want to ride south from here, down near the border. Little town down there I want to see, and some new country."

"Won't you ever settle down? Stay in one place?" Her hand was on his sleeve. "Why don't you stay here, Hoppy? Somehow— Oh, I feel so much better when you're near, and lately I've been almost sick when you were gone."

He avoided her eyes, reflecting miserably that she would probably be sicker if he stayed and then went. And he would go.

"Who lives in that house down the street? The one that is out farther than the others? On the corner almost?"

"That one? It's empty. Frager used to live there, they tell me. He was an outlaw, I guess. Anyway, when the Eagle closed, he left very fast."

"I see. Anybody been in there lately?"

"Oh, no! It's empty. It has been for days."

Hopalong Cassidy nodded, and his eyes gleamed in the darkness. The snow in the street where it had been walked over and run over was gone. There were still a few roofs that had snow, however, but they were the roofs of sheds and barns without inner heat. The houses where lights showed had no snow on the roof, for the fires within had helped to melt it away. There was no snow on the roof of the house in question, although there was snow on the porch, unbroken, untrodden snow.

"I'd better go," he said quietly.

"You'll come back?" Pamela pleaded gently.

"Yeah, maybe." It was better to say you would come back. Better than flatly saying no. It wouldn't work, he knew. Pamela was lovely, but he was a man who lived by the gun. She deserved better. Maybe she was a little in love with him, but he was not at all sure. And in a little while, if he was gone, there would be somebody else.

"Yeah," he said quietly, "I'll come back, Pam. After I go south."

He stepped quickly off the porch, intent now upon something else.

No snow on the roof. He smiled, seeing again a pattern of living and a pattern of going shaping itself. "So long, Pam! Tell Dick I got a little job to do down the street, but I'll be ridin' on right after."

Within the dark window of that house his eye had caught, in the moment he first stepped from the door of the house, a tiny fleck of light that might have been a suddenly extinguished cigarette. And it might have been his imagination.

He huddled his sheepskin coat around his ears but stripped off his gloves and shoved them into the capacious pockets. He walked slowly down the street. And then the door of the empty house opened and a man made tracks in the hitherto untracked snow. His boots crunched on the porch snow, and then he stepped down on the walk. He wore a heavy buffalo coat that hung open.

"A cross draw," Hopalong said to himself, "an' it will be fast."

Johnny Rebb stopped and watched the man approaching him.

He was young at this game, but good. He knew he was good. He was too young to have the feeling of going too often to the well, too young to have any premonition of death or to recognize it if it came. He was a young man of singularly basic emotions. An uncomplicated young man. His ideas were few, his tastes and desires simple. Right now he wanted to kill Hopalong Cassidy. Right now he felt he was going to kill him.

"Howdy, Cassidy." He spoke in a low voice, and waited.

"Yeah, Johnny. I been expectin' you. Fact is, I knowed you was here."

"How?"

Johnny Rebb was puzzled. How could he have known?

"No snow on the roof. Only houses with the snow gone are those with fires."

"Well, what d'you know? I never figgered on that." He chuckled. "You're a smart one, Hoppy. Too bad you have to go this way, but Sparr, he done me some favors."

"Do yourself one, kid," Hopalong suggested quietly. "Call this off an' beat it. You had luck. You beat out a tough game, so take the luck you have an' go someplace else. Start ranchin' or punch cows. This killin' won't get you no place."

"Talkin' too much, Hoppy. Them who talk too much are usually scared."

Hopalong's chuckle was dry. "Not this time, kid. I hate to see this happen."

Johnny Rebb's right hand lightly held the edge of his coat, only inches from his gun butt. "Sorry, Hop—!"

He turned his body at the hips with a swift motion that thrust the gun butt—the gun was in his waistband—right into his hand. Then he drew and fired. It was fast. Amazingly fast.

Hopalong, whose gun was in its holster, the butt at the edge of the coat, was an instant slower. It was a hair's-breadth difference caused by difference in gun positions and the edge of Hoppy's coat. But Johnny Rebb shot first, and he shot too fast.

He had failed to learn what those who live must learn—that the instant of deliberation before the trigger is pulled is often the only difference between life and death. His bullet tore a deep furrow along the top of Hoppy's sheepskin coat's shoulder. His second shot went through the thick fold of the coat within an inch of Hoppy's heart but failed to touch his body.

Hopalong's gun had swung up to hip level, and then he fired. He fired once only. He fired at the shining buckle on Rebb's belt, and the heavy lead slug hit the corner of the buckle and ranged upward. Hopalong walked forward swiftly to the fallen man. Rebb stared up at him, his eyes surprised and bitter. "You should have filed the shine off that buckle, kid," he said gently. "It makes much too good a mark."

People came running, and Pamela would be one of them. He edged away from the dying man, remembering that he had not picked up the buckskin yet.

"When Pamela Jordan comes out," he told a bystander, "tell her Cassidy was all right. I've got to see a man about a horse."

AFTERWORD

by Beau L'Amour

Reproduced from the Table of Contents page of the original magazine version of *The Rustlers of West Fork.*

HOPALONG CASSIDY'S WESTERN MAGAZINE

$\mathbf{M}$y father was Tex Burns. He's gone now, so I feel it's time to stop denying it. I really don't think that Tex ever did anything he needed to be ashamed of; all he did was lose an argument. Nonetheless, Tex Burns was persona non grata around our house.

In the spring and summer of 1950, Louis L'Amour wrote this and three other stories about Hopalong Cassidy. He used the pen name Tex Burns and the books were commissioned by Doubleday's Double D Western imprint. *The Rustlers of West Fork, Trail to Seven Pines, Riders of High Rock,* and *Trouble Shooter* were the first four novels that he ever had published.

But for the next thirty-eight years he denied that he had ever written any of them.

When asked, he told people that he had never written about Hopalong Cassidy, that he had never written as Tex Burns. At autograph sessions he would refuse to sign the Hopalong books that fans would occasionally bring. And for years he worried that these books which he tried so hard to ignore would be reprinted and brought back into circulation.

I first heard about the situation when I was ten or eleven. Dad had just returned from doing a radio call-in show and as we sat down to dinner he grumbled something about how he wished people would stop asking about Hopalong Cassidy.

I asked him what the matter was, and he gave Mom a look (the kind parents give each other when their children up and say something that makes people uncomfortable). He put down his fork. "A long time ago," he said, "I wrote some books. I just did it for the money, and my name didn't go on them. So now, when people ask me if they were mine, I say no."

"But you *did* write them, didn't you?" I asked. This sounded vaguely like a secret . . . very important to a kid.

"Yes," he sighed.

"And when people ask you if you wrote them, you tell them you didn't? Isn't that lying?"

"I just wrote them for hire. They weren't my books." A non-answer.

I had hit a nerve that youngsters seem to have a magical talent for finding. The Parent Paradox. To be a "good parent," Dad has to tell Junior not to lie, that lying is bad. Of course, everybody lies. The real issue is how often, and to what extent do you distort the truth—a subject too complicated for many kids . . . and some adults.

"But why don't you tell them the truth?" I asked. As a kid, you always suspect that adults have a whole other set of rules made up for themselves. Like all children, I found a lot to lie about. When adults would ask "who broke this?" the last thing that came to mind was what really happened. But I understood that kind of lying, there's a motive to it.

"Beau," he said, "I don't care for the books, and I don't care for the whole situation. Those books have no relationship to the work I'm doing now. They agreed that I could write them one way but then they went back on their deal."

"But you still wrote them," I protested.

Dad said something designed to shut me up and we went on with dinner.

Now, twenty years later, I understand his problem all too well. He had, at some point, begun telling people that the four Hopalong Cassidy stories he wrote were not his. After that, he had to lie to keep his story straight . . . so people wouldn't catch him lying. And when you're a dad, I guess that's the last thing you want your son to catch you doing. It's what you're trying to protect him from.

In following years the character of Hopalong Cassidy faded away into the past and Louis L'Amour became more and more famous. L'Amour paperbacks sold millions of copies while the novels about Clarence Mulford's cowboy-hero disappeared from the shelves. The triple-feature theaters, where the black-suited Bill Boyd used to appear, were turned into strip malls. And finally, after pioneering the airwaves and a decade of reruns, Hoppy vanished from television. L'Amour fans, however, still occasionally asked *that* question.

They had good reason to ask, because there was evidence. Somehow the copyright form to one of the stories ended up reading "Author: Louis L'Amour," rather than "Tex Burns." The United States Government knew who had written those books and the information was there for anyone to check. Trouble was, Dad still denied it.

He kept on denying it until he died. When Bantam's parent company acquired Doubleday, the publishing house that owned the books, he was relieved. Now Bantam could forever block the sale of the hated books. As I got older I learned that I was never going to get a complete answer out of him, and so stopped asking.

After his death we discovered some of his correspondence with the editors of the *Hopalong Cassidy* magazine. I read *The*

Rustlers of West Fork and *Trouble Shooter* (the first and last of his Cassidy novels), and began to put together my own version of why he couldn't admit that he wrote the books.

The story goes like this. . . .

Sometime between 1906 and 1908 (coincidentally the year my father was born), Clarence E. Mulford wrote a series of magazine stories that were collected into a novel titled *Bar 20*. It chronicled the adventures of Buck Peters, foreman of the Texas ranch, and others, including a rough-talking red-haired cow-puncher named Bill Cassidy. He got the nickname Hopalong aftcr he was wounded in the thigh by a bullet. Peters eventually left to run his own ranch in Montana and Hoppy became the foreman of the Bar 20.

Over the course of his career (roughly 1906–1941) Mulford wrote more than two dozen novels, the majority of which were about Hopalong Cassidy and the other characters from the Bar 20 ranch. In 1941 he published the last of his Cassidy novels, *Hopalong Cassidy Serves a Writ,* and retired on the money made by his extraordinarily popular books and the sale of their film rights.

In 1935 producer Harry Sherman had hired William L. Boyd to appear as Hopalong Cassidy in what would be the first of 118 films (including TV episodes) about the Cassidy character. From the first, Boyd showed a great deal of both concern and control over the image of Hopalong. Allegedly he insisted on the black costume, white horse, and nickel-plated guns that became his trademark in the films. The story is that he also consulted with the writers on cleaning up the foul-mouthed, hard-drinking, but basically realistic character from the Mulford books. The Hoppy of film and televison was a well-laundered gentleman who abstained from tobacco, alcohol, and profanity. He was a character who (though perhaps not at first) became more and more aimed at an audience of children. It is reported that Mulford was disappointed in the movies. "The only comment I have to make," he said laconically, "is that he is not properly dressed for the part."

Some thirty Hopalong Cassidy movies had been made between 1941 (when Clarence Mulford retired) and 1950. It seems that Doubleday began to feel that some new Hopalong Cassidy books could do well in a market that supported so many movies. They put together an agreement with Better Publications to release the stories in magazine form as well and asked Mr. Mulford to come out of retirement. For reasons of his own, he turned them down. He was, however, willing to license them the rights to the character so that another writer could do some new stories . . . and for better or worse he chose my father to be that writer.

Dad had been writing for the *Thrilling* magazines for about ten years. Before the war he wrote the very successful "Ponga Jim" Mayo series for *Thrilling Adventures,* while afterwards he built up a good career selling to the *Thrilling Western* and *Thrilling Detective* pulps. I assume that he, and probably several other writers, were recommended to Mulford by Leo Margulies, the editorial director of Better Publications.

Mulford chose my father. Now that I have read some of the original Cassidy stories, I am not in the least surprised, for they were soul mates. Although the sound and the flow of their writing was different, both wrote with boiling energy. When my father began a story he never looked back. He made it up as he went along, rarely planning what was going to happen. The stories of Clarence Mulford have the same feeling of spontaneity, the same sense that the writer was totally immersed in the world of his creation. Both seemed to be writing for their own entertainment as much as for that of the audience.

I know that my father was flattered at having been chosen.

Mulford had made it big as a novelist, and that was a world that my father hoped to break into also. Although he never mentioned it to me, I'm also sure that Dad read several of the early Mulford books as he was growing up. I've tried to imagine being asked if I wanted to be the literary successor to Ross MacDonald or Ray Bradbury, and the idea sends chills up my spine. Of course I want to write my own stuff, and so did he, but as long as that wasn't happening they sure wouldn't have to beg me.

They didn't have to beg Dad, because along with being flattered, he was hungry. He was living in Los Angeles, subletting a room from a family who had an upper duplex in the Wilshire district. I know he was having a tough time because he made no journal entries that year at all (Dad was always better at writing in his journal when he was both motivated and productive).

Mr. Margulies sent him copies of the Hopalong Cassidy stories and Dad studied up. I know that he had several discussions with the executives of both the magazine and Doubleday regarding the characterization of Cassidy. They were entertaining the idea of patterning him after Bill Boyd because of the very successful movies, but Dad insisted on Mulford's original and more colorful interpretation. They were probably eager to get the first edition out in time to coincide with the NBC premiere of *The Hopalong Cassidy Show,* which had been given a Sunday 6:00–7:00 P.M. time slot starting the 1st of October. They asked him to start immediately.

On January 4, 1950, Dad received this letter (which I've edited a bit).

Dear Louis:

I'm glad that you are interested in doing the Hopalong Cassidy Novels in our new magazine of that name. We are

*going to pattern the magazine novels after the Mulford books
and will attempt to retain as much of the Mulford character
as possible. You will notice in reading the very last of the
Hopalong Cassidy novels that he was a deputy sheriff. However, in my opinion, we should steer clear of any form of
lawman characterization, deputy marshal, or otherwise. I
think we should have him a free lance trouble shooter, drifting along and settling range, town and other western problems. We don't want him to lose touch with his old pals like
Mesquite Jenkins, Buck Peters, Jonny Nelson, etc. They
should appear in the stories now and then, but the stories
should not be tied in with the Bar 20 or any of the other
ranches established by Hopalong's pardners.*

*There may be a slight woman interest in the stories, but
it should be handled so that it is more of a case of hero
worship—Cassidy rides off into the distance and a gal looks
after him wistfully. I don't think Mulford used the limp for a
good many years, especially in his later stories. I know that
they don't have him limp in the movies, so let's forget the
limp.*

*The reason we are buying All Rights is because we are
merely being licensed to use the Hopalong Cassidy novels for
one time use in our magazine. Therefore it is necessary for
us to do business with an author from whom we can pur-
chase All Rights for a flat fee.* [Dad got $1,000 and his agent
took 10%.] *If you don't find that this arrangement meets
with your approval, let me know immediately so that we can
make contact with another writer who will be interested in
doing these stories on the terms we can offer.*

*We plan to do the magazine on a quarterly basis. Maybe
more than that if it catches on. The first one should be written as soon as possible, and if I were you I would plan a new
one every other month or sixty days apart. Please let me
know, and my best regards.*

*Sincerely yours,
Leo Margulies*

As you can see, when Dad said that it was just work for hire, he meant it.

Another detail, not mentioned in this letter here, was the issue of credit. Before the war, when Dad was writing adventure and sports stories, nobody had any objections to his using his own name. But in the mid '40s, when he started trying to sell Westerns, he ran into trouble. The management at Better Publications did not believe they could sell Western stories by a writer named Louis L'Amour. Westerns had to be written by a man who could have been a cowboy and everyone knew that cowboys had short, tough-sounding names: Luke Short, Max Brand, Will Henry, Brett Hart, Zane Grey. They told Dad that no one with a name like Louis L'Amour could ever sell Westerns—it was too hard to pronounce, too soft sounding, it was too, well . . . foreign. Irritated at having to use a pseudonym, he chose Jim Mayo, the name he had originally created for the hero of his South Seas adventure series. The "Ponga Jim" Mayo stories had been written under his own name, and so there was at least a slight connection.

When the issue of the Hopalong stories came along, the editors asked Dad to write under still another name: Tex Burns. I think another reason they did this was so that, if the publisher became dissatisfied with Dad, someone else could be hired to write as Tex Burns without the readers' knowing there had been a change.

Louis wrote *The Rustlers of West Fork* and *Trail to Seven Pines* very quickly. By June of 1950 he was about to finish *Riders of High Rock* when he received some bad news from the offices of Better Publications in New York. Doubleday was getting around to preparing their hardcover edition of *Rustlers* and it's my guess that they wanted to capitalize on the other version of Hopalong Cassidy.

The movies had turned Hoppy into a merchandising phenomenon, and the upcoming national TV release was expected to send it through the roof. By January of '50 there was both a radio show starring—who else—Bill Boyd, and a comic book that represented Cassidy with a likeness of the silver-haired actor.

In an extraordinarily canny move, Boyd had previously sold almost everything he owned to raise the money to buy the rights to all the early Hopalong films and was now selling them to television. As if that weren't enough, he was in the process of preparing yet another fifty Cassidy episodes aimed directly at the small screen. He was also selling Hopalong Cassidy clothes, breakfast food, towels, watches, bicycles, and candy.

In light of all this it seems that the publisher wanted a Hoppy that the masses would recognize, not the rough-edged character that no one had heard from in a decade. They wrote to my father and told him to change his stories to use a Hopalong in the Bill Boyd mode.

Now Dad hated rewriting, and he'd never liked to be told what to do. He had a lot of respect for Clarence Mulford and felt that he was doing his best to carry on in his tradition. Doubleday had been Mulford's publisher since 1925 and I think that Dad was deeply disturbed by the thought of being involved in selling out the writer to a company that ought to have had more respect for his work.

Unfortunately he was broke. Los Angeles, even in 1950, was an expensive place. The last third of 1949 he had spent writing *Westward the Tide* (a book that would not appear on the American market for twenty-seven years) and thus hadn't made his usual number of short-story sales. Dad's income for the year had been barely over three thousand dollars. Although more and more bothered by the entire situation, he went back and changed the manuscripts for Doubleday. Then he proceeded to write *Trouble Shooter* with a character that looked and acted like Bill Boyd. (An interesting note: *Hopalong Cassidy's Western Magazine* published the first two stories the way my father originally wrote them, but *Riders of High Rock* and *Trouble Shooter* used the revised description.)

In the following years Louis L'Amour went on to produce successful and respected work under his own name. And somewhere along the line a fan, or an editor, or a reporter, came up to him and asked if he was the guy who wrote those Hopalong Cassidy books back in 1950. At that point he had a decision to make, and not knowing that he would go on to become much more famous and thus closely scrutinized, he lied because he didn't feel good about what he'd done, and he didn't want to spend all night justifying his actions.

For the sake of consistency, he kept on doing it until he died.

Then one day, two years later, I pulled his old copy of *Hopalong Cassidy, Trouble Shooter* off the shelf and read it.

And it wasn't bad.

I liked it, and I am not uncritical of my father's work. I realized that, regardless of Dad's feelings about changing the description of the character, it didn't matter. He was obviously not trying to copy Mulford's (rather Victorian) style. The book was a good example of vintage L'Amour work, and one that I felt ought to be made public.

There. Now that that's over with, I have a few more things to say. First, about Clarence Mulford and my father: I found some interesting similarities between them as I was writing this afterword. Both men prided themselves on their research into the historical aspects of the West and both maintained enormous libraries to support their research habit. Each sold millions of copies and was extraordinarily successful for his day. Although he wrote westerns about other characters, Mulford's most popular books were about Hopalong and his friends. Dad's were the Sackett series. Lastly, both were exercise fanatics and eventually (late seventies for C.M., eighty for L.L.) died of lung disease. (I'm not sure but I think that Mulford's problem was also cancer.) Seeing that C. L. Mulford chose Louis L'Amour as his successor, it is interesting to note that the man who was perhaps the most widely read author of westerns in the first half of the twentieth century passed the torch to the man who was the most widely read author of westerns in the second half.

Besides Hopalong Cassidy, you will meet a few of Mulford's original characters from the Bar 20 stories in this book. Buck Peters, whose money Hopalong is delivering to Dick Jordan, was the original foreman of the Bar 20 ranch. Tex Ewalt (who is only mentioned in this book) and Johnny Nelson are also characters that date back to the novel *Bar 20* (1907). Johnny goes on to become the hero of both *The Man from Bar 20* (1918) and *Johnny Nelson* (1920). He also appears, in a more minor way, in several of the other stories. Mesquite Jenkins first appeared as a character in *Hopalong Cassidy Returns* (1925), and continued in *Hopalong Cassidy's Protege* (1926). Mesquite also appeared without Hopalong in his own novel, *Mesquite Jenkins* (1928).

Even though I discovered that the magazine version of this and the next Hopalong novel used the description of Cassidy that Dad had written originally, I decided to leave these stories the way Doubleday printed them—that is, with a Bill Boyd-like Hoppy. The reason is consistency. The last two magazine stories used the cleaned-up Hopalong and that's the way that all four stories appeared in book form.

Looking back on all the trouble Dad went to to keep his association with the Hopalong books a secret, there is surprisingly little difference between his original version and the "revised" one. Nothing but the physical description of the character, the occasional mention of his smoking, and the inclusion of the movie Hoppy's horse, Topper, has been changed. These changes were plugged in with no alteration of the surrounding text. At times you can catch Dad trying to downplay the Bill Boyd image; he mentions that Hoppy's silver guns were "worn", or that Cassidy wore clothes that were "no different" than other Western men might wear. The most glaring example of this is that Hoppy manages to abandon Topper at Sim Thatcher's ranch for almost the entire length of *The Rustlers of West Fork.*

It is my opinion that the reason for Louis's continued and emotional denial of the books came more from irritation at himself for having started that process of denial to begin with, than his anger at being told to alter the character descriptions.

Lastly, a request to you, the reader. As my father was finishing *Education of a Wandering Man* (this was only a couple of days before his death) he mentioned that he wanted to include a note in that book asking each of his readers to plant a tree. At the time I felt that this was somewhat pretentious of him and I did not follow up on his wish. Since then I have changed my mind.

Dad wanted to ask you, whoever and wherever you are, to go out and plant a tree. He didn't care what kind and he didn't care where you put it. He only cared that thousands of trees are cut down every day and few are ever replaced. Trees are cut to build your home, to clear land to raise cattle or crops, trees are cut to make this book you hold in your hands. Cutting a tree for profit takes less than half an hour, whereas growing a new one will take half a century. Louis wanted you to do this for yourself, to do this for your future.

I feel better now. I wish I'd done that a couple of years ago when I was asked to, but better late than never.

I wish to extend thanks from Kathy L'Amour, Bantam Books, and myself to the many people who helped bring this book back to press after so many years and to those who supplied me with the information I used to write this afterword: David R. Hastings II and Peter G. Hastings, Trustees of the Clarence E. Mulford Trust, Michael Marsden of Bowling Green University, Gene Autry Museum, Sybil Brabner, and Violetta Volovnikov.

I think that's it. I hope you had a good read.

December 4, 1990

ABOUT LOUIS L'AMOUR

"I think of myself in the oral tradition—as a troubadour, a village tale-teller, the man in the shadows of the campfire. That's the way I'd like to be remembered—as a storyteller. A good storyteller."

It is doubtful that any author could be as at home in the world recreated in his novels as Louis Dearborn L'Amour. Not only could he physically fill the boots of the rugged characters he wrote about, but he literally "walked the land my characters walk." His personal experiences as well as his lifelong devotion to historical research combined to give Mr. L'Amour the unique knowledge and understanding of people, events, and the challenge of the American frontier that became the hallmarks of his popularity.

Of French-Irish descent, Mr. L'Amour could trace his own family in North America back to the early 1600s and follow their steady progression westward, "always on the frontier." As a boy growing up in Jamestown, North Dakota, he absorbed all he could about his family's frontier heritage, including the story of his great-grandfather who was scalped by Sioux warriors.

Spurred by an eager curiosity and desire to broaden his horizons, Mr. L'Amour left home at the age of fifteen and enjoyed a wide variety of jobs including seaman, lumberjack, elephant handler, skinner of dead cattle, assessment miner, and an officer in the tank destroyers during World War II. During his "yondering" days he also circled the world on a freighter, sailed a dhow on the Red Sea, was shipwrecked in the West Indies and stranded in the Mojave Desert. He won fifty-one of fifty-nine fights as a professional boxer and worked as a journalist and lecturer. He was a voracious reader and collector of rare books. His personal library contained 17,000 volumes.

Mr. L'Amour "wanted to write almost from the time I could talk."

After developing a widespread following for his many frontier and adventure stories written for fiction magazines, Mr. L'Amour published his first full-length novel, *Hondo,* in the United States in 1953. Every one of his more than 100 books is in print; there are nearly 230 million copies of his books in print worldwide, making him one of the bestselling authors in modern literary history. His books have been translated into twenty languages, and more than forty-five of his novels and stories have been made into feature films and television movies.

His hardcover bestsellers include *The Lonesome Gods, The Walking Drum* (his twelfth-century historical novel), *Jubal Sackett, Last of the Breed,* and *The Haunted Mesa.* His memoir, *Education of a Wandering Man,* was a leading bestseller in 1989. Audio dramatizations and adaptations of many L'Amour stories are available on cassette tapes from Bantam Audio Publishing.

The recipient of many great honors and awards, in 1983 Mr. L'Amour became the first novelist ever to be awarded the Congressional Gold Medal by the United States Congress in honor of his life's work. In 1984 he was also awarded the Medal of Freedom by President Reagan.

Louis L'Amour died on June 10, 1988. His wife, Kathy, and their two children, Beau and Angelique, carry the L'Amour tradition forward with new books written by the author during his lifetime to be published by Bantam well into the nineties—among them, three additional Hopalong Cassidy novels: *The Trail to Seven Pines, The Riders of High Ridge,* and *Trouble Shooter.*